PRAISE FOR BHART

"At once a cautionary tale of culture-clash, a tender love story and a finely crafted tear jerker . . . an appealing debut . . . Kirchner proves a sensitive observer of India and the dilemmas of bicultural heritage."

—*Publisher's Weekly on Shiva Dancing*

"The author has created such appealing characters and has done such a good job of portraying her heroine's longings and struggle that we are kept guessing. Her descriptions of domestic customs are richly suggestive, adding color and flavor to an already evocative novel."

—*Christian Science Monitor on Shiva Dancing*

"*Darjeeling* is poetically told, artfully rendered story of the true test of blood loyalties, bringing a family to the brink and back again. There is a lot to love here."

—*India Currents on Darjeeling*

"Interwoven with themes of family, unrequited love, and forgiveness, Darjeeling is as strong as the tea itself and just as satisfying."

—*Booklist on Darjeeling*

"Bharti Kirchner brings privileged insight to bear in her fiction . . . This is a bittersweet story, as astringent and refreshing as a brisk up of tea."

—*The Seattle Times on Darjeeling*

"Sprightly writing, well-defined moral choices, and a wonderfully exotic sense of place . . . a page turner."

—*School Library Journal on their selection of Sharmila's Book in the category of "Adult Books for Young Adults"*

"Witty dissections of some of India's anachronisms . . . smart, swift and funny, with rich dollops of local color."

—*Publisher's Weekly on Sharmila's Book*

"Luminously evocative, if breathless, a tale of the cultural fissures that emerge as a very modern woman contemplates an arranged marriage. An affectionate grace note to the (Indian) subcontinent as well as a sensual feast."

—*Kirkus Reviews on Sharmila's Book*

"This is magnificent, classical historical fiction which is said to depict the life and work of the founders of Calcutta. An absolute must-read!"

—*Review by Historical Novel Society on Goddess of Fire*

"What really brings 'Goddess of Fire' to life is the huge quantity of vivid, compelling detail on literally every page. All the sights, sounds, smells and customs of the time and place are recounted here: the feel of a rich fabric, the aroma of spices, the jade-handled bamboo fans of the Nawab's attendants, the sound of conch shells and drumbeats, and the dreaded crackling of fire. Research and authenticity resonate in every chapter. This is a book that will transport you across centuries and across continents."

—*The Seattle Times on Goddess of Fire*

"Readers will look forward to seeing more of the astute Maya."

—*Publisher's Weekly on Season of Sacrifice*

"Indian culture adds spice to Bharti Kirchner's new Seattle mystery series. And her opening scene is a real zinger: two white-robed women set themselves on fire in front of the house occupied by the visiting Chinese foreign minister in Seattle's Green Lake district."

—*The Seattle Times on Season of Sacrifice*

Murder at Andaman

MURDER AT ANDAMAN

BHARTI KIRCHNER

CAVEL
PRESS

Kenmore, WA

A Camel Press book published by Epicenter Press

Epicenter Press
6524 NE 181st St.
Suite 2
Kenmore, WA 98028

For more information go to:
www.Camelpress.com
www.Coffeetownpress.com
www.Epicenterpress.com
www.bhartikirchner.com

This is a work of fiction. Names, characters, places, brands, media, and incidents are either the product of the author's imagination or are used fictitiously.

Design by Scott Book and Melissa Vail Coffman

ISBN: 978-1-60381-680-9 (Trade Paper)
ISBN: 978-1-60381-679-3 (eBook)

Printed in the United States of America

As always,

for Didi, Rinku, Tinni and Tom

for bringing joy to my life

"Look into any man's heart you please, and you will always find, in everyone, at least one black spot which he has to keep concealed."
—*Henrik Ibsen*

"Life is made of marble and mud."
—*Nathaniel Hawthorne*

ONE

With the gray hangover of a Seattle November morning spreading outside her window, Maya Mallick caught the headline on her iPad.

American Tourist Hacked to Death
in Port Blair, Andaman Islands Capital

Another sensational news item from the wire service, scandalous and already two days old. Best not to linger. Heart beating, finger poised to scroll down the screen, she registered the mention of Andaman. She knew that place, an isolated cluster of islands belonging to India, strung like a chain of jewels off the coast of Myanmar in the Indian Ocean.

After taking a deep breath, she dismissed her irrational reaction. *Must be a coincidence.* She heard the shower turn on and Alain singing. In French. Soft and seductive, with its elongated vowels.

Less than a week ago, she'd driven their close friends, Rory and Lee, to SeaTac airport. They were scheduled to fly to Port Blair, Andaman's capital. Prized for its natural beauty and reasonable prices, Andaman had become popular with both Indian and Western tourists. The mainland of India was 850 nautical miles to the northwest and the connecting flight from Mumbai would take five hours, all in all more than a day's flying time from Seattle.

Maya had wished them a splendid time in a cheery voice. It had struck her as unusual, even special, when Rory—red-haired, freckle-faced, fair of complexion and reserved—drew her into a light hug, saying, "You and Alain must come with us the next time."

Lee, short for Leena, her usual vivacious self, flounced up in a peony dress and lifted a light suitcase from the back of Maya's Toyota. She winked at Maya and said, "Swimsuits and a cocktail dress—that's all I've packed."

Only Maya knew that Lee was newly pregnant and had hoped for a son. *Tell your best friend, but not your husband; wait for a special moment.* The tradition went back to Lee's family, of waiting to share the good news with your husband at an auspicious instant, such as on a full moon night. On that day Maya was happy for Lee but kept her feelings to herself, content to imagine their joyful future. After Rory had finished his talk at the Andaman literary festival, on the topic of "Transparency and the Digital Age," Lee would share the good news. And what a perfect setting it would be: a soft sandy beach, azure waves, peacocks idling in the shadows of palm trees, and Lee, looking demure in a lacy black cocktail dress under the silver light of the full moon. The couple had been blessed with all the riches life could offer in their seven-year marriage, except a child. Time to celebrate.

The excitement in their voices as they said goodbye and dashed toward the departure gate lingered in Maya's ears. She looked at the screen, her jaw tight.

Port Blair police has identified the victim as Rory Thompson.

Oh, no, not Rory! Followed by, *Where's Lee? Why hasn't she texted?* Heart lurching, Maya returned her attention to the screen.

Publisher of Roaring Books, an independent literary house based in Seattle, Thompson specialized in edgy social and political exposés.

Maya tore her gaze away and shook her head. The familiar objects around her in her Seattle home—the glass surface of the accent table, the teal ceramic lamp, and the landscape painting of a winter storm—couldn't provide her any comfort. She straightened in her chair, experiencing more fight-or-flight alertness than when in her typical inquirer mode.

During the night, the authorities received a tip from an anonymous telephone caller that Mr. Thompson might be in danger. A search for him began. The next morning, the police found him slumped in the "alley of tricks" in the red-light district on the edge of the town, an area frequented by Western tourists. Mr. Thompson, who had multiple stab wounds to his face and body, was pronounced dead at the scene. His body was identified by his wife, Lee. Mr. Thompson's watch, wallet, gold ring, and credit cards were untouched. His smartphone was missing.

Our Rory? Killed? In an alley of ill repute far from his hotel? Maya's breath froze in her throat.

Thompson, 42, was scheduled to give the keynote address on Friday at the inaugural, three-day Andaman Islands Literary Festival. According to Andaman authorities, neither a motive nor a suspect has been found and no arrests have been made. A spokesperson confirmed that the festival has been proceeding as planned, though some distressed attendees are believed to have left.

A shot of adrenaline jolting her body, Maya pressed her hands on the arms of the chair. She stood up and paced the room, wishing she could take some action. The sound of her own footsteps disturbed her. Was Lee all right? But then, despite her warm smiles and social skills, Lee was a private person, shut tight until she was ready to open herself up, which could take days.

Rory's dead? As a PI managing the Seattle satellite office of Detectives Unlimited of India, Maya dealt with crime of all kinds, rape, theft, assault gun deaths and domestic violence. But to think that a close friend's husband would attract the wrath of a criminal and end up dead, far from home. Her hand touched her heart.

Rory, a dear friend, attractive man, and quiet soul, had a passion of Himalayan proportions for books, and a prodigious work ethic to go with it. In social situations, he often faded into the background, allowing his wife to shine, a slight elusiveness about him. But when the conversation turned to literature, he would become animated, for he loved the written word the way parents dote on their children. He also adored his wife. From the goofy, admiring glances he bestowed on Lee, he couldn't be mistaken for anything other than a faithful, devoted husband.

A strong gust of Pacific Northwest wind rattled the windows. Even though she was bundled in a fleece vest, an arctic chill ran through Maya's body. Her investigative mind shifted into gear. *His smartphone, a digital evidence, was missing.* Because the perpetrator hadn't stolen any of Rory's other valuables, mugging wasn't a motive. Might it be a case of revenge?

Hearing footsteps, Maya looked up. Alain entered, whistling and looking well rested. For an instant, if only to dispel her anxiety, she watched him, this man who had added much to her life in the last eight months. An American of French ancestry, Alain had a personal style, a result of spending his formative years in France and Belgium. He carried a few extra pounds, no doubt about that, and yet his size made him appear stable and important. This morning, dressed in pale blue shirt, charcoal jacket and matching trousers, he looked refined, well put-together, and professional. His light brown hair, combed flat except for an upsweep on the forehead, accentuated his clean-shaven face, which always brought a flicker of warmth to Maya's heart. At thirty-four, she was younger than Alain by ten years; the age difference didn't matter to her.

"Have to go, darling. A breakfast meeting at eight-thirty." Smelling of cologne, carrying a briefcase, Alain stood solid. "You have a full day, too, don't you? Have you decided if you're going to take the Sanders case or not?" Then noticing the stunned expression on her face, he stepped forward. Putting the briefcase down, he wrapped his arms around her. "You all right?"

Maya shook her head and handed him the iPad. He began browsing the news story. His forehead showed a small frown and his eyes were full of confusion.

"Good grief. Our Rory?" Alain placed the tablet on the desk and allowed several moments to pass before speaking again. "Someone harmed him? Near a bordello? No, no, he wasn't the type. This makes no sense at all. Perhaps they mistook him for someone else?"

Maya let herself hope. Then a sinking feeling overcame her, and she shut her eyes for an instant. "Hope you're right," she said. "For Lee's sake. Heavens! She's the sweetest, gentlest person I know, and she loved Rory."

Maya's voice broke as she considered Lee's pregnancy; how her joyous expectation would crumble, how she would have to tread a path filled with obstacles. How much sadder could it be that her baby, opening his eyes to the light of the world for the first time, would already be touched by the tragic loss of his father? Maya shook herself out of the thought. Best to discuss this matter with Alain when they had a little more time.

"Do you have any way to reach her?" Alain asked.

"Yes. I have her in my contacts and I know the name of the hotel where she's staying. It's evening over there. I'll call."

"Wish I could talk with her, but you're closer to her. Be sure to give her my condolences. Any help she needs. Leave me a message if you need anything, will you?"

Maya agreed. Hard to comprehend that she'd never again see the sparkle in Rory's eyes, feel his presence, or hear his voice.

Alain gave her a soft kiss, then let out a deep breath. "Don't worry too much yet, okay, darling? Get the facts." He headed to the door.

Maya heard the clattering of his footsteps on the front stoop and wished she could call him back. Since becoming a private detective two years ago, she'd handled complex criminal cases on her own. When first receiving a report, she'd listen with cool detachment, except when it involved someone close to her, except when it involved death. Death, a sneaky adversary, severed the hopes and dreams of a person. It didn't consider how it would incapacitate his or her family and friends. Maya's ability to react had become clouded.

A few shoulder rolls lessened the tension. She scooped up her phone from a side table and placed a call to Lee. When her call didn't go through, she tried the hotel number. Upon receiving the hotel room's voicemail, she left a brief message. All the while she wondered what it'd be like for Lee as she grieved and sought answers. How lonely and desperate she must feel in a resort surrounded by the paradoxical cruelty of beauty, leisure and luxury.

A truck rumbled somewhere. The cell phone sang. Maya answered the phone in a controlled voice.

Lee said hello from the other end, her voice choppy and edged with anguish. She mumbled something about having ingested an herbal potion, a tranquilizer prescribed by a local doctor. "You saw the news?"

How Maya wished she could reach out and hold her friend's hand. "What happened? What did happen?"

"I can't believe it." Lee described how Rory had worked for hours in their hotel suite, perfecting the speech he would deliver at the book festival the next day, practicing in front of the mirror and her. He considered it a huge honor to have been invited as the keynoter. He wanted to shine and had planned on giving an inspiring talk about his small, assertive publishing venture, his books and his authors. Around seven-thirty in the evening, looking wiped out, he told her he was venturing out for a bit. *"For a walk on the beach and a drink. For some air. To clear my head."*

"Did that surprise you?" Maya asked.

"No, he was a night-owl. At home he often stayed up till two a.m. And Andaman is considered safe for walking around at night, at least for a man."

Maya absorbed Lee's wavering voice. "You didn't want to go with him?"

Lee paused, as though trying to figure out an acceptable answer. "No, I was bushed. Jet-lagged that I was."

That raised a flag. Maya went on to ask another question. "Was Rory concerned about anything?"

"If he was, well, he didn't confide in me. An hour later, he wasn't back yet, and I was starving. Called room service. After finishing my supper, I went to bed, couldn't keep my eyes open. The last few days had been hectic, to say the least. Before I knew it, I'd fallen asleep. When I woke at about midnight and didn't find Rory next to me, I was in a tizzy. I rolled out of bed, left several messages on his cell. He didn't answer." Voice choking, Lee stopped speaking.

Maya, gripped by a feeling of being unsettled, said, "Look, you don't have to—"

"Okay, I'll call you back later." Lee hung up at the other end.

With heavy steps, Maya crossed to the window. The mist had softened, but a grayish cast to the morning lingered. The skeleton of a maple tree, shorn of its leaves, dominated the view. Winter had arrived, the season to execute the end of things.

TWO

ON MOST DAYS, EVEN IN WINTER, Maya started her mornings by slipping on her running shoes and finishing the three-mile loop around Green Lake. Upon returning home, her mood enhanced, she would shower and dress and fix a bowl of oatmeal. Then she'd peruse her to-do list, review the case file and tackle whatever work challenges lay in front of her. Today would have been no exception. Earlier this week, she'd wrapped up a kidnapping case involving a young bride, and she was ready for a new assignment.

After her brief exchange with Lee, Maya fought down a sense of being lost and crumpled. She didn't feel at all like the strong, composed, quick-thinking investigator she was. She decided to skip jogging and went to her home office. Sitting at the desk, she opened the cherry wood card box that held a supply of her biz cards and picked up one. Done in white linen paper with black lettering, the logo-free card proclaimed:

Maya Mallick

Private Investigator

Her business phone number and email address followed.

She put the card back in the box. Her gaze swept a geometric, silver-framed photo of her widowed mother, Uma Mallick, on the desk. A beauty in her fifties, Uma boasted porcelain-smooth skin, deep black eyes, and a mass of grayish black hair cascading around her face. Her bright eyes indicated she had smarts, too. Maya and Uma were close; they talked on the phone often or e-mailed each other. Maya could never thank Uma enough for pointing her to a career in private investigation.

She was a mother who could always discern what Maya needed even before she opened her mouth, such as her desire for an occupation that would not only provide a decent income, but also challenge her. Couple of years ago, much to Maya's surprise, Uma, through her network, had made the initial contact with a Kolkata-based detective agency—Detectives Unlimited. Uma's hometown, Kolkata, was tucked away in the eastern part of India, almost halfway around the world from Seattle.

"With your energy, toughness, and intelligence, you can do much more than your current nutrition consulting," Uma had said over the phone. "You're a go-getter. Why not fly back here and have a chat with this company? They're successful and they can afford to pay the industry rate. I have a gut feeling that you'll like the high-adrenaline work of a PI."

Uma was right; Maya had thought. She had a natural ability to jump into action, whenever necessary. But would it be that easy to become a PI? "But, Ma, I lack experience."

"Didn't you take criminology classes in college? Didn't you pay your way through college by working as an office assistant to a Seattle PI?"

"Yes, to both," Maya had replied. How fortunate that she'd picked up a repertoire of investigative techniques from her part-time work at the Hawk Eye Agency. Do your legwork, see, hear and smell, read the client, accumulate the facts and lie, if necessary, to find the truth.

"Think about what you bring to the table," Uma said. "A rare combination of American know-how and Indian big picture thinking."

"Ma—"

"Okay, you're wondering how you'll live in Seattle and report to an Indian outfit?" Uma interrupted her. "You'll have the best of both worlds, dear. Maybe you haven't heard the news yet. Our India is growing at an astonishing rate and our business tycoons are looking to establish a presence abroad. With all the expertise they have acquired and the cash they have on hand, what can they not accomplish? Working for an ambitious international company, you'll have opportunities you don't have now. Doesn't Seattle have a large Asian Indian population?"

"It does, but not a large number of crimes happen in our community though."

"Give it time, dear. Indians will become good at it," Uma said. "And yes, this outfit wants to have a face-to-face interview with you."

Maya had hesitated. Working long distance for a foreign company in a line of work that was new to her . . . she could be trapped, stabbed, kicked or shot at without her boss knowing about it. Yet, she could visualize herself on the street, wherever that might be, excited to be chasing leads and identifying culprits. Suppose she succeeded. One good break and you're made, as they say in the industry.

After considerable reflection, Maya had flown to Kolkata. On one of the top floors of a high-rise building, she'd met with the agency owner, fifty-something Simi Sen. Fit, well-groomed and elegant, dressed in a yellow silk sari and pearl earrings, Simi sat behind a high-gloss, executive desk. A strong presence lifted her to beyond-pretty level. Reputed to be a tough investigator, she ran an all-woman boutique agency. Behind her back, industry insiders called her "Iron and Silk."

"When I first started this agency, a one-room operation," Simi said, "a few pompous male detectives made fun of us. 'Those sari-wearing ladies would go nosing around on Kolkata's mean streets? They have no place for their guns.' The tide has changed. Look at us now. We celebrated our tenth anniversary last week. Women are better at it. Intuition, people skills, and resourcefulness are our strong points. We're inconspicuous. Nobody can beat us when it comes to probing pre-and post-matrimonial affairs, Internet romances, or cheating spouse cases. Our work is discreet, confidential and private. We're established as wedding detectives and we've expanded to nine cities. Now I want to branch out to Indian communities in the U.S. You know better than I do that Indians are one of the most successful minority communities there. They must have plenty of headaches. I believe that our Indian people will prefer to go to another *desi* for help, if one is available. They tend to be on the conservative side, if I'm not mistaken."

Maya had assented while Sen adjusted her sari at her shoulder and continued. "Probing has got to be in your genes. Your late father, Subir Mallick, the legendary detective with the Kolkata Police Department— who hasn't heard of him?"

Maya had lowered her face. Decades ago, when she was only nine years old, her father had been murdered. It remained an unsolved case. The loss of her father, a man who lived to help others, had provided her with motivation to be of assistance to those in need.

"I'm sorry." Sen had paused as a bearer served them each a glass of amber tea made from estate Darjeeling. "Here's a hypothetical situation. A bride's family requests us to find out if the groom smokes or not. Smoking is a big no-no in that family—her father died of lung cancer. The groom claims he's never touched nicotine. That raises some eyebrows. How would you prove or disprove him, if you were to handle the case?"

Maya had thought for an instant. "I'd shadow him, concealed with a mini-camera, and catch him off-guard in a pub, on the sidewalk, or even in a latrine. Disguised as a man, I'd videotape him as he lights up."

Sen had given a rare laugh. Her gaze on Maya's résumé in front of her, she'd said, "You helped your mom when a burglar broke into your flat in Kolkata and stole all your possessions? You gave testimony to the police. All that was reported in the *Statesman*. You were only twelve then?"

To which Maya had given a yes.

"I can tell you're an independent soul," Simi said. "If you work for us, you'll have autonomy as far as the cases you wish to look into."

How will I learn the trade so fast? Maya had wondered, even though she had an inquisitive mind. *You don't inherit those techniques from your father, do you?* From what little she could remember of her father—a tall, slender man with a mischievous twinkle in his eyes—he enjoyed his chases. Once, coming home late and bending over her, he'd said, "What do I do all day, my darling? I give bad guys a run for their lives."

"But to chase bad guys on my own . . ." she'd said to Simi.

"Would you like to hear we used whom as an operative? When we first started out—our eyes, ears and our sixth sense? Cabbies, servants, street vendors, friends and relatives, and neighborhood busybodies. The point is, Maya, we talk to people, work with information and collect evidence. You're good at all of those, aren't you?"

Maya had held her back straight and smiled. She'd always considered herself a good interviewer, someone who could draw a person out, listen between the lines, and look for the truth. People did confide in her about their feelings, about their personal secrets. She did gain her suspect's trust. Her part-time job during college days had trained her to be persistent and to notice details in any situation.

"What's your success rate?" Maya asked.

"We hit sixty to seventy percent, whereas our competitors barely come close to the fifty percent mark." Sen had smiled. "You're interviewing me?"

After a lengthy conversation, she'd offered Maya a position as a private investigator based in Seattle. "You may have to keep long, unpredictable hours. We'll give you all the support we can offer from here. We have informers and plenty of databases at our fingertips, should your searches lead you back to India. When can you start?"

At that moment Maya had experienced a sudden burst of happiness. Silently, she'd thanked her mother. Given that she was a U.S. citizen, over eighteen years of age, and had a job offer, she could apply for an Unarmed Private Investigator License. She'd have to take pre-assignment training in such matters as court systems, confidentiality and legal powers, and pass a State exam. She replied to Sen, "It'll take two or so months to complete background check requirements and be licensed by the Washington State Business Licensing Services. A few more weeks to obtain a liability insurance policy to cover client lawsuits. About three or so months total."

"Rent an office space. Hire a smart assistant. Build a business website." Sen had offered Maya a signing bonus to help pay for all three.

Once the official paperwork was completed, Maya opened the Seattle branch of Detectives Unlimited. She didn't look at the clock as she spent hours preparing a business plan, complete with an industry analysis, services, competition, fees and other financial matters. Simi was on her side when she decided that, lacking advertising dollars, she would depend on word-of-mouth to secure new cases. For the most part she liked to help women, pulling them out of troubled situations and using compassion to deal with them. In the two years since her hiring, she had handled several criminal cases, including homicides. Because of her empathy and resourcefulness, she resolved issues and closed a fact-finding process faster than expected. Far more than providing a paycheck, this job had provided her with unexpected satisfaction, an excitement that propelled her throughout the day. Her interrogation skills continued to improve. She could tell when a suspect's story didn't hold up.

THREE

STANDING AT THE WINDOW OF HER HOME OFFICE, Maya pictured Lee: tear-streaked cheeks and quivering lips, heart-wrenching questions about her dead husband torturing her mind. They'd become close friends after having been introduced at a neighborhood house party. Both born in India, both naturalized American citizens living in Seattle, they mirrored each other's looks: big, dark and expressive eyes; straight lustrous black hair; skin on the olive side. At five feet five, Lee had a couple of inches on Maya. At thirty-six, she was older than Maya by two years.

They huddled together often, to catch-up, laugh, joke, and share each other's lives. They texted each other throughout the week. Both liked to try out new places for lunch. As a part-time consultant to Rory's budding publishing house as well as other small outfits, a "numbers guru" as she was often called, Lee oversaw financial planning, evaluated new fiscal strategies, and offered advice on investments. "No nine-to-five schedule ever for me." Less career-oriented than Maya, Lee wanted to have children, stay at home, and raise a family. "I'm a mom by nature."

Now that Lee was pregnant, she'd be able to fulfill her dream of nurturing; the very thought cheered Maya. She didn't want children, at least not now. She wanted to build her career as a PI, be a worthy daughter to her detective father, and some day able to solve the case of his mysterious assassination.

Meantime, she appreciated Lee's company. A social creature by nature, if somewhat reserved, Lee contrived to meet Maya whenever she could make time for lunch or tea. "You're the most stable of all my friends," she'd once said. "I cherish our closeness. I find it easy to open up to you. I like it that I can speak with you anytime I want. You make time for me and understand me. You're one of the few who will keep my secrets."

At the end of a crazy morning, wracking her brain trying to figure out the psychology behind a culprit's behavior, Maya enjoyed listening to the bell-like quality in Lee's voice. Lee, a friend who stood by her, who had her best interest at heart. She shared her deepest feelings about Alain with Lee, and her alone. She trusted Lee that much. She valued their kinship, the boundless affection and goodwill they had for each other. A saying she'd heard as a child in India came close at describing it: Deep as the seven seas.

Maya's investigative mind went to work. Could she recall any nugget of intelligence Lee had revealed about Rory that might be considered unusual? Yes, a talk about a month ago on a rainy day at Café Bolan might be worth considering.

Lee, her arm draped on the table, displayed a set of stone-studded, yellow gold bangles. Gold suited her. It spoke of her comfortable existence, almost a birthright. Unlike Maya, who had grown up in a middle-class household, Lee hailed from an upper crust family in India. *They have crores stashed away.* That was how people would describe the family's means, using the Indian numbering system. "I'm like anybody else," Lee would insist, always staying her humble self.

On that day, when their identical order of potato pierogi had arrived, Maya smiled, her appetite awakened by the rich scent of olive oil mingling with that of sour cream. She noted Lee's expression, which matched the drab sky outside the window, and her smile vanished.

Eyes downcast, her abundant eyebrows arched higher than usual, Lee fussed with the dumpling on her plate. Then, intuiting Maya's concerns, she lifted her chin and said softly, "Rory."

"Is something the matter?"

Lee's face tightened. "He got sad."

"Over?"

"No, SAD, Seasonal Affective Disorder. This is the season for SAD and sad he is. He's acting more grumpy than usual."

How well Maya understood the effect of weather on people. SAD, the winter blues, was normal in Seattle, a region far from the equator, where the light level diminished during the winter months. On the plus side, crooks hibernated in that period, which resulted in a lull in crime, making her case load lighter.

"Although Rory prefers to keep his condition hush-hush even to me," Lee said, "he's someone who's sensitive to weather. He sneezes if the sky is cloudy, dozes off if the air feels moist, and drops and breaks things as soon as it starts raining. He only eats carbs—rice and pasta. And I couldn't say this to anyone but you. There are days when he even loses interest in love making, doesn't come near me. Me—I'm the affectionate type."

Shouldn't he see a therapist? Maya would ask that question later at a suitable time; she didn't want Lee to be more upset. For now, she disguised her reaction with a pleasant face and replied in a lighter vein, "Why don't you guys jet off to a sunnier spot like Arizona, Palm Springs, or Hawaii?" She paused. "Which might boost his libido?"

Lee blushed. "Looks like we'll be able to lie in the sun, after all. And . . . have intimacy. Rory travels to Andaman Islands alone several times a year for business. This time, I insisted and he's taking me with him." She looked up at Maya. "And Alain? How's he doing?"

Maya felt close enough to Lee to answer, "He's always full of surprises. I gave him hugs and kisses and more when he presented me with a fresh flower bouquet yesterday for no reason. Along with that came a funny card that said, 'Life is never dahl when you're around.'"

Lee laughed. Then a small frown appeared on her lips.

The cell phone jangled. The scene vanished from Maya's mind. She snatched the phone at the first ring.

"I'm back, Maya," Lee said. "Sorry to have cut you off like that. But, well, I . . . to tell you the truth, I wish I was dead."

Startled, Maya said, "What?"

"Better to be dead than half alive, which is what I am. I'm made of nerves and tissues and tears. It doesn't matter if I eat or sleep or bathe. Each day hangs like a bloodied sword. Each moment is like swallowing a bottle of poison. I couldn't sleep at all last night—I'm terrified of darkness. It's pure hell."

Maya could only imagine the depth of her anguish. "Lee—"

"Let me tell you the rest. That night . . . at one a.m., seeing that Rory wasn't back yet, I went down to the hotel lobby and spoke with the manager on duty. He called the police. They had no clue, as you might expect. Back at our suite, I was a nervous wreck. Called my mother in Kolkata and woke her up. I justified it in my mind by thinking it's only an hour from here by plane. Talked to my sisters. Didn't hear from the police until around six in the next morning. They told me Rory was no more. 'What are you saying?' I asked. 'I don't believe it.'"

"And then—?"

"They said, 'Come with us, Mrs. Thompson, please, and identify the body.'"

Did Rory ever receive the good news about Lee's pregnancy? That he'd become a father? Maya couldn't quite ask the question. Facts about Lee's family popped up in Maya's mind: distinguished, with a long lineage; owner of a mansion, several fancy cars, a chauffeur and servants. "Is your family there? Anybody to look after you?"

"Yes. My mother and siblings flew here. They're kind and loving, but I can see it in their eyes, the shame they're drowning in, the weight they have in their chests. The news has hit Kolkata. I can only imagine the blame, mockery, and pumping they've been subjected to by their relatives and neighbors. 'Your in-law died near a whorehouse?' People will gossip for years to come."

"The Andaman cops," Maya said, "what are they doing?"

"The officer-in-charge found Rory's body. He and his technicians collected whatever on-site evidence they could gather."

The Indian system. Maya had spent her first seventeen years in India, with her mother, a schoolteacher, and her father, a well-known detective in the Kolkata police department. He was murdered when she was a child. Given that background, she knew a little something about how law enforcement worked over there. She went over the procedure in her mind. The officer-in-charge, upon returning to the local police station, would register a First Information Report or FIR, their initial step in recording a crime. Then he would send the report to a local judge. Lee's quavering voice drew her back to the present.

"The officers came to our hotel room, seized Rory's laptop and all the paperwork he had in his suitcase," Lee said. "What will they do with that laptop? Do you know?"

Maya noted Lee's worries. "The usual procedure is this. A forensic computing expert will make a copy of the hard drive and restore the deleted files. They'll look at Rory's e-mails, check the websites he'd accessed, and any other work he'd done on that machine. The laptop will be returned to you." She paused and asked, "Any arrests? In India, the police can detain a person without a warrant if suspected of a murder.

'Guilty until proven innocent.'"

"No arrests. An officer grilled me for hours, like I'm a principal in the crime." Lee's voice had a catch. "I'll be frank with you. I wish you were here."

"I'll fly over there to visit you as soon as I—"

"I need more than that. My sisters are doing all they can to make me comfortable. Can't complain about the hotel management, either. Like clockwork they respond to all my needs. They even did away with the reporters who were camping outside my suite, looking for a tip, a scandal, so they could blab to the media. You're the friend I feel most free to share my concerns."

"I'll alter my schedule to be able to stay with you for a while."

"Call me selfish, if you will, but allow me to make an offer. I'd like you to fly down here and launch a private investigation on retainer. How would that be?"

Such a stunning prospect. Maya hadn't quite expected it. She could almost see the angle of Lee's face, her strong chin and vivid, expressive eyes. Even when traumatized, Lee could focus on the present moment and stay true to her purpose. But then a somber thought crossed Maya's mind: Lee was too much in control.

The thought evaporated. *What has happened to you, Maya? You don't trust your friend? Of course, she keeps going, putting in order whatever she can, given the circumstances. She's that type of a person.*

"You mean that?" Maya asked. "You didn't call me right away."

"I apologize. I didn't feel strong enough to talk on the phone. I was incoherent. Glad you reached out to me. I mean it. I'd like you to come down here and catch that bastard."

Maya understood what Lee had in mind for her to do: Gather all the evidence while it was fresh. Break the case wide open, bring to light Rory's murderer, prosecute the felon, and clear Rory's name, with the result that Lee and her family could again stand up in the community. Her husband was an honorable man, a brilliant man with a vision. He ought to be remembered that way.

Maya remembered the importance of "First 48 hours," when looking for evidence in a murder case. It was already past that period. "You said the police were at work. Won't they object to my joining the hunt? It's a little late already."

"You work fast. You operate on your own. You'll catch up. The police—they're within the system—they drag their feet. I won't hold my breath waiting for them to apprehend the killer any time soon." More than a little dissatisfaction was evident in Lee's tone. She sounded isolated, desperate, and disturbed. "Out here they're called 'slow boat,' not without reason."

Maya understood. Although the criminal justice system in India was said to be improving, she heard numerous reports of corruption, bribery, torture, delays and failure of the judiciary. She'd experienced that first-hand when she was twelve. Her mother's flat in Kolkata was robbed, "house-breaking" as it was called. Upon returning home from a short excursion, they'd found a ransacked flat; all their possessions of any value—cash, jewelry, expensive rugs, and memorabilia—were gone. The investigative officers bungled the evidence from the crime scene and the case was never closed. It sat in a dead file and was there to this day, if Maya were to make a guess. Even prior to that—and it tore up Maya to recall that now—the mysterious, cold-blooded assassination of her father, Subir Mallick, had never been solved. That case, too, remained open. As did a huge wound in Maya's heart.

A part of Maya wanted to catch the next plane and stand by her friend's side. To help her deal with the mourning. To give her a hand so she could return to a daily routine. To hunt down that murderer and bring him to justice. But there were a few practical considerations, such as introducing a financial transaction in their friendship, which could cause friction.

Lee broke the frozen silence. "If you're hesitating, I can fully understand that. You have a mortgage to pay and it's not cheap living in Seattle. What if I pay your full fee, an extra allowance for an overseas assignment, and roundtrip airfare?"

"It's not the money, you know."

"I know, but I want to sweeten the deal, given the major disruption it'll cause you. I'll put you up in a nice big hotel suite with an ocean view. You won't believe how crazy beautiful the scenery is here."

"Wouldn't it cost you a fortune?" Maya asked.

"Only a fraction of what it would cost in the States. A close friend of my father, who owns several luxury hotels and other businesses in this island, is giving much of it to me almost free." She paused. "Perhaps you'd like to bring your administrative assistant here, too. I'll reserve a room for him at the same hotel and offer him a stipend."

"Hank would jump at the chance, but—"

"You'll be closer to your mother in Kolkata."

"My mom would like that."

"I know it's a long way for you to travel to an unknown territory," Lee said, "but you're cool-headed. You'll land on your feet, figure out who to talk to, who or what to avoid. Port Blair is well developed. It's easy to travel around by taxi and the mobile reception is acceptable."

Maya stared at a photo of her and Alain on the desk. They stood, smiling in her backyard in full summer, surrounded by yellow bursts of sunflowers. Alain had his arm around her waist. Maya almost smiled, feeling the same closeness she'd felt toward him on that occasion. Why hadn't Lee mentioned Alain? To leave him for an indefinite period would be the biggest sacrifice Maya would have to make: his warm eyes, his embrace, the love and closeness they shared. How could she leave him, with their relationship in a budding phase?

"It's the timing, Lee. I'm about to negotiate a new retainer agreement. Besides, Alain wouldn't want—"

"Don't listen to Alain."

"Why do you say that?"

"How long have you two been together? Only eight months? Let's talk about him another time. I don't need an answer from you right now. It's a major commitment, far away from home. But I've seen you go out of your way to help women in distress. Please think it over, Maya. I need you."

Maya considered her handicaps: First, of not being familiar with the Indian Penal Code and the criminal justice process. All her training and experience in crime analysis had taken place in the U.S. "I have another concern," she said. "I left India when I was a teenager. Thugs try to bypass the legal system over there. A PI has to be current on present laws in India, to the changes that have been introduced."

The line went quiet for a moment. In the pause, Maya considered the situation further. A second objection: In whatever country it happened, a homicide was always complicated and emotionally demanding. A man, alive and kicking one day, then someone did him in. His suffering might be over, but those who loved him would never be the same again. Maya, who had investigated homicide cases before, was aware of the difficulty of balancing the loved one's needs with the duties of a private detective, Lee being her best buddy.

A second objection: Maya's lack of confidence in herself—if she were to admit it—given that she was new to this game. This homicide case could be way over her head. She might put herself in harm's way by confronting the perpetrator in a land no longer familiar to her.

A third objection: Maya hadn't been able to keep up with all the changes India had undergone in recent decades, the tremendous economic growth it had experienced, much less that of Andaman. Settled in the last few decades, Andaman, the remotest state of India, operated like the newer version of an ancient land. The physical distance alone had a lot to do with the difference. Andaman was situated in the Bay of Bengal, closer to Myanmar than India. Maya, who had visited the place only once as a child, drew a blank when it came to any other details about it.

But most important of all: she'd have to overcome her inner reluctance to immerse herself in this tragic case, one so personal that it could compromise their friendship and tear her to pieces.

"Are you still there?" Lee asked.

"Yes." Maya didn't want to burden Lee with her insecurities. "If I were to take this case, I'd have to understand the legalities, what I can or cannot do, and whether or not the evidence I gather would be admissible in the Indian court."

"You might not have missed much." Anger amplified the torment in Lee's voice. "I'm told they're using the Police Act of 1861. It goes that far back. A sick joke, you might call it. At any rate, those are mere technicalities, aren't they? You work for Detectives Unlimited, which is headquartered in Kolkata, only an hour's flight from where I am. They're an efficient bunch, you've mentioned that yourself. Won't they be able to help you with legal and technical details, if needed?"

"I suppose. My boss gives me a free hand as to the types of cases I want to take and she'll respond if I ask for help, but . . ." The phone to her ear, Maya paced the room again, her mind caught in a tangle of thoughts. She ran her fingers through her hair; questions about Rory lurked in her mind. What was he about? Did she know him? Had she overlooked clues all along? Had Lee?

"You're quiet," Lee said. "What are you thinking about? Any other concerns?"

"Yes, I'll be frank with you. I don't want to lose you as a friend." Maya contemplated the word victimology, common in her profession. "During the course of my inquiry, I'll have to stick my nose in Rory's private affairs, dig around to put together his full story. I'll be forced to ask you questions about your marriage, Rory's sexual habits, and his financial status. I mean . . . I mean stuff you might not want to share and I . . . I wouldn't blame you if you didn't, if you tried to throw me out, never wanted to see me again. You see, I don't want our friendship jeopardized."

Maya mulled over her own situation with Alain. As tight as they were, there were a few things that weren't quite right. What if she ever had to confront what Lee was facing?

Quietude crept in, dense and impenetrable, but Lee cut through it. "I want the truth, my dear friend. I want to make peace with it, even if it wounds me. What can be worse than the shame and humiliation I'm going through? As for sensitive questions . . . our friendship is more durable than that. I'd rather confide in you than be interrogated by those cops. They're kinda scary. They give me horrible looks, like I've done something wrong. And the pushy media types. They seem to be bent on finding only negatives about Rory."

Maya pressed her lips together. These were only the preliminaries. Lee, sweet Lee. She hadn't been exposed to the cold, cruel criminal world—the deep pit she might have to descend into in search of the answers to a homicide. If Maya didn't take the case, Lee would be hurt, and that could end their closeness. Lee, who took such good care of Maya when she had to have minor surgery and Alain was out of town. Maya had even said to Lee, "I'll give you a kidney if you ever needed one." To which Lee had replied, "I'll give you my eye."

"This borders on being intrusive," Maya now said, "but I have to ask you a pretty personal question. Were you happy?"

"Of course. He was my one and only love."

Maya couldn't be sure. She decided to change the topic. "You're all alone Do you feel safe there?"

"Funny you ask. It has occurred to me—and my stomach is in a knot as I speak—that I might be the next victim of the crazy guy who took Rory's life."

Maya's shoulders shook. "You have reasons to believe that?"

"Yup. Yesterday evening, I . . . I took a long walk by myself along the seashore to take the evening air. No one was about. How perfect. Even so, as a woman, should I have ventured out alone in the evening? I suppose not. But I wasn't thinking. I went to where Rory might have strolled. I could almost see him, walking, contemplating, and looking at a distance, his hair blown by the wind. 'Rory,' I called out. 'Rory, my love.' He didn't answer. "Honey, can't you hear me?' Not a sound. I started crying. But being out there—the breeze, the lapping of the waves, the chirping birds, the white sand, and the open space—calmed me down. On my way back to the hotel and it was dusk by then, I heard footsteps. Coming closer and closer. You know how the air feels thicker when someone stalks you? How the sky changes color? How your heart starts drumming before you've sensed anybody's presence? I turned and gave a glance, hoping it was Rory."

"What did the guy look like?"

"He was a stranger, tall and well-built, with a hood over his head. I couldn't see his face. My eyes were full of tears and my knees were like jelly. I kept hearing the steady footfall, only felt a strong intention in him. My mind blanked out. By the time I turned around a second time, frozen but ready to scream, he'd disappeared into the shadows of a coconut grove.

"Spooked as I was, I managed to run the short distance, stormed through the hotel entrance, and shouted to grab the bellboy's attention. They sent out a search team, but the stalker couldn't be found. The manager said it was a lonely, harmless guy. I didn't believe him. It could have been a pervert or a murderer. I couldn't sleep that night and had to pop several pills."

Maya gripped the edge of the curtain. Raised by a single parent, she'd been fending for herself from a young age. She always looked about her. Lee, on the other hand, had always been well taken-care-of by her family. Comfortable and well protected, she didn't expect trouble. Nor would she know how to handle trouble. That stalker could come back again and this time he might strike.

"Leave Andaman and take the next flight back to the States, Lee. Call your travel agent or let me—"

"No, Maya, I can't leave Andaman until Rory's assassin is brought to justice. How can I? He loved these islands, felt at home here, this is where he spent his final days. Besides, if I leave, the police will drop the investigation and call it quits."

Maya couldn't blame her friend. Lee, the ever-devoted wife, held on to her husband's memories, like snuggling a silk pillow.

"I can see your point," Maya said, "but for safety's sake—"

"Rory joked a few days ago that he wanted to be buried here." That reference must have triggered a fresh wave of sorrow in Lee, for the line went soundless.

"Lee?"

"Sorry, Maya. Will you, please, give it some thought? I'm asking a lot. Be aware of what you'll be involved with. If you do, however, decide to accept my offer . . . I'll owe you big time."

"I'll give you an answer in a couple of days." Her throat tightening, Maya envisioned a murderer's tentacles reaching for her friend. "Meanwhile, don't go out alone, okay?"

FOUR

AFTER CLICKING OFF HER CALL TO LEE, Maya walked over to the window and looked up at the grayish blue November sky. Nearby, a motorcycle thundered, deafening her for an instant. Rory's image stood before her, a six-foot tall man, his intelligent eyes holding a spark. He had connections to India. He loved that country. Why was he murdered there? Might his interests offer any clues?

Always open to new adventures, Rory would fly anywhere in the world to meet with a prospective author and hash out the feasibility of a book. A trust-fund his grandmother had left him financed his trips, which he claimed as business expense. Lee, his wealthy wife, chipped in whenever necessary. India, even a brief mention of the country, brought a flush to Rory's face. He flew to India several times a year, calling it "a second home, a retreat of the soul." An editorial team based in New Delhi polished and proofread his manuscripts. Their work had proved to be low-cost but high quality.

Rory dubbed the country a "silver mine for ideas, know-how, and human-interest tales, a place I never quite understand and where I catch a bug at least once each time, a place that grabs me by the collar." He would even say, in that guttural voice of his and with a slight smile, that in his next life, if he was going to be reincarnated at all, he would like to be born in India. "Raised in a sunny spot, surrounded by a loving tribe, and adored like God Krishna—the prankster, the baby celeb."

Lee would give him a mock look of exasperation and fire back, "Do you have any sense how difficult it is to grow up there, if you're not born in a family of means, if you're not everybody's favorite baby God? It's better to admire the country from a distance, you know, what they call the 'idea of India,' the mythical space to philosophize over endless cups of chai. Better to visit once in a blue moon and call yourself an Indiaphile and let it go at that."

Lee might have been right. But now, she, too, was in trouble. Concern about her friend deepening, Maya picked up her cell phone.

First order of business: Examine the locale where the crime took place. As a homicide investigator Maya made it a point to analyze the site, which often provided her with worthwhile information. But she wasn't in Andaman yet. Hank, her young, imaginative, administrative assistant, would be able to do preliminary data-gathering on that beautiful but now cursed island on the Net. It sickened her to talk about it, but she called Hank, explained the situation, and tasked him the assignment. Hank should also start an online document, with the working title of "Rory Thompson Murder Case," where all the details of the investigation would be recorded.

She concluded by saying, "I'll meet you at the office in less than half an hour."

Within fifteen minutes, keys in hand, Maya rushed out the door. She wove through a series of streets coated with black ice, skidding. The temperature was well below freezing, a rarity for Seattle, and she came close to being hit by an SUV. *Better focus on driving, Maya. You won't be of any help to Lee if you're in a coma.*

Somewhat shaky, she arrived at a low-rise office building, Future Space, in the Green Lake district. She took the elevator to her office in #106, situated next to a row of other small firms, and paused at the door.

A brass plaque spelled out in bold black letters—Detectives Unlimited of Kolkata.

And below that in a smaller script—Maya Mallick, Private Investigator and Manager, Seattle Branch.

Most of the time, she got a charge when she viewed the nameplate, but not today. A vision of Rory filled her head: dressed in a pale blue shirt and navy trouser his lifeless body slumped over in an alley, red hair coated with dust. He'd left myriad unanswered questions behind him. A ripple of anxiety passed along her spine, as though she wasn't safe, either.

After looking around, she grabbed the keys from her purse, and stepped into the two-room office. Call it habit but she inspected it because of that dreadful feeling within. The cleaning lady had gone over the wood floor and dusted the file cabinets, the desk and the chairs. She'd straightened the oil painting that adorned the right wall. Through the smudge-free picture windows on the back wall, Maya viewed the evergreen courtyard. A handyman hired by the building superintendent swept up the scattered foliage debris, which somehow added to Maya's discomfort. She shrugged it off and walked into the back room.

Equipped with a desk, space for extra storage, a coffeemaker and a dwarf refrigerator, this snug back chamber served as a work area. Hank sat at his desk by the window, his hands on the keyboard; an empty coffee cup squatted in front of him. Dressed in a T-shirt and jeans, he sported sleek, combed-back hair. Two years ago, from a pool of a half-dozen candidates, she'd selected the mild-mannered MFA student, and they'd clicked. He had had no previous experience in the field of criminal investigation, but Hank, a short story maven, fit in his part-time role rather well. When not busy with his thesis—a set of linked short stories centered on dating—he acted as the first line of communication for her. He'd proved himself to be reliable and trustworthy.

"Morning," Hank said. The expressive blue eyes of the 24-year-old blond dominated his pale, narrow face.

Maya returned the greeting. Her voice was off, she could tell.

Hank stood up and gave her a hug. "How're you doing?"

Maya said, "Trying to cope."

"When you told me about it, I was like . . . I was shaking. Never met the man, but I know how close you were. I totally understand what you're going through."

"Can't believe I'll never see Rory again. Wish somebody would tell me it isn't true."

"You're really, like, upset," Hank said.

Maya walked over to the coffee maker, poured a cup, then regretted it—because she didn't feel like drinking it—and slipped herself into a chair.

"It happened when my father died. I was very young then. It's like losing parts of yourself. You keep asking, 'But why?' There's no answer."

"Anything I can do for you?" Hank leaned toward her, his forehead creased, eyes cloudy in sadness. "Get groceries or drive you somewhere—?"

"Thanks, Hank, that won't be necessary. I must pull myself up, stay strong for Lee. Better to keep busy with daily chores."

"Tell me more about Rory."

Maya took a deep breath. "He was a generous person, kind to his friends, and even people he didn't know. Every Christmas he sent boxes of books free-of-charge to the prison system for the inmates. They were returns but, even so, not every publisher will do that. The postage cost him a pretty penny." She drew a profile of the man and his publishing enterprise, now in its seventh year. Rory, who employed only a small staff, insisted on quality and produced a maximum of five hardcovers a year.

His latest title, *Poisoned Plate*, started with the health crisis and eventual discovery of wheat contamination in Afghanistan due to the undetected presence of a toxic weed in the crop. It dealt with other wheat crop challenges, such as the environmental impact the world over. According to a book critic, the volume had "as many hair-raising moments, as many twists and turns and misdirection as any fine thriller." Even though the book spent a few weeks on the *New York Times* best-seller list, an Afghan agriculturalist wanted to sue Rory.

Maya concluded by saying, "Regardless, Rory was always on the lookout for exciting ideas. His authors, who had excellent pedigrees, came from everywhere."

"Where did he find them?"

"He 'discovered' them in odd locales, the way film directors used to discover starlets at soda fountains." Maya went on to say that Rory loved to travel, his favorite phrase being, "Let's go." Once, when visiting Timbuktu and crossing a pasture, he met, due to an accident of fate, a smart, educated cattle herder reciting poetry in his native dialect. Rory approached him through an interpreter. The simple meanings of those poems enchanted him. With the poet's permission, he had them translated by a native speaker of English. Later, he'd publish them to high acclaim in a volume on domesticating animals. He would establish a fund for the cattle herder to go to college.

"He must have been popular with his authors," Hank said.

"Yes, I've heard it said that he listened to his authors and treated them well."

"A small indie publisher, who loved books, who took care of his authors, who stood up against the giants and made it, while being a good guy. How cool is that? If I had any talent in nonfiction, I'd have knocked at his door."

"You know what Rory used to say?" Maya replied. "'A few bucks and a few hours of your time, and a book opens a new life. Which is why I work so hard.'" After a few moments, she asked, "What do you have for me?"

Hank turned his laptop, giving Maya a full view of the computer screen. "Andaman—I like the sound of that name. These islands are tops of mountains that lie under the ocean. Can you believe that? Andaman is too beautiful, too cool and too isolated to be a site for a murder."

"Don't you think it'll be easier for a criminal to hide in a remote locale? Lee is there. Who knows what kind of danger is lurking nearby for her? I'm troubled about it."

"I feel for you."

Maya turned her focus back to the monitor. With the help of a stylus pen, Hank located Sumatra on a map of Asia and traced the Andaman and Nicobar Islands. They lay directly north, dotting the Andaman Sea, like emeralds broken loose from a necklace, on the east side of the Bay of Bengal. "There are five hundred of these islets," Hank said, "heavily forested, and, for the most part, deserted. Only about thirty are populated. Are there any major cities?"

As Maya studied the map, the only metropolis located in South Andaman jumped out at her. "Yes, there is, Port Blair," she said, pointing. "Often visited by Rory, and the scene of the crime, and now it's Lee's operational base."

"I don't know why, but Andaman feels a little creepy to me," Hank said.

"No surprise. Let me share with you what I studied in history books when I was growing up in India." Maya explained how the British Raj used Andaman as a penal colony for Indian freedom fighters. Thrown into tiny cells, they were given little food and forced to live under horrible conditions. "They had nothing to live for and no way to escape. Thousands died."

Hank sat back in his chair. "I wonder if the place is haunted. I always dug ghost stories. I could seriously go there. Did Rory talk much about Andaman?"

"He did, from time to time." Maya elaborated: On this visit Rory had been invited to speak at the Andaman Literary Festival as a celebrity publisher in what would be a Bollywood-style glittering affair. However, he made several forays a year to Port Blair on his own, his objective being to look over the work of a small commercial printing company. It did the printing, binding and shipping of his books. His last published tome was a hardback with a cover design of golden wheat and a varnish finish. "It looked quite rich."

"Andaman is an outsourcing destination? I had no clue. But then, I've never ventured outside the U.S. Sounds like he marketed his books worldwide?"

"Yes, and he was beginning to show profit." She paused. "Any calls?"

"Yes, a Ms. Irene Sanders is dying to know if you've reached a 'decision point.'"

"That boating accident case in Ballard. Irene Sanders insisted from the beginning that her husband was murdered—poisoned—by her son Nick. Nick, in turn, gossips she's crazy. The poor woman is fighting the battle alone."

"She's heard of the Sylvie Burton case we handled last year," Hank said. "She asked me all sorts of questions about the scientist who had self-immolated. She sounds like money."

"Correct," Maya said. "She's loaded. Money will not be an object. I was almost sure I'd take on her case. Now, with Lee in this terrible mess—"

"You have to revisit what's important to you?"

"Right." Maya stood up. "Which way do I go?"

"I can put Irene off for a couple more days, if you need a little extra time."

"I appreciate that. There's something else I want to share with you." Maya elaborated Lee's offer to Hank, for him to visit the island as well.

"Why sure, I'll take her up on it. What'll be my job there?"

"As far as I can see, you'll do research for me, like you do here. Document the crime, as necessary. Figure out the surroundings."

"I'm excited. I'll never have a chance like this. Will start making plans." Hank leaned and adjusted a framed new photograph on his desk. Maya's glance fell over the image of a young pretty Eurasian girl. Dressed in skimpy shorts and a décolleté top, she looked animated and held a mischievous smile. She looked at Hank with a question in her eyes.

"That's Sophie, twenty, a total babe." A brief smile lit up Hank's face; it put an extra sparkle in his eyes. "We're back together again—social media official."

"Congratulations."

"Sophie is part-Aussie and part-Thai," Hank said in a proud tone.

"This week she's visiting her father Down Under. She calls me almost every hour she's awake. She'll fly back tomorrow. She's a proper jetsetter. I'll have to catch up somehow."

"I'd like to meet her."

Hank's eyes shone in excitement. "I'll be sure to arrange that, boss."

Maya asked the usual question she had for him. "How's the short story coming?"

"I was doing surgery on the story when you called. A murder? Of someone you knew? That made me twitchy. I almost had a panic attack. Like they're coming at the whole writing community, at me, with their machetes."

Maya smiled. "No, they're not coming at you."

"You know this incident woke me up to a flaw in my writing," Hank said. "I don't do a good job with crisis, conflict, and obstacles, three biggies. I stink at them. When I stoop down to the nitty-gritty, I play safe. It's unconscious, involves more work, but I must dive into the right mental groove to make my stories sizzle."

"You're rethinking your craft?"

"Yes. I don't mean to sound cold and opportunistic, but this homicide has left me feeling anxious and inquiring—I realize that now—which is what I need to vent in every sentence I scribble."

Maya half-turned and waved. "Let me read the story when you're done."

"Perf, boss," Hank said, his trademark good-bye. "Perf."

Before starting her car in the basement parking garage, Maya summoned up her voice messages. Of the seven received, she clicked on the one from Lee.

"Guess what, Maya?" Lee's sad, weary, hysteric voice rang out. "My passport was stolen from my hotel room. I had hidden it in my suitcase inside a pair of jeans. Nothing else was touched—cash, credit cards or jewelry. Man, I'd rather lose all my money than my passport. Now I'm trapped. And I'm running a temperature."

Maya fell back on her seat. Without travel documents, Lee wouldn't be allowed to leave Andaman; she'd be a virtual prisoner. Was that a deliberate action on the thief's part? Again, Maya gazed around, saw no one. In this dank underground lot, she had a sense of being squeezed tighter and tighter into a closet, of not having enough oxygen to breathe and no soul to turn to for solace.

FIVE

Late that afternoon, Maya received a text from Alain saying he'd like to meet her at Pagoda for dinner. She smiled for the first time today as she wove through drizzly rain and drab evening sky toward Ravenna Boulevard. They both liked the food and the ambience of that neighborhood joint, a little off the radar of most people. If Alain at all suspected her of having had a trying day, he'd cup her face in his strong hands and suggest, with a twinkle his eyes, an activity—dinner out followed by a show, a visit to an art gallery, or a walk in the park.

They'd met eight months ago at the corner grocery store—somehow started talking—and had been inseparable since. Alain had been the best lover and most attentive and loving companion she'd ever had. They had the same taste in food—both were on a quinoa kick, preferred veggies galore and a daily ritual of green tea. Both shunned animal protein. As far as spare time went, they spent it attending concerts and readings, sharing gardening chores, or catching foreign flicks. Best of all, they helped mend each other's emotional wounds. Maya's stemmed from losing her father at an early age and having to fend for herself. Alain had lost his high-school sweetheart to a kidnapping incident.

Maya entered the restaurant. Her anxiousness faded in the calm ambience created by soft lighting, wood-beamed ceiling, and walls decorated with Chinese silk scrolls. A musty wine smell clung to the air. The waitress beamed a smile of recognition and whisked her to a corner table where Alain was already seated. Eyes low, he nursed a glass of water, his hands large and soft. The mere sight of him caused a yearning in her. As she stepped toward his table, he sensed her presence and rose, his face brightening. She couldn't help but notice a shadow in his eyes.

"Darling!" He gave her a hug and a kiss and waved at the chair facing him. "I figured it'd be best to spend time outside the house. I suppose you have a lot to tell me?"

"Right, yes." She wanted to pour out her feelings. About this morning, about enduring this calamity together, how much she'd missed him all day. She paused as the waitress ambled over and handed them their menus before drifting away. Amid the tinkling sound of silverware from a nearby table, her voice going scratchy at times, Maya related the details of her call to Lee. She left out the part about Lee's wish—more like an insistence—to retain her as a PI. That needed some back and forth and could wait for later.

Alain sat in stunned silence for a few moments. "Oh, Lord. It really was Rory?"

Maya reached out and clasped his hand. "I'm afraid so, dear. But if you ask me, we're far from knowing the full story."

"We saw them on most weekends and at least one night during the week. Together we vacationed in Maldives. He arranged the whole thing, the busy guy that he is. We were close—I mean, we knew all there was to know about each other, right?"

"This makes me wonder . . . can you ever know a person? I mean the total person—strengths, weaknesses, and all the peculiarities that make him who he is. We think we do. Let me ask you this: Did Rory ever pass on anything to you that might explain—?"

"Nothing that I can think of. All day long, I've been going over our conversations."

"Like most people, there were two aspects to Rory's life, business and personal." Maya touched the napkin on her lap. "His publishing house was often in the news and he became all bubbly when a new book came out, but his intimate personal life? I don't mean to press you, but did you two ever have a guy talk, where he opened up and shared?"

Alain took a swallow of his drink. "No, that'd have been out of character for him, reserved as he was."

"Never? I mean you must have chatted about your personal lives."

"Yes, there was that one time when we were having a beer at The Elysian. I told Rory how happy I was to have met you, how I wanted nothing more than to spend the rest of our lives together, go gray together."

What? A marriage proposal in the making? Maya could hear the longing in Alain's voice. He'd talked about wanting to settle down. Did she believe him? Was she ready? She wasn't sure of either. Although she cherished those words, in trying to respond, she choked and stayed mute.

"Rory narrowed his eyes and gave me an envious look," Alain continued. "That made me think. He had a gorgeous wife and he was doing what he wanted to do with his life. When I pressed him, he said, a bit poetically, 'Oh, the strangling vines of unfulfilled desires.' I asked him what he meant. Bigger house, expanded business, relocation, or kids? He didn't deny any of it, only looked uncomfortable and changed the subject."

Unfulfilled desires—that could have been all talk on Rory's part, a fleeting feeling, or a genuine concern. Maya wanted to explore the topic further, even though a discussion about him only intensified her sadness. "No inkling from Lee that they weren't happy. I mean . . . she shares a lot with me. Rory may have been hiding his frustrations from her and us." She drank from her glass. "He didn't have roving eyes, not that I ever saw. I mean he wasn't the type—at least not when he was with us. We'd have seen the signs, don't you imagine?"

"No argument from me."

Seeing Alain's face turn even more grave, Maya held her tongue for a few seconds. "What else did he talk about when he was alone with you?"

"Mostly routine business issues. First and foremost, concern about finances, which every small business has. Other than that, he would mention the difficulty of selecting viable exciting projects to work on, keeping his authors happy and productive, and pushing them to submit their manuscripts on time." Alain shrugged his broad shoulders. "How's Lee? How's she holding up?"

"She's not a complete wreck—the woman is too strong for that. She's staying her level-headed self. Even so, I can't be too sure. Andaman might not be a safe place for her. She would have to count on the local police force to keep her protected. Will they do their part? Her answers indicated to me that she wasn't convinced. Neither was I." After they ordered their food, she laid out the details of Lee's offer. When she was finished, she noticed Alain's eyebrows arching in astonishment.

"She wants to retain you?" Alain asked. "She's thought things through. That's a lot calmer and more together than I'd expected her to be. Do you suspect that she . . .?"

"No, not unless I see more evidence." Maya paused and concentrated on how difficult it'd be for her to be apart from Alain. "You know I can't think about going to Andaman for an indefinite period, not with you here. No, no, that's too much for me."

She studied Alain's face and expected to encounter a wall of resistance: *It's too far away and too isolated a location, not to mention dangerous. Lee's right. You need to think it over. If you have the slightest doubt, reconsider it.*

Alain nodded at the waitress who had come bearing their orders. Their attention shifted to the multitude of colors and flavors on the platters before them. Pangs of hunger gnawing at her stomach, Maya stabbed her fork into a tangle of hand-pulled noodles that was doused in sesame oil and sprinkled with ginger, scallion and seaweed. She took a small mouthful and gazed up at Alain. She liked listening to him on any topic. He was wise and had depth. His opinion mattered to her, even though she didn't always agree with him.

"Is Lee close to her family?" Alain asked.

"Not as much as she once was. She's been away from India for fifteen years. You change and grow during your absence, and the next time you meet your relatives, you don't relate to them the same way. I suspect that's what has happened to Lee. I'm sure she feels alone, in a strange environment, which is a lot to cope with, and I want to lend a hand. My heart is crying out for her." All the concerns bottled up inside her came tumbling out of her mouth. "But it's a daunting case in an unfamiliar location, far beyond what I've handled up to this point. And—and it'll take a while to delve into, not to mention the disruption it'll cause to have to travel. Can you imagine? More than a day's journey to reach there? I'll have to let go of the Sanders case, which has the potential of building up my business in this town. But the worst part is having to leave you here all alone."

Alain, deep in thought for an instant, dove into his plate of pillowy noodles loaded with mushrooms and topped with a soft-poached egg. His voice firm and low, he said, "Don't worry about me. Go ahead. Accept the offer."

Maya put her fork down. "Do you . . . mean that? You wouldn't mind?"

"Look, only you can console Lee and give her the kind of support she needs. You two are sisters. You're going through what she's going through. You feel the same urgency she does."

"I do, but . . ."

"My gut feel is you're the woman for the job. You got the smarts. Didn't you once tell me that a murder is a history book? The victim's antecedents are wrapped up in it. His habits, family, friends, work and hobbies could offer zillions of clues. The cops in Andaman have no idea whatsoever who Rory was and what he was about. They'll conduct a routine check and go nowhere." He took a sip of water, then put the glass down. "By the way, Rory had a friend in Andaman, I remember him saying. If so and if you can locate him, he might be of help to you."

"A friend? Interesting."

"However painful this is for you, however difficult in terms of execution, you'll do a good job," he said. "Your approach is rational when it comes to probing a crime. That's what I've noticed. One of your appealing traits is you're enterprising. As for the Sanders case, let it go. Now that you're known in the Puget Sound region, there'll be others."

"And yet—"

"A secondary point, this would be the adventure of a lifetime. You're drawn toward action and danger." He pierced a mushroom with his chopstick. "I did my homework this afternoon. Read a series of articles on the internet about Andaman."

"What all did you find?"

"It's one of the few places left to explore in India. Port Blair, the capital, is touristy and offers a host of amenities, but the outer islands are another matter. Some are undeveloped and remote, reserved only for the Andamanese, world's oldest indigenous tribes. Yes, they go quite far back and only a few of tribes are left. Believe it or not, some live in the forest, use bows and arrows to hunt and kill. Others live in huts, caves, or tree houses. You'll need special permission to visit their areas. Of course, you're not going there as a tourist and you might not even have the time or inclination to take on any side trip, but I must say overall that this is a most unusual opportunity. You might regret it if you pass it up."

A well-informed response considered from diverse angles. He wasn't trying to be obstructive. Given that they'd never been apart since they met, she asked, "What about us?"

Alain searched out her eyes. "I have a confession to make, Maya. I'll be on an overseas assignment for several weeks myself. I didn't want to travel, not at this juncture, but it's company business. When least expected."

Company business. Maya thought about what that meant. Alain

worked for a nonprofit that refurbished hand-me-down laptops and tested them for reuse, then sent them overseas, to be donated to orphanages in third-world nations. He'd visit these orphanages and teach computer skills to the children. *"You should see how quickly these boys and girls pick up the skills,"* he'd say. *"How rewarding to work with them."* And no, he'd insist, it wasn't E-waste dumping. Rather it was straight charity work, satisfying at that, humanitarian effort that changed lives.

Maya squeaked out, "Where to?"

His eyes wavered. "Borneo."

Rainy, rugged, a remote undeveloped island, home to wild animals, crocodiles and modern-day pirates. All Maya could remember reading about Borneo. That and occasional outbreaks of terrorism that had cropped up in the eastern region in recent years. "My job is risky, but yours is, too? Isn't it a bit dicey for Westerners to travel to parts of Borneo right now?"

"I don't want to go, but my boss—"

"When are you leaving?"

"Tonight. I'll be in cell phone contact, as always. You can leave messages."

So soon? Disquiet pricked at her from inside, but she managed to say, "At least you won't be too far away."

"That's right," Alain said. "It's a blessing of sorts that we'll each be focused on our assignments and be apart, but not too far apart. I'll join you in the Andaman chain at the first opportunity. I won't have a moment's peace until then. Yes, I'll help you in any way I can. Rory was dear to me, too." He paused and checked her face. "You look upset."

Did he really owe her more of an explanation? Her logical side said no. Her emotional side, however, remained raw and tender. "Didn't mean to burst out like that."

"You've had a trying day. You haven't even eaten, have you?"

Maya gave a low yes, dug into her food and finished it without tasting the flavors. They carried on a conversation about routine matters—he would have to pack; she would drive him to the airport; he would call as soon as he arrived. All the while, it crushed her insides, the fact that they'd soon part, the fact that he was encouraging her to travel to Andaman. Why did he seem big on it? Her rationalization: because he was going away himself that he wasn't concerned with her departure. Chances are, he already had his bags packed.

She regarded him now. He wore a closed expression that concealed how he felt inside, this even-tempered man. *I don't have worrying genes in my body*, he'd said to her once. *I thank my father for that. He chattered away at the nurses from his hospital bed right up to the end.*

They ordered her favorite dessert: sticky rice with mango. Maya viewed the plate, which contained a mound of shiny glutinous rice topped with coconut sauce, flanked by luscious yellow mango slices. They had a ritual of sharing a dessert—their forks meeting each other—to end the meal as a couple. Maya took only a small bite of the dessert, which laid flat on her palate. She couldn't stay seated.

She retrieved her phone, excused herself and exited the restaurant, colliding with the door on her way out. Standing on the sidewalk, Maya texted her boss Simi and mentioned Alain's impending business trip. A routine update to her life. As she shoved the phone back in her purse, she noticed the emptiness of the street and shivered.

She reentered the restaurant and bumped into the reception counter. *Not again.* She drifted back to the table, feeling the flush on her cheeks and the burning behind her throat, but managed to collect herself. She chatted with Alain for a few more minutes and paid their bills. Exiting the restaurant, they headed for their cars, the air sharp as a blade on her forehead. Evening had descended; the trees had lost their shapes. It would be easy to bump into one and bruise yourself. Even the night sky was painted in a deeper, bluer hue than usual, the overall effect unsettling.

Alain put his arm around her, a loving look in his eyes. Back to being who he was, his pleasant scent comforting, making the pavement feel more solid, snatching her away from her over-thinking mode.

The tension subsided. Her legs became looser. The edges of the landscape softened about her.

SIX

THREE DAYS LATER, AT ABOUT ELEVEN-THIRTY A.M., prior to landing at Port Blair's Veer Savarkar International Airport, Maya looked down below at the alien seascape through her plane window. A deep, majestic ocean spreading out a turquoise canvas; sunlight sparkling over the waves; a chain of islands surrounded by greenery and golden sand; the home territory of Rory's killer and the most isolated spot she'd ever been.

Her chat with Simi, conducted on the evening before her departure from Seattle, arose in her mind.

"I must warn you about Andaman," her boss had said. "The roads are narrow. Be careful if you drive. Don't stay out late on the beach—not enough lighting. Be aware that there aren't too many places where you can exchange foreign currency. Most important of all—the Andamanese like to preserve the good reputation of their island. They have a saying, 'Andaman likes to keep its secrets.' If something goes wrong, people may not tell you about it; you're an outsider. Not an easy place as far as investigative work goes."

Maya walked toward the Customs. Having spent a day on the plane, with stopovers in Amsterdam and Chennai, she found it a relief to breeze through the formalities. At least that part was easy. A little before noon, sleepy-eyed, she entered the crowded arrival hall. There she heard the hum of languages that reminded her of her childhood and smelled the salty sea air mixed with body odor. She rolled her heavy suitcase down toward the exit, without any expectation of being met by anyone. With

Rory's funeral service taking place this morning, Lee would be occupied. Maya had already assured her friend on the phone that she'd reach the hotel on her own.

Therefore, it put her on alert when a smiling, white-uniformed taxi driver, acting as though she was expected, pushed toward her and boomed a namaste greeting. He gestured with a hand, while grabbing her luggage with the other. "This way, Madam."

Clean-cut, of medium-built, the thirty-something man spoke fluent English and had a genial expression on his face. His features were unremarkable—he'd be invisible in a crowd, but for a hairdo of a tall cool pomp. Beneath his thick eyebrows nestled a pair of shiny eyes that made full—maybe too full—eye contact.

"Who sent you?" Maya asked, her tone guarded. "What's your name?"

"Nobody. Welcome to A and N, that's what we call the Andaman and Nicobar Islands. Latitude eleven. Our winter is mild and pleasant, as you can see, the best time for a visit. You can even swim in the ocean. Areas that are crocodile-infested are marked." He leaned toward her. "My name is Kal. My taxi is a Maruti Swift. It's less than two years old, metered and has A.C. I'm passenger friendly. Any humor I provide is free. Are you ready?"

"Yes," she said, the cloying heat of the island subduing her, and wishing to reach her hotel. As they walked outside the terminal, a few eager cabbies pressed closer, but she waved them away. Blinking in the blinding sunlight, taking in the fresh air, and registering shrill honking of cars, she named her destination to Kal.

"We'll be there in no time. Let me also mention to you that our island is known for its colors. The ocean is various shades of blue, depending on where you are and the time of day. Our forests are called 'green gold'. The sky changes from orange red to violet blue. We have three-hundred species of birds, from white-headed sterling to purple moorhen."

Maya settled herself on the backseat and took note of the colorful details in her head. She didn't sense any immediate threat from this talkative cabbie but noted the taxi registration number and texted it to Hank. The vehicle zoomed out of the airport and bumped along a palm-lined, wide boulevard on which cars, buses, trucks, bicycles, and auto-rickshaws jostled with each other.

A large billboard proclaimed a tourist slogan: Emerald Blue and You. Another billboard said: Untouched and Irresistible Forest Greens.

"How was your flight, miss?" Kal asked.

"Too long, but pleasant otherwise." She'd never liked being called a generic "miss." She gave him her first name.

"Maya—lovely name, an important concept," he said, adjusting to the slowing traffic. "In our culture, maya means illusion, wisdom, and magic. Philosophers in ancient India said, 'It's all maya,' which means don't take anything too seriously. Our material world, like this traffic congestion, is transient."

Her parents had chosen that name for its deeper connotation.

"Would you like a scenic tour of our town, Miss Maya? It'll take only a few extra minutes."

"Why, sure." He'd pump up the meter. So what? She needed to be orientated to this town. That is, if she were to have any chance of bringing Rory's killer to justice. Soon Kal veered off the main road. Perched on the backseat, cooled by the air-conditioning, she looked out the window. Port Blair rolled out before her. At first blush, the city appeared to be neither a backwater, nor a modern resort, but suspended in an in-between state. Paved roads, pruned bushes, and boxy modern buildings greeted her eyes, as did a deer wheeling toward a dense jungle, suggesting that civilization ended not far from here.

The vehicle wound its way along the seashore. Maya's head cleared at the glimpse of turquoise water. A peacock strutted on the beach, its plumage spread like a ceremonial fan, displaying colors such as, indigo, jade, lilac and peach. A red-throated bird, with olive plumage, chattered on a tree branch. Sidewalk vendors sold fresh coconut water and coconut meat. Children tossed balls back-and-forth under palm trees swaying in the wind. Maya had the feel of being enchanted.

"Your first visit to Andaman?" Kal asked, navigating the twisty, narrow streets. "You're from the U.S.?"

Eyes on a far-away white sailing boat, she gave a low yes to both questions. She could see herself through his eyes. A Westerner, who claimed to be of Indian origin, paying a pilgrimage to her ancestral land; one who was a simpatico and a good tipper, but demanding of service, pissed off too easily, and too much in a hurry. One who was here to do the town, shop for mementoes, and sunbathe. No, she wished to convey to him that her reasons for being here were different. Not to hunt for artifacts, shoot pictures, or take in the beaches, but to figure out a horrific crime. An entrepreneur loved by his community had been stabbed to death for unknown motives. His wife, her best friend, was in trouble. She had a hard time sitting still.

"I'm from the mainland." Kal shot her a glance over his shoulder.

There was more to this chauffeur, if his clever eyes were any indication. After having spent her youth in Kolkata, Maya was aware that India was a land of contacts. As an investigator, she understood that to accomplish your goals here, you must be in touch with the right person, who would pull strings for you. You might have to grease palms. And taxi drivers were reputed to be purveyors of facts and gossip, the tabloid journal of a town. Quite often, they created links. She must strike a friendship with him—standard operating procedure.

"What brought you here?" she asked.

Kal yelled at another driver cruising in the opposite direction and waving. Both slowed. A torrent of banter in a language unfamiliar to her flowed, followed by a fury of wild hand gestures. In the end, they exchanged ear-to-ear smiles.

After regaining his speed, Kal replied to her. "Worked in IT in Ahmedabad. I was a nerdy computer programmer, a cubicle professional, as they called me. When my company folded, I relocated here. Couldn't find a coding job right away. Started driving a taxi. Twelve hours a day. Not much money, but no boss. I didn't have to spend long hours poring over the computer code, trying to figure out the glitches, wasting my eyes. Living in a calm, beautiful place close to a tropical rainforest did me wonders. I was reborn, you might say."

"How is Andaman different from India?"

He smiled. "Andaman is—what you might call—a mini India. People of different faiths, speaking funny tongues, people from places you've never heard of, call this archipelago their home. One major difference is: it's a classless society. I'm sure you know the Indian attitude. 'Are you a Brahmin, fella? If not, clear out. I won't speak with you. I won't even want to breathe the same air as you do.' In A & N, my adopted home, we're pretty much equal. We cross paths with everyone. Except for the few with deep pockets, who stick to each other, throw exclusive parties, argue about how to pile up even more money and how to hide it from the government. The rest of us, plebs, we're happy with what little we have."

"Are there any drawbacks to living here?"

"Yes, an abundance of tongues, thirty-three when I last counted. They buzz in your ears—Hindi, Bengali, Tamil, Telugu, many tribal languages and English, of course. They can make you feel stupid and helpless. Most people either speak Hindi or at least understand it. Often in public you start a sentence in one language, continue in a second, and finish in a third. You can keep your secrets that way." He paused. "This is a different society. I mean, different. You must follow its rules."

Her ears perked up. "What rules?"

"For you to find out, Madam."

She could see challenges before her, circuitous as the road on which she now traveled. Soon they approached a series of villas grouped around a modern building, a glass-and-chrome job, with a dazzling saffron exterior. The tri-color Indian national flag, mounted on its top, fluttered in the wind.

"What are those villas used for?" Maya asked.

"That's where our literary festival took place," Kal said. "It was a glitzy affair, included music and dance performances, as well as panel discussions. Brought readers, writers, students, and thinkers from all over the world. For those who were lucky enough to have registered, it must have been a once-in-a-lifetime thrill. The rest of us were glad for the business. We had no time to sleep, ferrying as we did those who landed here and couldn't wait to get to the beach."

An image of Rory appeared in Maya's mind's screen; her heart ached. "Did you ever give a ride to Rory Thompson?"

The happy-go-lucky cabbie's voice tightened. "No, Madam. I did hear about his murder, which was all over the news. May his soul be blessed. May he rest in peace." He cruised past storefronts vending saris—a forest of colors and designs—and announced, "We're entering the business district."

Maya viewed an ornate, triangular-shaped temple, characterless office plazas, bustling open-air markets, houses made of brick and cement, teenagers engrossed in their cell phones, a gent's saloon, roaming goats, and the Good Women's Gun Shop. The smell of batter-fried onion rings rose from an open stall. On the pavement, women vendors squatted and sold piles of tiny fresh fish. How familiar the customary dust, din, scents, and rhythm of India and the cloud of near chaos that often settled over an Indian street. But the similarities ended there. She could feel the presence of something inscrutable in the atmosphere of Andaman. This wouldn't be an easy place to chase down the perpetrator of a crime.

"The funeral mass for Rory Thompson is being held this afternoon," Kal said. "I heard that on the radio."

Maya felt a flutter in her stomach. "How far are we from that church?"

Kal went silent, negotiating the cab through heavy traffic. Maya went over the details of the service and the burial in her mind. She pictured Rory as he was put in the ground to his final resting place: the coffin lowered into a pit and covered with soil, then being sprinkled on top with flower petals by the mourners. She almost heard the church bells, absorbed the priest's deep sad voice and experienced the solemn atmosphere. Hymns, reflections, organ music, and sermon followed, as did private prayers. Despite her wish, Maya couldn't have been in attendance. Her flight had arrived a little too late for that. Besides, Lee had informed her earlier on the phone that only the primary family of the victim and those with prior security clearance would be allowed at the funeral.

"We're not too far from the church," Kal replied a moment later.

Maya glanced at her watch. Past one o'clock. The service should be over by now. Despite that, she wanted to be there. "Can we take a detour and drive by there?"

"No, Madam. They don't allow too much through traffic in that area. Had to do with suspected arson in the church a few months ago, which caused property damage. It's a blessing that no one was hurt. But they haven't caught the guilty party. Can I take you straight to the hotel?"

"Let me break this one rule today, okay?"

"Very well. I'll slow down and you can have a look." Kal took a U-turn, drove for a few minutes, slowed, and stopped in front of a church.

Maya looked through the passenger's window to take stock. The well-maintained, fort-like façade of the church, one that could hold a few hundred people, exhibited a fusion of Hindu and Christian architectural motifs. That included a pillared entrance and several stained-glass windows in popular jewel tone colors. If Maya were to guess, the flooring had been done in marble. A green lawn extended in the front.

"They're leaving," Kal said.

Indeed, a crowd of funeral guests streamed out in a hushed procession. The first batch of twenty bereaved appeared to be publishing professionals who had stayed on to attend the service. The next ten were friends and relatives of Lee; Maya guessed from their anguished appearance. Among them were an older, Irish-looking couple, perhaps Rory's parents, who had flown from Pennsylvania after receiving the news. And now Maya spotted Lee. Glassy-eyed, wearing a white sari—the widow's garb—her abundant black hair tamed into a chignon, she accompanied the couple. She walked as though in a trance, her body slimmer, posture bent, sorrow slowing every move she made, looking more miserable than Maya had ever seen her. All three drifted toward a parked car.

Weepy-eyed, Maya settled back in her seat. Her gaze picked up another trickle of people emerging from the shadows cast by the church building. A late-fortyish European woman escorted by an aide or relative strode toward a vehicle. Face aristocratic oval and complexion radiant, she exuded confidence born of wealth. She was tall, in fact, quite tall, and sported mid-length brown hair gathered into a ponytail. She held a disdainful expression and didn't seem burdened by woe. Only a tad weary. Decked out in severe form-fitting black, she'd pulled off a fashionable, even a romantic look, by wrapping a scarf—a sheer lavender cloth flecked with gold—around her throat. One thing became clear. Stylish, distinctive, and a woman of obvious social standing, she belonged to the high society in New Delhi or Lahore, not this remote, nearly forsaken island. Who was she and what brought her to Rory's funeral?

Maya took another look at her regal posture, expression of detachment, and way of carrying herself. She retrieved her smartphone and snapped a picture of the woman. As she drew closer, Maya observed: She wasn't married. Maya could tell her own kind.

"Do you know her, by any chance?" Maya asked Kal.

"You noticed?" Kal smiled. "They say a woman figures out another of her tribe far quicker than a man ever could. Her name is Esme Peterson. That tall man walking with her is her younger brother Jorge."

Esme Peterson: In her iPhone, Maya tapped in that name. She paid close attention to Esme's male companion. Pale, fair-skinned and frowning, the man resembled Esme but didn't appear to be as impressive or as sharp. In fact, he seemed rather clueless. He took orders from his sister, if Maya were to make a guess.

"Not sure I've figured out that much about her." Maya made her voice light. "You can fill in the rest, if you like."

"Esme Peterson, an elite member of the Port Blair society, lives in a sea-side mansion with her brother. To me, elite means complicated, lots of headaches. In IT we used to talk about baklava code, have you ever heard of that? It means a tangled set of instructions, layer upon layer. When you try to debug the instructions, you can't help but be frustrated.

What we have here is, in my opinion, the social equivalent of that."

How Maya would like to meet that enigmatic woman and have a long chat. To listen to her view of the town, how it operated, who the important players were, and what the complications were, if any. But she was aware of Indian protocol. Without proper introductions, she would go nowhere.

"Why did she come to the funeral mass?" she asked Kal, looking for a thread of connection.

"Her Highness could have been there for any number of reasons. It doesn't have anything to do with the funeral. She does charitable work in these islands. The idle rich trying to amuse themselves, you might say. She drops lots of rupees for her favorite causes, all of which are channeled through the church."

"What causes?"

"Rescuing women from being beaten up every night by their drunk, asshole husbands."

Maya made a note of that, too. *Have Esme been abused herself?* In minutes, the cab drew up in front of an oceanfront hotel. Named Jahar Palace, the villa, with acres of greenery around it, exuded a feeling of lavishness. On one side of the gravel driveway rested flowerbeds in pink and purple. There was also a lounging area set with benches and a barrier of lofty trees with leathery green leaves and egg-yellow blossoms. On the other side stood a tennis court. The place had the aura of being private, if a little too secluded, even a little eerie.

Kal deposited her luggage at the check-in desk of the hotel lobby and uttered cheerio, then hurried out through the main door, only to vanish in the greenery. Strange—he hadn't handed her a business card or try to solicit more business, as taxi drivers were wont to do.

She asked the desk clerk, "Do you know that taxi driver by any chance?"

"Why? Did you leave anything behind?"

"No."

"Okay, good. Please don't be concerned but our biggest headache here is tsunami. You know about tsunami? My son recites his school lesson this way. 'High waves caused by earthquakes under the ocean, bringing along strong winds that hit the shore and destroys it all.' If you see any dead, uprooted tree, chances are that's due to a tsunami. We have a saying, 'A tsunami reshapes your life like nothing else could.'"

"Thanks for warning me," Maya said, alarmed.

Once the registration was completed, a bellhop escorted Maya to her quarters, a large suite on the second floor, where he stowed her luggage in the closet. The suite was neat, and all the surfaces were clean and polished. She began scanning the layout, which she always did upon her arrival at a hotel. Her investigative self would demand that. Could anyone break in here? Yes, they could. The doors weren't exactly sturdy, and a petty thief could access the windows with a ladder from outside.

Maya put those concerns out of her mind and traversed her suite, which consisted of a bedroom and a spacious living room. The mellow citron-hued walls of the living room were decorated with a pair of scenic paintings. Past the brocade sofa in reds and oranges and harmonizing chairs stood a desk equipped with pen, paper and note cards.

A hand-written card from the hotel manager said: "This is your home. Let me know if you need anything. Biren Ghar."

A note from Lee lacked her usual strength and beautiful penmanship. In it she mentioned she was staying at the Emerald Villa about half-a-mile away and apologized for not being there to welcome Maya. Rory's parents were there for the service. Rory's mother, beside herself in shock and regret, had suffered a nervous breakdown. Lee needed to comfort her in any way she could. "Let's text each other," Lee had written before signing.

Maya held the note, feeling the pulse of her friend, and texted a reply, saying she'd be in touch several times a day. Following that, she left a message of safe arrival to her mother in Kolkata.

As she put the phone down, she smelled a pungent, sweet aroma. Her attention went to an arrangement of mixed tropical flowers—intricate enough as to remind her of the difficult road ahead of her—that graced the coffee table. A card tucked inside the bouquet was signed by the florist named Flower Lady of Andaman. She'd addressed Maya by name, the words "Welcome" embossed in green script. What a lovely gesture. How did the Flower Lady of Andaman hear about her arrival?

Maya could see why Rory loved it here. At least on the surface, the town was hospitable, providing warm attention to visitors as well as offering small personal touches.

She resumed her tour. The bedroom was furnished with a queen-sized bed and an ornate dresser. Made up with velvety white linen, the bed was loaded with fluffy white pillows. On top of the pillows—and this captured her breath—lay a withered, thorny, long-stemmed rose. How odd. Who put a withered flower there? Couldn't be the hotel staff. She picked up the stem and dropped it on the dresser. The mirror in the dresser showed a duplicate image of her with the dead flower. Torment twisted inside her; she called the hotel manager.

"This is a first, Madam," Biren Ghar breezed on through the phone. "I'm so sorry. We don't put dead flowers on our guests' beds. It could be the work of the maid's young son who, I'm told, plays pranks. I've never caught him. I'll put security on alert. From now on, I'll have a second maid double-check your room." He apologized again and concluded with, "Your dinner is on us. Please call the room service when you're ready."

As she thanked him and rang off, Maya recognized the disbelief in her own voice. She opened her suitcase and began unpacking. The doorbell buzzed. To her ears, plugged from a day-long flight, the sound vibrated with an ominous quality.

Who could it be?

She cut through the length of the suite; her heart palpitated. "Who is it?"

"The police."

She frowned and hesitated, then opened the door a crack.

A heavyset policeman loomed before her.

SEVEN

MAYA SCRUTINIZED THE WELL-GROOMED, DIGNIFIED OFFICER, whose graying moustache spoke to his high rank in the Indian police service. Dressed in a khaki uniform and polished brown shoes, he had an insignia on his shoulder. A matching beret couldn't shade out his sharp eyes, which regarded her with interest.

He flashed his badge. "My name is Mohan Dev." He pronounced each word with eager politeness in British-accented English. "I'm the Inspector General of Police for the Union Territory of Andaman and Nicobar Islands. Our motto is 'With you, for you, always.' I've spoken with Mrs. Thompson. She's told me she has retained you, that you'll work on this case as a private investigator, and you'll arrive today. It's my pleasure to welcome you."

Maya cringed inside. The vision of Dev's uniform flooded her with long-ago memories of Indian law enforcement. Her father—a highly regarded police detective known for his compassion toward victims—was assassinated when she was a child. Years later, as a teenager, she'd had to deal with the authorities after a burglary—a "house-breaking"—at her mother's flat. They never gave her a straight answer, if they bothered to answer her at all. In her follow-up contacts with the police, she'd continued to encounter an infuriating attitude of indolence, arrogance, and corruption. *With you, for you, always.* With her feet on Indian soil, in the remote outpost of Andaman, she wondered: Would this officer of the law be any different?

"Please call me Maya." She recomposed her face, motioned the inspector to an armchair in the living room, and dispensed with the salutation.

"You can call me Mohan."

An analysis of the crime as it happened was on top of her list. She asked him to nail down the time and location of the murder, two high priority items for her. In reply, he mumbled about the "alley of tricks," but couldn't offer the specific time of death.

"How was Rory murdered?" she asked.

"It was a nasty attack, Maya. Madness, pure madness." His voice grave, Inspector Dev related how a stranger, wielding a light weight, sharp-edged machete, struck Rory from behind, hitting him in several vital places. Judging by the precise slashes, the attacker was adept at using a machete.

"Was there a fight?"

"Nothing to indicate so. My guess is Mr. Thompson was unaware, with little power to resist the blunt force. He suffered—and I saw the horrific sight myself later—large lacerations to his face and fatal wounds to his head and back. One needs a strong constitution to bear it. We ruled it a homicide."

Maya sat stunned for a minute. "Do you think he might have been targeted? None of his valuables, except for his smartphone, was stolen, which suggests a personal motive. Rory's not the type to have enemies. It's also puzzling that the murder happened far away from his hotel. From what I understand, you don't have a high crime rate here, do you?"

"You're right," the inspector responded. "Few bad things happen in Andaman—mugging, pickpockets, occasional credit card scams are about it. We have one of the lowest cognizable crime rates in India and we'd like to keep it that way. Our Andamanese people aren't an aggressive lot. A few nut cases, alcoholics and political dissidents make their home here. That's about it. This homicide has damaged our good name. And the media—those scumbag crime reporters and bloggers—they're pounding at our door, looking for an update and a cute quote. 'A visiting American publisher, an international star, chopped to death?' they're saying. 'When will you have this sorted?'"

"Yes, when will you?" Another priority for Maya was to create links between the victim and his surroundings. "And who have you interrogated?"

"We've interrogated more than thirty people Rory Thompson had contact with at the literary festival. They included both authors and festival organizers. We've ruled them out. If we look beyond the festival, the question we might want to ask is this: Could this be the work of a disgruntled author trying to take revenge? Well, that could be. But like I said. No one has given us any reasons to be suspicious."

"You've spoken with Lee Thompson." Maya inhaled deeply. "Her alibi?"

"We did receive Lee's testimony. Our security cameras show that she was in her hotel room all evening, except for a fifteen-minute period when she went out of the premises."

Lee hadn't mentioned that brief absence of hers. In her astonishment, Maya leaned back in her chair. She decided to switch directions, obtain an answer to the "First Sighting" question instead. "Who first saw the body?"

"The son of one of the prostitutes," the inspector answered, "a boy of five, quite early in the morning."

"And the timing of Rory's death?"

"Around three a.m."

"Is that the location where the murder happened?" Yet another important part of her research. She'd like to visit the site. "Any drag marks or other signs on the body?"

"We don't know. No drag marks."

It pained her to ask, "Did any of the women recognize Rory?"

Inspector Dev stretched out his legs. "He looked familiar, they said, but how could they be sure? Countless foreigners pass through their doors."

At least the answer wasn't in the affirmative. "The women must feel threatened by all the grilling. Did you give them enough assurance that they wouldn't be punished if—"

"Are you here to give me the third degree?" A small, sarcastic smile played on Dev's lips. "My constables know how to deal with them."

The constables might have taken their questioning too far, Maya surmised.

The inspector noticed Maya's distressed face and said, "This is your first visit to these islands? You're operating in the mode of a big city in the West? As you will soon see, the Andamanese rise with the sun, live their stories, and retire as the sun sinks into the ocean. All activities must be squeezed in between. They follow an ancient rhythm here which, I'm sure, you're not used to, and I'm not, either. I'm from the mainland. For years I was posted in the great capital of New Delhi. Transferred here three years ago. My wife is very understanding and doesn't complain much. But my kids haven't adjusted well. They miss their friends. They miss the traffic congestion. They miss the polluted air and even the dirt of Delhi. Can you believe that?"

Maya's travel fatigue prodded her to end this conversation. "Mohan, I've been on an airplane since yesterday morning. I'm as anxious as anyone to know more, but I—"

The inspector's forehead creased, making it obvious he wanted to close the subject too. "Why don't you go have dinner, Maya? We offer several excellent cuisines here—Thai, Burmese, Bengali, South Indian—and the freshest seafood ever to delight a person's mouth." He kept speaking, as Indians were wont to do, giving the low-down on the local dining scene. "First rule of dining—you must try our lobster. It's succulent, it's a treat. Often captured by hand-picking. There's this little spot called Lobster Mania that my family loves. We find all sorts of occasions to celebrate there."

Maya adopted a confident posture and peered up at him. "I have no doubt the cuisine is fine here, Mohan, but this is a brutal murder of someone very close to me. I have a personal stake in this matter, and I'd like to put all my effort on this case. Look, I bring something to the table. Rory was a friend. I have knowledge of his background. And, I've had previous experience in dealing with homicides."

"No one will question your competence, Maya."

Maya stared out the window. The blue calmness of the ocean hid the currents below the surface. The old-school inspector was politely brushing her off. As a woman, she was at a gender disadvantage. As a newcomer and a private detective, she wouldn't be trusted with classified dossier. Such was the police culture in India. She choked, stung by the extra layer of obstacles, but overcame it.

"And yet you're hesitating to divulge more," she said. "It's been almost a week since the episode, and you have no suspect. The media—don't you wish they would stop bugging you about this celebrity murder?"

The inspector gave a tiny reluctant nod.

"If you want to maintain the reputation of your district as being a safe spot for visitors, you might consider . . ."

"Your point is well taken, Maya." He hunched forward. "How can I be of assistance?"

Drawing her shoulders back, she made sure her look demanded an answer. "Is there a person of interest?"

"No."

"Any eye-witness?"

"No."

Maya reminded herself of the two major tools used in a death investigation: evidence collection and subsequent analysis at a crime laboratory. "There's a common saying in our industry, "Every contact leaves a trace." What about forensic evidence—blood, hair, fiber, or cosmetics—at the murder site? What about prints?"

"We were drenched with unexpected heavy rain that night, which contaminated the site and caused headaches for our fingerprint guru. There wasn't much for him to work with. We photographed the corpse and the surroundings, took notes, and drew sketches. Our crime lab has the clothing. The only blood was that of the victim. However, our crime scene examiner swabbed the body and harvested some DNA evidence."

"I suppose you've created a DNA profile of the suspect?"

"Yes, and our DNA analyst ran that profile through the database of genetic information but didn't come up with an exact match."

"That would limit it to felons and those who had been previously arrested, wouldn't it?"

"Yes. The DNA and polygraph tests rule out the hookers and Mr. Pande, the brothel keeper, as being the killer. There are no loopholes in their accounts, either—it appears to be an outside job. What I'm saying is we can't build a case quite yet against a suspect. Our Privacy Act makes it laborious."

Maya wondered if money had changed hands or if local politics made it difficult to pursue a criminal matter. "Given that Rory's smartphone was stolen, have you received the records from telecommunication service providers as to his incoming and outgoing calls?"

Inspector Dev shook his head. "We don't have access to voice data."

"Could you ask for necessary permission?"

The inspector lowered his head. "You know about Indian bureaucracy, don't you?"

Maya nodded. In order that she could analyze any physical evidence of the crime that was left, she said, "I'd like to pay a visit to the woman and her son who first spotted the dead body. Could you arrange that?"

The air in the room tensed. "Those 'Ladies of the Night' are tribal women, Maya. They're out of their reservations and living amongst us. Most have had some schooling, but they're vulnerable. The Tribal Welfare

Division of Indian government wants to protect their land, their culture, and their rights. We the police try to build trust and do our best not to interfere in their affairs. There have been accounts of poachers trying to lure young girls away from their homes, which has further eroded their confidence in us."

"I'd still like to have a talk with that woman."

"Be aware that there could be language or accent barriers. Around here you'll hear at least five major Indian languages spoken, on top of various Andamanese dialects. You might need an interpreter. What languages do you speak?"

"Hindi, Bengali, and English." How Maya preferred not to have an intermediary between her and the suspects or witnesses she wanted to deal with, but there appeared to be no choice. "Any recommendation for an interpreter?"

"We have a competent one, yes. I can put you in touch with him. His name is Hindi-Man."

He'd be someone in the inspector's camp and therefore not trustworthy, but it might work. "What an unusual name."

"A Hindi speaker, he's fluent in a number of tribal dialects. He's the right sort when it comes to dealing with our indigenous brothers and sisters. They trust him. Tribal children tease him by calling him Hindi-Man and that name has stuck. He's too humble to change it." The inspector paused. "The chap is an excellent negotiator, what we call our 'contact party,' a go-between and a guide. If you ever visit one of the smaller islands, then it'll behoove you to have him accompany you. He's picked up a bit of American slang from working with tourists."

"Yes, I'd like to hire Hindi-Man for that visit as soon as possible." Seeing the inspector tilt his head in affirmation, she added, "I also rise with the sun."

"Okay, then. Before I make the necessary arrangements, I should remind you that few women of your upbringing, other than our social workers, ever visit that 'bawdy house,' in an unsavory part of the town. What you find might shock and embarrass you. Are you sure you want to go?"

"Yes, it's a necessary part of my job. And, oh, one more question to ask. Did you track Rory's activities in the past when he made regular visits here on business? Where he stayed, whom he hung around with, which places he frequented?"

"No. no," he said, voice rising. "Where would I find time to get down to beat the streets or do such dirty surveillance work? I'm out all-day long. My men and I patrol for illegal fishermen on the beaches, plead with the tourists not to damage the coral reefs, and monitor the sand-fly population for the Forest Department."

Her voice turned ironic. "Doesn't sound like too bad a life to me."

Inspector Dev stiffened his broad shoulders and resumed a ramrod position. "Thank you for allowing me the pleasure of meeting you in person. Please call anytime you need my help." He reached into his breast pocket, drew out a business card with a fleshy hand, and handed it to her with a grand gesture.

You haven't spilled the whole story about Rory's whereabouts or your investigation into his passing. She wanted to stop him and question him further, but he'd disappeared through the door.

She headed for the shower, where she lathered her weary back with the hotel's fragrant sandalwood soap. Warm water washed away the grime and frustration. Wrapped in a terry cloth dressing gown, she stood before a steamy mirror and combed through the wet strands of her black hair, which she would allow to dry naturally.

Her stomach grumbled with hunger. She placed a room-service order for a veggie burger, a fruit compote, and peppermint tea. Her dinner turned up on bistro-style blue-rimmed china, accompanied by a lace-bordered white napkin. Along with the food, there came a slender crystal vase containing a long-stemmed single red rose, a fresh one this time. She stared at the arrangement, hoping it would lighten her mood, but it failed to do so. She hadn't dined alone since meeting Alain. To her, a meal meant smiles, jokes, stories and sharing. He'd have laughed at the size of her dinner. *Why such a small order? Where's the wine?* Not having heard from him, she hoped he was well. She'd seen what Lee was going through. She didn't wish anything like that to happen to Alain. She picked at her food, then pushed herself away from the table, and looked out the window. The stars were as clear as she'd ever seen, given the area's minimum light pollution.

Next order of business: to pull out the e-reader from her carry-on. Prior to leaving Seattle, she'd downloaded a selection of books published by Roaring Books onto this e-reader. Did the books have any relation to Rory's murder? She'd also made note of a couple of YouTube interviews with Rory. She'd researched all this to obtain a clearer idea of the professional side of the man. Who was Rory as an editor, a publisher and an entrepreneur? What did he want to achieve? What were his hopes and fears? What might have caused him trouble? Despite their close friendship, Maya now lamented, she was in the dark about certain aspects of his life. Might his books provide a clue as to why he ended up the way he did? She hadn't read his entire offering because of her excuses such as: *I don't have the time. I'll take these books with me on my next vacation. Or I don't care about this topic.*

She eased herself into an armchair and dove into the books. What a variety of subjects his authors had introduced to the public, all in an accessible manner. A book about how China's culture shapes its destiny; one on the love habits of ancient civilizations; a third on the women of Burma. She chose the book on Burma and read the first fifty pages. The writing had a lusty quality, at odds with the gentle sedate reputation of modern Myanmar. She closed the book and dove into selective passages from other books, all the while pondering the meaning of the weighty topics and relishing the exercise. After two hours, not being able to discern any obvious connection to the crime, she put the e-reader aside.

Next, she clicked on her laptop to watch the YouTube video of an interview with Rory. It was conducted by an up-and-coming regional author, Christopher Jensen. A slight, wiry man, he sat hunched across from Rory. Maintaining a straight posture, as though breathing from his diaphragm, Rory exuded a certain confidence, which must have flowed from his passion for the world of books.

Jensen asked about Rory's philosophy of publishing.

"Giving the readers their money's worth—that's what my publishing venture is about." Rory held a smile. "Relevant topics, talented authors, and books that are given every possible attention from our editorial end."

Jensen: "That shows a love for the written word. Did you always know you'd pursue this line of work?"

Rory: "No. I worked as an editor for a global publisher and saw how they short-changed their authors. I vowed to myself that'd never happen if I ran a publishing company, which I did a few years later. And I've kept to my promise. Several of my authors have gone on to have successful careers."

Jensen: "Indeed. Your authors sing your praise. But aspiring writers complain about rejection letters from your house, including myself."

Rory: "Smile at your rejections and say, 'One less.' That's what I did in my early life. My parents were Irish immigrants. I had an underprivileged childhood. Fell down dozens of times but lifted myself up every single instance. For sure, I have scars that haunt me at night, but I'd rather not show them in public."

Jensen: "How big is the financing issue for a small business like yours?"

Rory: "It's the biggest issue. I like to pay my authors a decent advance but can't always. And I can't match big publishers as far as the wallet goes. A small business is a risky proposition, which makes funding difficult, if not impossible."

Jensen asked a few more questions, then ended the interview with, "We're proud to have you in our fair city."

Maya clicked off the laptop. She thought about Rory, his successes and his scars, the inspiration he was, and pondered his answer about financing. It was often said in her line of work that a money trail often led to clues to a murder. Might that be the case here? She cast her eyes about the room in vain for an answer. It was then she noticed the local daily placed on the coffee table.

As the last act of the day, she sat up in bed against the headboard, covered herself with the blanket and scanned the daily. Not a news junkie, she liked to scan the paper. With the curiosity she had about her new surroundings, she breezed through the headlines, and stumbled across a paragraph on Page 3.

The Bookish Murder Case Gets a Boost

The murderer of U.S. publisher Rory Thompson remains at-large. Port Blair police confirmed that no arrests have been made. Our residents continue to be tense. Thompson's widow, Lee Thompson, has retained a U.S. private detective, Maya Mallick. This, according to a source close to Mrs. Thompson's family. Ms. Mallick is noted for solving the double murder case last year that included Sylvie Burton, the prominent Seattle malaria scientist. Mallick is expected to land in Port Blair today.

The word about her arrival had reached the press, which explained why she received the extra attention and why Kal had shown up at the airport.

As she was ready to put the paper down, Maya's gaze hit upon another news story. Yet another earthquake, albeit a minor one, had occurred in the nearby islands of Indonesia. Folks here insisted the ocean was angry, according to this report.

She couldn't help but recall the warning from the hotel reservation clerk: that the Andaman chain was vulnerable to the earth's periodic tremors, and that another natural calamity wasn't beyond question.

She put the newspaper away. Alain's face sprang up before her eyes. She wondered what time it was in Borneo. She opened her laptop and brought it awake. She keyed in a lengthy e-mail to Alain in which she described her plane flight, her hotel room, her dinner and her present situation. After sending she waited and buzzed with anticipation about his reaction.

Minutes ticked by. No reply came, nor did her phone sing with an excited voice saying, *Maya, My darling.*

She nestled in bed and drifted off to sleep. Then thunder rumbled and a nightmarish vision of a high ocean wave rolling into Port Blair, like what the hotel clerk had described, jerked her awake.

EIGHT

THE DAY AFTER HER ARRIVAL IN PORT BLAIR Maya woke early, six a.m. On this winter morning, she went for a jog on the beach in time for the sunrise, the sand powdery under her feet. Birds cooed; the sun, a brilliant golden disc, pushed up from the shadow of clouds; waves rumbled; a sense of calm prevailed. As she began jogging, Maya considered the day ahead of her. She'd welcome Hank, who was supposed to arrive this morning, and bring him up to date.

One major task: She'd like to figure out how Rory spent his time in this island. Did he make any friends? Any enemies? What places did he frequent? Inspector Dev had skirted her question on this topic, adding an extra layer of gravity to it.

The three-mile run helped rejuvenate her and acclimate her to the local time, which was twelve and a half hours ahead of Seattle. She finished with a short walk to her hotel, the air warm, moist, salty and, at times strong, about her. As she entered the lobby, she spotted a man poking his head through the front entrance and casting a long look at her. Medium height and lean, dressed in white, sacred beads around his neck, he targeted his attention to her, even though other guests were milling about. Before she could react—catch the bellboy's attention—the man had disappeared. In a frenzy of anxiety, she walked toward the elevator. She hadn't quite figured out how this place operated. Her boss Simi's warning about Andaman wiggled in her mind.

She slipped through the door of her hotel room. While checking out clothes in her closet, she heard a gentle but definite knock on the door and opened it.

A young Eurasian girl, about twenty years of age, poised on spiky heels, beamed up at her. Wet hair cascaded in stringy tangles around her stunning, sloe-eyed face. "Hi, Maya, I'm Sophie, Hank's girlfriend."

This was Hank's off-hour preoccupation, this girl in high-cut denim shorts and a skimpy black camisole top? Maya had seen a picture of her, but never met her. Her outfit could be considered a bit risqué for Port Blair's conservative society dominated by settlers from the Indian sub-continent, who frowned on exposed female flesh. And why had Hank brought her, a young girl barely beyond her teens, to a place that might prove unsafe?

"I was expecting Hank today," Maya said. "I had no idea you were coming, too. Did he ask you to join him?"

"No, he didn't." Sophie brushed a stray hair out of her face, her silver bracelet flashing. "I decided at the last minute to come and bunk with him. He needs some looking after, you know."

Would she stand in the way of Hank accomplishing his tasks? Maya couldn't be sure. Nor did she feel charitable toward this newcomer. "Where's Hank?"

"Taking a shower. This is his first trip abroad—he's amped. We're on the first floor, room 110. Arrived here only a few minutes ago. A friendly cabbie picked us up from the airport, chatted nonstop, told us what's clicking in this town. We thought you'd sent him. But he said nope."

Maya detected a pattern and took an unsteady breath. "Is his name Kal?"

"Yes, the dude tried to flirt with me," Sophie tossed in. "Took us a bit out of the way on a road where we saw a lumbering elephant."

"He was my chauffeur, too. But no, I didn't send him. Did he give you his business card?"

"No."

Maya's mind became burdened with questions. The cabbie denied having Rory as an acquaintance or a fare. Was he lying? Who did he work for, if anybody? What purpose did he serve in the scheme of things? She'd like to get a line on him.

"Hank has read all the texts, all the updates you sent him," Sophie said. "He's dying to know what else you've been up to. Would you like to join us for breakfast?"

While Maya deliberated, the petite girl looked down the corridor. She was incapable of standing motionless for more than a few seconds at a time. Maya begged off, explaining her morning schedule and promised to meet them later in the day.

Sophie waved a goodbye, twirled in her high heels, and hurried away toward the staircase. Maya stared at her vanishing back. She shook her head, feeling responsible for the girl's safety and closed the door. She texted Hank, asked him to rent a car and locate the taxi stand where Kal parked. He could also speak with the hotel staff and gather any gossip on Kal.

MAYA REGISTERED THE SOUNDS OF TELEVISION, a nasal voice belting out a song, even before she rang the doorbell of suite 110. Hank must be up. It was nine a.m., a day later. Time to receive an update from Hank on the job assigned to him: to get a run-down on Kal. Maya went solo as far as her investigative work was concerned but depended on her administrative assistant to perform routine tasks. In her Seattle office, he answered phone calls, composed e-mails and did searches to make her life easier.

A good researcher, Hank would often jump out of his chair when he came across pertinent material, saying, "Bam! Got it." Although not a techie by any means, he employed tools and technology and dug into professional-grade databases. What he lacked in training, he made up for by using his imagination, a necessary component of a short story writer's toolbox. He interacted well with her clients. "I like working in an office," he'd say. "I like co-working."

"Maya, Come in." Hank opened the door and moved aside for her to step in. He was dressed in light tan cotton trousers and a wine-colored T-shirt that proclaimed: Adult-ish.

"Can't sleep late here," Hank said, "even though it's freakin' quiet."

Maya returned the greeting as she stepped into the two-room suite. She could hear Sophie in the bedroom, humming. This is the first chance Maya had of being alone with Hank. Unsettled by Sophie's arrival and with concern for her safety, Maya asked, "Why did you bring Sophie here?"

"Didn't mean to complicate things for you," Hank replied, apology in his tone. "She insisted. She argued that, in exchange for this vacation, she'll pay for my food and incidentals. I won't have to dig into my savings."

Maya decided to drop the topic for now. Hank was happier with Sophie. He had that awe-struck look in his eyes whenever she was around. Maya turned her attention to another matter: to scope out Hank and Sophie's accommodation. Keeping her thoughts to herself, she did a security check. They'd received a suite as well. Smaller and minus the feature of a grand ocean view, it faced the courtyard. Situated on the ground floor, the suite was, however, a tad too accessible. The killer could be anywhere—on the beach, in the hotel lobby, sneaking in dead flowers to a guest suite, acting as a welcoming cabbie.

Maya's eyes traced the living room. At the center stood a flat-screen television playing a Bollywood extravaganza. It sported a female dancer who wove her hands, eyes, and feet into a sinuous movement. Jewelry dangled from every exposed part of her body; her lips synced with the lyrics. The music, dancing, and fantasies from her childhood tugged at Maya.

She recovered and said to Hank, "These skin-and-dance flicks are an addiction, aren't they?"

"True. In between watching those flicks and checking out this town, I text my squad in Seattle. They're green with envy. When I tell them about this hotel, they say, 'It's so extra.' My mom's also driving me nuts. She wants to crash here on her vacation." Hank paused. "How's your friend doing?"

"Lee is scared, upset and grief-stricken, as you might expect" Maya said. "I've talked to her on the phone several times. We text each other throughout the day. We'll be able to spend more time face-to-face when Rory's parents fly back to Pennsylvania later in the week, or so Lee says." She paused. "I wonder if she isn't trying to avoid seeing me. That hurts."

"Guilty complex?" Hank asked.

"Could be. How did your venture go, trying to locate that cabbie?"

Hank lowered his voice. "I'll spill the tea for you—I haven't shared it with Sophie yet. She's ruffled easily and I'm extra careful with her. Yesterday, after dinner, I dragged her out to look for Kal and see the sights of this town. I followed the directions you'd given me about the approximate location of the rest spot where he parked his taxi. We drove around for a while in my rental car, went all over the area, never found what I was looking for and ended up in a remote part of the town. Through the car window, I saw what must have been a tribal dance. Man, it was epic: drumming, masks, flying bodies, and chanting. At first. I said, 'Aww, yeah!' Then I saw a dude holding a skull and whirling it in the air. I was freaked, zero chill, my buddies would say, and managed to drive back to the hotel. Sophie had already crashed in the passenger's seat. She had had couple glasses of wine at dinner, too many for her. I didn't tell her where we were headed for and, in any case, she didn't notice. Or else she'd have freaked out, too."

A creepy sensation passed over Maya. "Shall we put a hold on that search until we gather more of a run-down on that cabbie?'

"The bellboy said that there are several other rest spots where cabbies gather when they're off-duty. Let me try one more time."

"Watch out," Maya said. "Some places are off-limits to the outsiders."

NINE

SHOWERED AND DRESSED, Maya perched on a couch in the glass-and-gold hotel lobby the following morning. She consulted her watch: fifteen past nine. Her guide, Hindi-Man, hadn't turned up yet. She was killing time when she could be out there, putting her finger into things. Impatience wiggled inside her, given that an interview was coming up, making her bite her nails. She hadn't heard from Alain, either, which made her more anxious.

Where was Hindi-Man? His telephone message said he wanted to meet in a public space, when he could have come up to her suite for a more private conversation. Maya clutched her sari train. For this morning's appointment, she had donned a sunny-yellow crepe silk sari with a red border—arty but not flashy—to appear less foreign. "Keep a low-profile," was her mantra as a sleuth. "Go native if you can." She wore no make-up. Now it dawned on her. Given that "Be prepared" was her other mantra, had she remembered to bring *bakhshish*? Part gratuity, part bribe, it paved paths through treacherous territories of complex human interactions. The practice went quite far back in history, to the Mughal kings, maybe even further back, her family in Kolkata insisted. "Grease! Grease! Grease! We've always greased palms. It works." To ensure she'd conformed to the tradition, she opened her purse, drew out two red, letter-size envelopes stuffed with rupee notes, and slipped them back into their places. As always, the purse contained a folded paper bag, her "evidence" bag, and plastic gloves, for the safe keeping of any DNA evidence she might come across. It also held a 4x6 headshot of Rory.

"Hello, Ms. Mallick, I am Nagraj Pillu," a male voice announced. Well-fed and dressed in tapered jeans and a casual shirt, he appeared to be about thirty years of age. His voluminous black hair lay in neatly combed waves. An elaborate silver ring graced his finger. "But the people we'll be dealing with call me Hindi-Man."

This was the ace interpreter? Maya greeted him. Then, following good manners as the locals practiced it, she initiated a personal question. "Are you from this island?"

"Yes, my heart and soul belong to this place. My father and grandfather walked the beautiful trails here. They could think of living nowhere else." In keeping with his reputation of being humble and self-effacing, he didn't offer any more about himself, but continued to observe her with alert, thick-lashed eyes.

"Are we set to go?"

"Yes, Madam." He gave a nervous laugh. "This will be an adventure for both of us. Never have I taken a client to the red-light district. Nor do I expect to run into any language hurdles there. As a reminder—we're allowed only a short visit. Mr. Pande, the 'daddy,' will be out running errands. We'll take advantage of his absence and sneak in and out of his house. He mustn't see us. Do you follow? He'd raise the hell if he caught us talking to his 'girls.' He's criticized enough by local social workers who are in the business of fighting human trafficking. They insist he helps traffic tribal girls and he's touchy about that. They've threatened him with litigation. He's mad. Do you have your watch with you?"

"Yes. I'll be as quick as possible," Maya replied. "What can you tell me about the woman we'll visit?"

"My contacts tell me she's a tribal, who has had some formal education. Smart and articulate, she speaks Hindi with an accent. She's known to be difficult to deal with. 'Too spicy,' some say. 'Too much of a warrior.' Others insist there's a shred of *junglee* left in her. You know, a forest dweller, wild and unpredictable, with a nasty mouth. I've been told not to 'fuck' with her. Pardon my language."

Maya was charged with curiosity. It'd take patience and finesse to deal with such a person. "I suppose that's one of the rules of this island? Behave in such a manner that our indigenous brothers and sisters aren't ticked off with us?"

"Correct. As for me, I've never interpreted the words of a sex worker, much less that of a spicy, *junglee*, warrior-type." Hindi-Man smiled.

"Something new for me."

In trying to lighten the situation, Maya said, "Should we say new normal?"

Hindi-man gave out a laugh.

"Please interpret whatever she says or does," Maya said. "Every little nuance, every little gesture. Okay? I'm sure you understand the gravity of the situation." At Hindi-Man's bow of affirmation, she added, "Will you also show me the exact location where Rory's body was found?"

"I will. There has never been a murder in that spot before. I've heard it said that bad spirits haunt that alley, which lies between two houses of ill-repute. Whatever. We can spend a few minutes there before our visit."

Maya inhaled. She'd have to have her wits about for this encounter. "I've brought a little *bakhshish* to make things smooth. Hope that's okay."

"*Ek dum sahi*." Perfect. "Regardless of what others say, I like the Americans. They do their homework and are always ready to act. I dig that." Hindi-Man beamed and waved toward the exit. "My car is outside. Please follow me."

TEN

MAYA WALKED THE PERIMETER, then paused before the mouth of the narrow, unpaved, "alley of tricks." Wedged between two flat-roofed, brick-and-cement buildings, the rough patch of earth was worn and dusty, strewn with stones, rubble, and filth and it smelled of trash. Torn police ribbons indicated that the spot had been designated as a scene of crime and secured.

She took a jagged breath, almost seeing Rory's fallen body and the glint of a broken liquor bottle. Sprawled in the dirt, his face caked in mud, his white shirt a flag of some sort, through pouring rain, Rory had taken his final resting position here.

The sun, much hotter now, burned the tip of her nose. She knelt and murmured to an invisible friend. "Both Alain and I are heartbroken, dearest Rory. We love you, we miss you, and I promise to bring the killer to justice." A gust of wind surged into the alley and swept through Maya's hair as she tried to listen to Rory's reply.

"We can go inside, Madam."

Hindi-Man's voice snapped Maya out of her reverie. One last look at the alley and she followed him. Eager faces popped out of the second-floor windows as though a circus-type curiosity—what they called *tamasha* here—had arrived. A young boy chanted a Hindi film song. A girl gave Hindi-Man the eye. Two crows cawed in unison from atop a tree, perhaps signaling another imminent disaster.

Upon entering the adjoining, two-story building, they took a left to the living room. It housed a cot, a couch, a few chairs, and a large television. The air smelled of bidi—like cigarette smoke, only stronger and cruder—along with alcohol and sweat. A bright oil painting on the south wall depicted an incongruous scene from ancient times: an over-dressed king perched on a garish throne, being attended by bejeweled, scantily dressed maidens. Sunlight sifted in through the two windows facing the street.

A young woman flowed into the room, her movements deliberate, a colorful bead necklace sparkling at her throat. She folded her hands in a *namaste* and offered Maya a faded armchair, all the while giving her a look of appraisal. Hindi-Man perched on the cot. He cleared his throat and introduced the woman as Zarina. He added in English that it was her "trade" name.

Dark and slender, with high-cheekbones, flexible as a whip, and aged about twenty-five, Zarina would be considered attractive by most people. She'd covered her hair with the end of the brownish-orange sari, an act of modesty she might have acquired living in a metropolis. Free of any artifice, she displayed an attitude by the upturn of her chin.

To kick things off, Maya said a warm hello to her.

Eyes fixed on Hindi-Man, Zarina unleashed a torrent of words in a tribal tongue, her large ring-shaped earrings swaying. She gestured with an arm, causing her sari to bunch up over one shoulder.

"What is she saying?" Maya asked Hindi-Man, perturbed by the fact that she couldn't understand a word.

"'Posh women who live in big houses look down upon us, like we're dirt under their shoes. Do they have any sense how difficult it is for us to have any kind of life? Social workers who try to 'save' us exploit us so they could have jobs. University students come to do research, like we're animals.'"

Stumped, Maya paused, pulled herself together, and gave Zarina another close look. Frustration, even a shade of aggression, poured out of her—this from the way she gestured—as did sadness. She had some strength as well, perhaps buried deep below. Once again, Maya reminded herself she would have to tread with caution.

"I understand and sympathize," Maya said in Hindi, giving a kindly look at her hostess. "I'm not a posh woman. My best friend's husband has been murdered. Can you imagine what she's going through? I've come a long way to help her find out what had happened. Can we talk about that? Will you, please, sit down?"

Zarina began chattering with Hindi-Man, while Maya squirmed in her seat. Following that, Zarina eyed her female visitor and affected a kindlier expression, but she remained standing.

"She notices genuine distress in you," Hindi-Man interpreted. "She likes it that you're there for your friend who's in hot water. That you dropped everything and flew here to be with her. But the cops have already put her and her cohorts through a lot. She claims that you can ask her any question you like. She'll decide whether to answer or not. Out of respect for us, she'll stand."

"Let's start," Maya said to Zarina in Hindi, leaning toward her in expectation. "About what time did you notice the dead body?"

"Let me think—must have been around eight a.m." Zarina slipped into accented but fluent Hindi, her face gloomy, voice tense.

Maya needed a few moments for her ears to become used to Zarina's heavy accent. "Can you tell me more?" She leaned forward and paid close attention as she listened.

"My child wakes early and goes outside to play with his toy truck," Zarina replied. "He didn't have to go too far before he spotted the dead man. He became scared. He started screaming and crying and ran back inside. By then, I was awake. I rolled out of the bed, consoled my child and peeked through the window. From what I saw . . . I shook all over. Everything revolved around me. I, too, couldn't help but cry out. 'What the fuck your son is crying about?' Mr. Pande shouted as he came rushing. His bedroom is upstairs. He said, 'I must discipline him.' He shook my son's shoulders."

"What did you do?"

"I trembled, drew my boy closer to me and pointed to the alley. Mr. Pande ran outside, almost slipping. He's out-of-shape. I followed him. His eyes bulged out, like he'd never seen a dead body, started reciting a prayer to God Ganesh in Sanskrit. All the women were up, and they gathered outside. 'Who's this dude?' Mr. Pande asked. 'Who did him last night?' No answer. He called the police. The uniforms came and knocked on our doors. They grilled us."

Maya conjured the mess, almost experienced the pain Rory must have endured. "Did you—?"

"Neither my son, nor I, had anything to do with the murder."

"Did you hear any noises earlier that night?"

Zarina shrugged. "Didn't I tell you I was sleeping like a log?"

"Think hard. Did you hear the crunch of tires of a lorry or a car? Voices? Shouts? Sounds of a fight? Any kind of disturbance that woke you? The alley is right next to this building."

Zarina gave Maya a stony look. "You ask a hell of a lot of questions. I think you already know the answers."

"If I knew the answers, why would I be here? Please, Zarina, I don't mean to pry or be rude, but this is of utmost importance. It concerns the brutal murder of someone you might have met. He left many loved ones behind. Wouldn't you like to see the perpetrator, who's on the run—?"

"I'm sure it was nothing, but I did hear a car stopping and some muffled voices. It was raining hard." Sadness creased the corners of Zarina's eyes. "The sound of rain and thunder washed my sorrow away."

"About what time?"

"About four a.m., I think, a guess on my part."

"Did you think it was unusual?"

"Yes. This place is quiet at night. We're all exhausted by the time our clients leave. The voices scared me—I didn't make the slightest move. They lasted, not too long."

"Any sounds of fighting or resisting, any arguments?"

"None. Pretty soon the noises died, and the car drove away. It was all quiet again. I snuggled the quilt and fell asleep."

"Will you be able to identify the voices?"

"Nope."

Not an encouraging response. One piece did, however, snap into place for Maya. Rory had been assassinated elsewhere. His corpse had been hauled in and dumped in an alley in an unsavory part of the town, to tarnish his good reputation. Which would also make it difficult to preserve the scene of incident. She saw it now: Rory's death entailed more complications, more deliberations than she'd imagined; it involved more than one person.

"Why didn't you wake up the house, I mean, if the noise scared you?" Maya asked.

"Simple, Lady. Drunks, druggies, or those who can't keep it up come back and loiter around here. They sing, blabber and whistle. They try to barge in, like we're always available, like they can get therapy. We girls don't have to be concerned. This house is locked from inside and only Mr. Pande has the key to the doors. No one can go in or out. He opens the doors at nine a.m. sharp." Perhaps noticing Maya wince, she added a remark to Hindi-man in her tribal tongue.

Hindi-Man cleared his throat, bringing attention to himself, and said, "According to Mr. Pande, it's for the safety of the women that he keeps them locked in all night, Madam. Social workers, who come to visit, object to this 'locked stable' policy. But Zarina's son can climb a window and jump out. He can also come back in."

"You didn't tell the police about the voices you heard?" Maya asked Zarina.

"Why should I?" Zarina said, her chin jutted at a certain angle. "They didn't ask. Mr. Pande advised us to give away as little as possible. As it is, our business has fallen since last week. We're in deep shit. Mr. Pande might shut this place down and kick us all out. What'll happen then?"

Maya wondered if she could help Zarina in any way to escape this wretched existence. This was no place for a determined young woman and her son to spend their days. "Do you feel safe here?"

"I've made this shitty place my home. Sort of. But safe? No, I don't feel safe anywhere."

Maya pulled out Rory's photo from her purse and held it out before Zarina. "Did you ever meet this man?" She waited for the answer.

Zarina pressed a glance at the photo, looked away, and gave Maya a rueful stare. "Is that any of your damn business?"

"Yes, it is now."

"Plenty of dudes pass through our doors, Lady, wanting 'to have fun with the babes,' but really to abuse them. Who can remember them all? Most tourists look alike to us. Pale face, blue eyes, light hair, smiling too much. This house isn't lit too well in the evening. We can't tell one from the other. Besides, the dead man's face was cut up . . ." Zarina left the point unfinished. Her voice, now muffled, trailed off.

Hindi-Man consulted his watch. Not much time left before Mr. Pande showed up. *Get the answers to the questions you've come here for, Maya.*

"Are you sure about that?" she said to Zarina, the air hot and stuffy about her. "You don't recognize him?"

Zarina took a step back from her standing position, her expression wounded and bitter. "No, no, no. Your questions bleed my heart. Enough of this grilling, Lady. Get the hell out of—" Her voice cracked. Without finishing her sentence, she stormed out of the room, her sandals clatter-ing on the floor.

Stung by Zarina's abruptness, Maya swallowed and sat, her gaze to the ground. *How could you be so callous, Maya?* She'd hit Zarina at a vulnerable spot, pushed her into a corner. Her emotional outburst revealed that. It proved that there was more to her story, much more, and somehow Maya would have to access the core of it.

She sprang to her feet. After gathering her purse, she put a *bakhshish* envelope on the chair and said to Hindi-Man, "I'm sorry. Is there any way to apologize to her?"

"Let me try through a third party. Hope she cools off. Hope she doesn't turn her tribemates against us."

"What'll happen then?"

Hindi-Man's expression hardened. "You don't want to know, Madam."

A feathery fear passed across Maya's back. Did Rory somehow incur the wrath of one of the tribes? What connection, if any, did he have with them? Why might they want to do away with him, if that was, indeed, what had transpired?

ELEVEN

SETTLED ON THE BACKSEAT OF HINDI-MAN'S CAR, inching its way through heavy traffic, in a cacophony of vehicle and construction noise, Maya checked her watch. Eleven o'clock. Her visit with Zarina had led her back to square one; for she was no longer on Maya's suspects list. Instead it had generated more questions. Where was Rory killed and why? Who had a serious grudge against him in this town? Were there any accomplices?

She texted Hank, gave him an update, and sent a similar report to her boss Simi. As she took in the passing scenery, she decided to plot a new course. That wouldn't be easy, with only a few suspects and no witnesses. What if she called on Inspector Dev? On their first meeting, Dev had acted cool toward her. Nevertheless, he'd offered her a pertinent insider perspective. He'd mentioned an anonymous caller, without much elaboration. Where there was reticence, there was a story. Her experience now dictated: *Go for it.*

She said to Hindi-Man, "Drop me off at the *thana*, will you, please?" Local police headquarters.

"As you please, Madam."

As he crawled along the road, Maya thought about Alain. She wished she could discuss these details with him. He listened well, whether he could offer a solution or not. The fact that he hadn't returned her calls or replied to her e-mails thus far preyed on her. Was he alright? She kept seeing his face in her mind's eye. She could almost touch him, could experience his breath on her cheeks, on her breasts. She felt more concerned about his silence than she'd expected, given the uncertainty caused by Rory's murder.

Within minutes, Hindi-Man stopped in front of a multistoried brick building. It had a gated courtyard, which sported a badminton court on one side and a flower patch on the other. A police jeep was parked in front of it. He turned to look at Maya. "Here we are. I prefer to stay outside, if that's okay with you."

"I understand," Maya said. "I might as well confide in you. The inspector hasn't been open with me."

"The uniforms aren't usually."

"I'd like his cooperation." Maya made a point to open her purse. "Could you share any gossip about him?"

A smile flitted across Hindi-Man's lips. With mischief in his gaze, he said, "This is between you and me, Madam, but . . ."

"Please continue."

"I think . . . I . . ."

"Anything, anything at all?"

"I might be able to share an R-rated story."

"Yes?"

Hindi-Man cleared his throat. "It's hard for me to articulate this, but here it is. A high-ranking police officer—yes, a top one—was seen entering a house in the red-lantern district. Plain clothes. No uniform. Middle-aged. A family man and an important person in the community. Here's the kicker. Someone took a picture of him on his cell phone. As you might expect, the officer wouldn't want this to become public."

"I can make a guess who it is," Maya replied.

"You don't have to mention any names."

"Thank you," Maya said to Hindi-Man, slipped him the *bakhshish* envelope and climbed out of the car.

He waved and wished her good luck, the smile returning.

Maya entered the building. Inside, the station was bright and well lit; the air smelled of fresh paint. She rolled her shoulders down to overcome her nervousness, the touch of fear she harbored when she had to deal with the police. Especially in India. She stepped to the guard's desk, introduced herself, and announced her wish to see Inspector Dev.

The pockmark-faced attendant greeted her in English, his expression far too serious for the level of work he performed.

"Your passport, please." After completing the formalities, he said in a rough voice, "The sahib arrived only five minutes ago, Madam. He's behind schedule. He can't see you."

"But I must." Maya studied her watch. The inspector beginning his work-day at twenty-five past eleven? Regardless, she must speak with him. How? She hated herself for exploiting her late father's name as she said, "I am Subir Mallick's daughter."

The attendant looked impressed. "Subir Mallick? My son, who's in school, is studying a book about him. You're his daughter? Only child? No son? Please have a seat over there for a minute," he said pointing, expecting no answers.

Maya walked toward the visitor's area. The inspector would keep her waiting to establish his superiority over her. She'd stay put, yet her throat was dry. She wished for a cup of tea, but such a request might not be accommodated in a police station. Sitting in a hard chair, the rumbling of a bulldozer from a construction site in the next block puncturing the air, Maya read the inscription on the opposite wall. It described the motto of the police force: "We protect, and we serve." That took her back to her youth. How reluctant her mother and aunts were to visit the police station even when a serious crime had to be reported. "Those officers won't listen to us women," they complained, clutching the pallu of their saris. "Those *goondas* don't serve or protect, they harass us. They show us the door, saying, 'It's all in your heads, ladies.'" Maya vowed to herself she wouldn't let that happen. Yet she couldn't help but notice the slowness with which things moved around here.

The same attendant approached, double-cupped his hand in the *aadab* gesture of politeness and showed her into the inspector's office, with the proud declaration of, "The inspector-sahib will see you now."

"Hello, Maya. What brings you here?" said the top cop from behind his desk, raising his eyes from a printout and waving a hand toward a guest chair. Calm and formal, comfortable with his midlife bulk, he anchored his elbows on the desk, a small movement, measured and definite. Here was a man who played by the book except when making a trip to a brothel.

Maya returned his hello, took her seat, and surveyed the room. The airy space had undecorated white-washed walls, with files and ledgers stacked on a large shelf. On top of a sturdy desk stood a laptop computer, a phone, a framed family photo, and a gold pen. The picture window afforded a view of the street crawling with traffic. A car honked.

"Can we have a word?" she asked.

"Will it take much time?"

"Not too long."

"You've already had your morning excursion, I suppose."

"Yes, and I've found at least one thing of interest." Maya reported how Rory was killed at another location. Then his body was transported to that alley and dumped there. "The whole affair was well planned. More than one person was involved."

The inspector raised an eyebrow at her. "How did you come up with all that?"

Maya outlined her visit to Zarina, leaving out some of the details, not sure whether the walls between her and the inspector had broken down yet. Being that he remained wordless, she added, "Did you use a medical examiner? Are there elements in his report that could throw light on this matter?"

The uniformed man, with shiny insignia on his lapels and penetrating eyes, didn't spare a word.

"Look, Mohan, you're not making any progress. No leads. No suspects. How much longer can you . . .?" Receiving no reply, she said, "I wonder if the Governor General might be interested in hearing the rumor that a certain member of the police force . . ."

His face paled. She had him. "Okay. Section 53 of The Code of Criminal Procedure allowed us to use a forensics medical examiner," the inspector said. "His report indicates Mr. Rory hadn't been sexually messed with. Nor did he have intercourse with any girl in that house in the hours before his death." The inspector looked up as an aide brought a pitcher of mango nectar and settled the glasses down on the desk. He waited until the aide had departed, his voice reduced to a whisper. "You might already have picked it up by now—with no disrespect to Rory Thompson, mind you—but he visited the pleasure district quite often during his once-a-year trip to our island."

Maya stared at the floor. Even though, she'd suspected as much, this new revelation was hard to bear. *Rory, you had another side to your personality that you hid from us and Lee?* How would a loving wife, who gave her all to her man, take this?

The inspector gave Maya a shrewd glance. "I'm sorry, knowing how close you were to Rory Thompson. How much that must hurt you and what suffering it'll bring to his widow when she hears about it. You must be aware of the amount of interdependence we have in our society. We're close-knit, you might say. And personal reputation matters. Nobody would blame you if you dropped the case and—"

"No, Mohan. I'm not going to leave. I have a job to do, an urgent reason to be here. I'll see this case to an end however difficult it might be."

The inspector, at a loss for words, stayed quiet. Maya forced down a swallow of her beverage, despite the luscious fruity scent. Never a quitter, she found the toughness inside her asserting itself. She'd have to come at this questioning from another angle.

"Moving on to another topic, that anonymous caller who tipped you off to Rory's disappearance? I read about him in the news report." She recalled Alain saying something about a friend Rory had here. "I'm sure you've found his identity. What can you tell me about him?"

"He's one of Rory's Indian authors. Real name is Palkivala, Nitindra Palkivala, he goes by the pen name of Nemo Pal."

"What else?"

"He's a big name in Indian literary circles. Moves in high society. Makes his home in Gurgaon, near Delhi, but retreats often to the Rock of Wrath—we call it the Rock."

"The Rock? I've never heard of it."

"No surprise. It's a tiny isolated island south of here, shared by a nearly extinct tribal group, the Badungs, and a few mainlanders, retirees for the most part. Nemo flies down here, then takes the ferry over to the Rock to his rented cottage. He does this several times a year. It helps to write in a quiet atmosphere. Or that's what he says."

The lead she needed. The guy would be a gold mine, especially if he was a friend of Rory. "Who took the call from him?"

"A dispatcher in our control room."

"Do you have a recording of that exchange? I'd like to hear it."

"Not sure. I'll have to check." He made a scribble on a piece of paper with his pen.

Maya could wait on that recording but couldn't wait to pop her next question. "Why did Nemo Pal make such a call?"

"He claimed he'd been in phone contact with Rory, who would publish his next book. They were close friends. Rory had rung Nemo that afternoon, with a promise to discuss the status of Nemo's manuscript later that evening."

"Did that call ever come?"

"No."

"And that concerned Nemo?"

"Yes. He said it bothered the hell out of him because Rory was a man of his words. Nemo's writerly ear had picked up a trace of agitation in Rory's voice. He considered that unusual since Rory was being honored at the literary festival the following day, which would have been a big moment for him. Why did he sound disturbed? Nemo waited and waited for his call, then went to bed. At first, he couldn't sleep, then had a nightmarish dream, scary enough that he fell out of bed and stubbed a toe. Or that's what he reported."

"He called for help because of a bad dream?"

The inspector produced a tight smile. "I don't understand the mad genius types, either. Nor could I tell you what he smokes, but that's what he claims. The chap was incoherent on the phone. Kept mumbling, 'Rory, Rory, something bad has happened to him. Please send out a search party.' At first the dispatcher couldn't take in what Nemo was trying to convey. He could have dismissed him. The dispatcher doesn't act on every single call that comes through after hours, not with a few loonies and stoners around, but in this case, he flagged it urgent. He phoned me, woke me up, and brought it to my immediate attention. I came to the station and arranged for a call out, that is, broadcast the incident over the radio. I still get my hands dirty with homicide cases. You know the rest." He made a motion to rise. "Are we done?"

"Please, could I have a bit more of your time?" Maya drew another question from her mental list. "Does Nemo have an alibi?"

"Yes, but not a solid one. Let me back up a little. On the Rock, Nemo rents a cottage, one of the few reserved for mainlanders, and he takes his meals there. The call to our *thana*, indeed, came from the Rock. According to his landlady, an elderly woman who takes care of her boarders, he'd been in his room all day, writing, playing the guitar, and singing. He's quite the guitar player. His landlady likes listening to him as she does her chores. She says she served him dinner at around eight p.m. Since she can't remember how many grandchildren she has or what their names are—I don't trust her story. Nemo is supposed to have retired to his room around nine p.m."

"If that's true, then no way could he have sailed to Port Blair after that and killed someone. I assume the catamaran ferry doesn't run at night."

"Correct, but he could have had an accomplice in town."

"What could the logical justification be on his part in harming Rory?"

"These writer types—their heads are like a bowl of spaghetti. You know what I mean? Who can tell what their schemes are?"

"Did he show up for breakfast the next morning?"

"The landlady said she served him his uppama as usual at half-past eight, the way he likes it, with raisins and cashews. But then, as I mentioned, she gets people mixed up."

"Why in the world did Nemo make the call to your station anonymous?"

Inspector Dev studied his watch. "His rationale is this, Maya. He likes his privacy. Doesn't want his name connected with any sort of criminal matter. At the same time, he cared enough about Rory to take the initiative. Is he paranoid? Someone who imagines all sorts of possible outcomes of a situation and let them run wild in his mind? You know the 'what if' game?"

"Does he have any record?"

"None."

"Any chance you'll share Nemo's phone number with me? I'll find it out one way or the other. Can you give it to me?"

"If you insist." Inspector Dev tapped on his cell phone, scribbled the number on a scrap of paper, and handed it to Maya. She shoved the paper in her purse and thanked him. He took a quick sip; he was perturbed. "You're not going to visit him on the Rock, are you?"

"I'm pondering it."

"I'll advise you against that, Maya." He drained his glass and stared into it as though collecting his thoughts. "Most of that islet is settled by tribal folks, hunter-gatherers named Badungs, who have no use for our way of life or technology. Our government has tried to bring them to modern ways of living. We haven't succeeded. They resist any help we offer. They warn us off if we try to visit them. It can turn even worse. A week ago, two fishermen were found dead in their boat docked on the eastern shore of the Rock—the wrong side, I should say. They were drinking palm toddy and had dozed off. Hours later, they were found by another cruise—they'd been showered with arrows, which might have come from tribal members."

Maya contemplated: Did Rory end up on the wrong side of a tribe and was killed for that reason?

"The Badungs don't care for outsiders, except for Nemo and a few other mainlanders," the inspector was saying. "They're retired folks, who take a trip there on a regular basis, confine themselves to the west side, and don't interfere with the tribe's stone-age life." He paused. "You're new here, not aware of all this and a woman. I'll be frank with you. We won't be able to guarantee your safety if you happen to be on the Rock and find yourself in harm's way. If I were you, I would stay away from that islet."

"I'll bear that in mind. Do you know if Nemo ever shows up here, in Port Blair? Did he attend Rory's funeral?"

"Funny you ask. He's been spotted in our fair city in the last couple of days. Shopping, carousing with friends, I suppose. He might be hanging around."

"If he's in the vicinity," Maya said, "I might be able to find him. Are you, by any chance, keeping an eye on him?"

Inspector Dev looked up toward the smoke-gray window, pushed his chair back, and stood up. In a routine voice, he thanked Maya for stopping by.

Ah, he'd answered her question. She studied him. His bulky body and impressive uniform denoted power. A smile of condescension indicated he'd found a convenient prime suspect in Nemo and with that a way to thwart the hungry news media.

Maya stood, planted her feet on the ground. "May I request a favor?"

"Sure."

"Can you hold off arresting Nemo Pal until I've had a chance to speak with him?"

TWELVE

ABOUT EIGHT A.M., MAYA PULLED ON A PAIR of jogging tights and a long-sleeved red T-shirt. Time to get cracking. She'd been here over a week, doing her best to familiarize herself with the island. Not for a moment had she forgotten about Rory's murder. It had become obvious to her that in order to move forward with the case, she needed a better connection to this town. What secrets did it have? How best to ferret them out? Who held the real power here? What role had Rory played in this community and how that might have affected his safety?

Checking her cell phone, she found no message from Alain. That disturbed her. As a diversion, she browsed the headlines in the daily newspaper.

The phone rang and it was a call from the hotel desk. "I don't mean to over-worry you, Ms. Mallick," the night manager said, sounding over-worked and exhausted. "Our security noticed a suspicious character, a woman, loitering near our hotel this morning. As a precaution, we'll have the bellboy accompany you to your taxi. We're keeping an eye on your room, of course, to make sure no unauthorized person enters it."

Maya kept her voice calm. "Can you give me a description of the person? Have you tried to identify her?"

"No, I don't have the details. I work nights."

Did she believe him? No. She thanked him, ended the call, and crossed to the window. A single faint cloud skulked on the horizon. The vast indigo ocean, sparkling at a distance, spoke of the unknown. A boat lolled in the distance.

Then she spotted the graceful form of a woman down below. Esme Peterson. Yes, that was she. Arms swinging, hair loose, feet encased in sandals, she ambled on the seashore, her well-exercised body disciplined under a clingy floral dress.

Maya rushed out of her room, elated by the opportunity to meet with a mover-and-shaker of this town. She descended to the ground floor and zipped through the back door, her legs feeling loose and strong and taking an access path to the beach. Waves murmured, the sun blazed from a river of pink, and the water shimmered. Tourists with sun-burned faces lounged on beach towels. A clot of teenagers bantered back and forth. A young girl stumbled on the sand, then lifted herself up and laughed. An ideal setting to meet and chat.

She modulated her breathing and voice so this sudden appearance wouldn't threaten Esme. She approached Esme, smiled and introduced herself.

"You're the private detective?" Esme's voice was husky, and traces of a British accent showed. Up close, even this early in the morning, she had a weary look about her. Like she hadn't slept well. "I've read the coverage of your arrival in the paper. What a pleasure to meet you."

Maya drew in the smell of salt and fish, sea foam at her feet. "The pleasure is mine."

Despite an exclusive quality about her—after all, she was the town's royalty—Esme exuded warmth. She took frequent glances at Maya. "You're an early riser," Esme said in a honeyed voice. "Are you staying in this hotel?"

"Yes. Wonderful location. Sunbathing, swimming, snorkeling, coral viewing, all are available. If you have the time."

"It's sort of secluded, if you ask me. For a woman alone. I don't know if I'd want to stay here by myself."

Maya registered the note of warning in Esme's voice. For an instant Maya watched waves move along the sandy shore, a routine motion that soothed her.

"Would you like to join me in my little excursion?" Esme asked, her voice carried an undertone of command. She was rather strict and formal, Maya guessed, and expected everything to be done the way she wanted.

"Yes, I'd love to," Maya said. "That'll be my warm-up before a jog."

"You jog? I wish I could."

As they walked, they fell into a chat about the relative benefits of jogging vs. doing a walk.

"That's my brother Jorge over there." Esme pointed to a tall man of about forty. "He jogs."

Standing at a short distance and wearing exercise briefs and sandals, he was engaged in a conversation with two other men. He peered sideways at Maya, a sharp look. Maya would have to check him out.

Esme, taking purposeful steps, blinked against the sun's rays. "How did you know who I was, Maya?"

"I saw you at the church right after Rory Thompson's funeral." Maya watched Esme's reaction. Had Esme been acquainted with Rory? Maya sensed that she wasn't willing to give anything away. It'd be best not to question her about the murder, not quite yet. Maya didn't want to shock or frighten her and destroy the fragile bond they'd created. "Of course, everyone knows you. It's a coincidence that I'd run into you here."

Esme smiled, her attention turning to a muscular young man passing by. Caressing the hunk with her gaze, she moistened her lips. "Sooner or later, you meet everyone on the island," she said. "We like to become familiar with a person, establish a connection with him or her. Before long, you become one of us."

On this gorgeous day at the beach, open and expansive, a boat rocking far away from the shore, Maya was willing to go along with that. With the intention of drawing Esme out, she said, "You do volunteer work with the church?"

"Yes. More than volunteering, it's a commitment. There's enough family history here."

Family history. Didn't that say a lot about a person, especially in this part of the world? "I'd love to hear it."

"My grandparents—they were the most kind and generous of all people. Grandma Elizabeth, who had been tutored at home, was progressive. She cared. She looked after those who didn't have much. Together my grandparents started an organization called The Women's Place, which rescued abused women and provided them with a refuge. You know those who are beaten up by their husbands, who had no voice, no money, and no one to protect them. The organization, which was run through the church, tried to empower them. It was a brave proposition. 'Whatever social and constitutional rights you have,' the women were advised, 'you must claim them.'"

A powerful message. "How long did that project go on?" Maya asked, musing how much this snippet of information had enhanced the character of this island, as far as she was concerned.

"It ran for decades, benefited hundreds of women and children. My father took over at some point. He continued in the same tradition. After he passed, it fell to my generation. Now we have an army of women activists in this town and benefactors for these types of efforts. The organization has since been renamed Wings. It's no longer affiliated with my family." Esme's voice was laced with regret. "I'm active in it on a limited basis, the work is needed, and they've kept me as an honorary chairperson."

"Growing up in Kolkata," Maya said, "I saw hordes of families where girls weren't treated half as well as the boys. A common saying was, 'From womb to tomb, women suffer.' I've been away from India for a while. Have conditions improved any since then?"

"I'm sorry to say it hasn't. In villages and small towns, girls are told: 'Fetch the water. Dust the furniture. Feed your baby brother. Why do you want to go to school?' Even married women are not spared. Only the other day, I listened to Madhu, a middle-aged woman, a victim of domestic violence. She talked about her husband, who's a big shot in a large firm. 'I loved him, you know,' she told me. 'He was my temple, my God. I worshipped him. You can never make yourself believe that your God will give you life-threatening injuries. I had several operations before I gathered up enough courage to leave him. What did he do then? He stalked me, threatened to kill me.' I was horrified to hear this, Maya. And she's not the only one with a story like that."

Esme was more forthcoming than her appearance and manners dictated. "What kind of support does Wings provide?"

"First and foremost, we offer shelter to the sufferers. We give them vocational training and help them become e-literate. They get counselling, life skills, and medical care. Thank goodness, most blossom over time. You wouldn't believe the changes. Once they become self-sufficient, they often give back by becoming volunteers. They stay in touch with us for years. They become part of our tribe."

Zarina flashed in Maya's mind, the young, feisty sex worker, who wore neon colors, who had ample potential but who rotted away in a terrible place. With her son. Perhaps such an organization could assist her, help transform her life and that of her son. She could move up to where she wanted to belong. The very thought cheered Maya.

"What about trafficked women and their children?" she asked. "Does Wings have any programs to rehabilitate them?"

"Yes, we've taken on several sex workers and sex slaves. You should hear the stories they have to tell."

Under the brilliant sky, kicking at a tangle of seaweed, smelling the tang of the ocean, Maya made a vow to herself to find out how to help Zarina and her son. They deserved a better life. "How would they go about it?"

"You're serious, aren't you? Well, they'll have to take one small step." Esme fumbled in her purse, pulled out a business card, and handed it to Maya, saying, "Here are the contact details for Wings. Anyone can give the organization a try by ringing them or, better yet, showing up at this address."

Maya thanked her companion and shoved the card in her pants pocket. Yet another assignment for Hank: To check out the organization. For now, she concentrated on walking along the shoreline with Esme, the marigold sun burning about them. Ahead, an enormous wave drenched a rocky outcropping.

"No doubt you're dedicated," Maya said. "What, if I may ask, motivates you?"

"You're astute." Esme observed. "Yes, my interest is both personal and professional. I might as well admit it. There's been plenty of abuse in my family. The horror of it. You never forget those shameful, grim moments. Because of that, I've found it difficult to have a long-term partner. There was a time when I couldn't even venture out of the house. I'd be afraid of a rapist being out there, watching me and scheming."

Why Esme was willing to share that much, trust her with that side of herself? Maya gazed up and sent her companion a look of sympathy. Here was a scarred, forty-something woman, with an emptiness in her eyes. Maybe that explained it.

Seagulls shrieked and soared above as they strolled for a few minutes in companionable quietness. Two little girls squealed. Esme bent down, picked up a shimmering pink shell and examined it. "I have to turn around now," she said. "Hope to run into you here again soon. Next time, you'll have to talk about yourself."

As a PI, Maya found it necessary to guard her privacy and disclose little about herself. However, in this case she might make an exception.

Mist from the ocean caressed Maya's face. "Shall we meet at my hotel coffee shop one morning this week? It's quite cozy."

Esme hesitated, then said, "Why, yes, that'd be a nice way to start the day."

They settled on a date and time. Esme said goodbye, turned and waved over her shoulder. Listening to the rumbling of the ocean and pondering this fortunate encounter, Maya broke into a jog, the solidity of earth beneath her feet. She noticed that Jorge watched her from a distance.

Why did he have to scrutinize her? Her legs stiffened.

THIRTEEN

IN THE LAST FEW DAYS, HANK HAD DONE MUCH research on Wings, an anti-trafficking organization, which helped rehabilitate women at a safe shelter. Maya, thankful to Hank, paid a visit to the Wing's office this morning. At eleven a.m., the hour-long meeting over, she stepped onto the sidewalk, her purse full of paperwork, head brimming with details. The day sparkled before her now that she was better equipped to help Zarina. That is, if Zarina would be willing to make an enormous change in her life and leave her job as a sex-worker. Zarina, in turn, might provide Maya with more specifics about Rory's yearly visits to Andaman, which could offer clues to the case. Heretofore, she'd been rather guarded about this topic. Yet another incentive for Maya: The killer was still at-large and Lee felt unsafe, as did the whole town.

Maya had an additional reason for making a foray to this neighborhood, situated far from her hotel, not known for any major attraction. She wanted to check out the taxi stand where Kal, the cabbie, parked his vehicle. Hank had located the stand, but he didn't speak Hindi and hadn't been able to chat with other cabbies. Maya would catch Kal and have a word with him, if he happened to be there. Or she'd speak with whoever was present. Thus far, she'd gathered that Kal had a connection to Rory. He wouldn't admit it and as such he aroused both curiosity and suspicion in her mind. "You never know where a lead might take you," was an axiom she believed in. "It's worth following."

Her cell phone sang. She whipped it out of her pocket and answered it. Her boss, Simi Sen, who headed Detectives Unlimited, was calling from Kolkata. Maya trusted her and they were almost friends.

After they'd exchanged a few niceties, Simi said, "I have some particulars for you. Let me click to the right screen. I had it here a minute ago. Hold on a sec."

While waiting, Maya meandered down the winding street, taking in the local rhythm of life. This working-class neighborhood was dotted with small businesses located in single-story buildings, as well as multistoried residences. How different from where Simi was.

Maya pictured her now: Dressed in a stylish pink or yellow silk sari, her favorite colors, Simi would be sitting behind an executive desk in her glamorous office on the fifteenth floor of a tower in Kolkata. In Maya's opinion, Simi's character, charisma, and competence gave her face a glow, an extra twinkle in her eyes. Her organization was said to be the agency to run to if you needed a detective for "matters of the heart."

Maya, based in Seattle, had extended her services to homicides, and Simi approved of that. "A murder is the ultimate puzzle, in my opinion," Simi had said. "If you can solve one, you have it made." A shrewd detective herself, Simi could always be counted on to provide an insight into a person or situation. Maya took advantage of her gifts.

"Ah, here I am." Simi's voice came through the line. "Any update on the murder case?"

"Yes. I'm broadening the scope of my investigation. Rory was killed at a different location in town and his body was transported and dumped in the 'alley of tricks.' That indicates he had an enemy, not one of the women in that house. Who had contacts with him in this town? Who might want to hurt him? Did Rory's finances have any bearing to this crime? These are the questions I'm grappling with."

"Who are your suspects?" Simi asked.

"I have three. Kal, the taxi driver, is the primary 'person of interest.' I'm yet to meet Nemo Pal, the author, who was close to Rory. The police are keeping an eye on him. And I find it hard to admit but there are a few questions in my mind about Lee. We text each other, that's about all. She makes excuses why she can't get together with me and that bothers me. Like she has things to hide. We're such good friends. I've set up a regular confidential call with the manager of her hotel. He gets a generous *bakhshish* for keeping a tab on her and telling me of her activities."

"How's Andaman treating you?"

"Met the royalty, Esme Peterson. I lucked out and made an initial contact. I'm told the lady holds the key to the island." Maya was distracted by a man who passed by, carrying a rose-ringed parakeet in a cage. The poor bird squawked at the jostling crowd. "My gut feel is this: If the place has any secrets, she probably knows them. She's friendly enough that she might help me."

"Smart move," Simi said. "I did a load of looking for you. Good news is Kolkata isn't far from Andaman, only an hour by jet plane, and I have plenty of contacts there. A good many of them know Esme Peterson and her brother Jorge Peterson."

"What all did you find?"

"Father Australian, mother Anglo-Indian, culturally European," Simi said in a factual voice. "Born and raised in Andaman in a traditional environment, both went to a British school in Delhi, and they never stop talking about their 'home' in Australia. Both the kids were wild in their school years. Now they're well regarded by the Andamanese society. They keep an appearance of being old-fashioned, conservative, socialite types."

Maya heard the clip-clip of scissors from a street-side barber. "Wealthy, from the sounds of it?"

"Positive. The elder Petersons, who were Aussies, were timber barons, made millions in Andaman. Timber, as you probably know, was once the life blood of that island chain. High-quality wood products, such as flooring and furniture were made there, and the Petersons flooded the markets all over India. But word has it that part of the fortune made by that clan was black money."

"That's the illicit money people earn on the black market, isn't it?" Maya walked past a noisy open-air, fresh-produce market, inhaling a fruity fragrance. "An underground economy, where you're reimbursed under the table and avoid paying taxes to the government?"

"Correct. It's shady dealings."

"Esme looks and acts classy, like she's a VIP. There has to be more than money."

"Right you are. She's a principal of her family business. The family either owns a local bank or is invested in it. They're the proprietors of several bars and a shopping mall, which was shut down several months ago. As you might expect, their net worth has fallen. It's not public knowledge yet. In her role, Esme, the family matriarch, entertains the major players in Andaman. Anybody who's important, who can do for her what she wants done is welcome in her circle."

Maya slipped down a side street on her right. On a clean spot at the end of the trash-strewn lane, a vendor, with receding gray hair, had set up a concession stand. His chai-making wares and clay cups rested on a counter. An accompanying sign read: "We brew happiness for you." A homey aroma of tea leaves and milk flowed out of the stand. How Maya wished Alain was with her to share a cup.

"Does Esme have any love interest?" she asked Simi.

"If there's any, she keeps it under wraps. One thing is known. She's a friend to women's charities. Did that come up?"

"Yes," Maya replied. "She spoke about it in bits and pieces. Said most of her work benefited disadvantaged and battered women. It's curious that she told me about abuse she's suffered in her own home, which was what motivated her to take up this work. Even though she'd met me that morning, she was quite forthcoming."

"The islanders tend to make fast friends, which might explain it. Wings, the women's group, loves her, calls her Esme-ji, 'Beloved Esme,' or even Esme-mother. She's a planner and is well organized, orders people to do things for her. That's her public side. Port Blair isn't big, and the residents pretty much keep track of each other, but I'm told she's rather aloof. You know the nose-high-in-the-air type."

"What else?"

"She's supposed to be clever, crafty, and a control freak. You might have noticed her elite taste, a weakness for expensive clothes. She orders wine, caviar and chocolate from foreign sources."

Maya's gaze swept to a shoe repairman doing brisk business in a roadside stall. "What can you tell me about her brother Jorge? He gives me the creeps."

"You're not the only one. Jorge—that's not his real name, but the name he goes by— defers to his sister. Rumor has it that he suffered a serious brain injury in his teens in a mountain-climbing accident. A bully, he's said to have shown enough negative behavior in school to be considered troubled. He underwent therapy. As an adult, he picked up sword-fighting as his hobby. The man has cognitive limitations—is a bit off, you might say—not to mention depression and anxiety. It's been said that he likes girls much younger than him. Nobody talks. The brother and the sister are supposed to be very close. People do talk about that."

"Did Jorge ever do time?"

"No, and no criminal record, either," Simi said. "By the way, the Andamanese make a lot of hullabaloo about their parties. They're supposed to be great hosts."

"Noted."

"That's all I have," Simi said. "What else is cooking?"

"Something's bothering me a lot—it has to do with Alain. I haven't been able to reach him for days. I've sent at least five emails, left numerous messages and texts on his phone. No answer. That's not at all like him."

"Panic time?" Simi asked. "Shall I look into it?"

"Yes, please, he's supposed to be in Borneo."

"Borneo? I'll buzz you back as soon as I gather any input."

After terminating the call, thoughts about Alain percolating in her mind, Maya took a left, expecting to find a taxi stand, and walked right into it. A few cabs idled in front of a small shelter, which looked as though it served as a rest stop. Three men, ranging in age from young to middle-aged, stood by a lamp post and conferred. Maya looked for Kal, but he wasn't to be seen.

A turbaned cabbie broke away from his group, approached her and clasped his hands in a namaste gesture. "Which hotel, Madam?"

Even though she'd been born and raised in India, she was a foreigner to them, and that frustrated her. Swallowing her feelings, she concentrated on the matter on hand. "I don't need a taxi right now, but I'd like to ask you about a fellow driver of yours, if I may."

"Sure. This is a rest spot for us, one of several in the city. Nobody comes here looking for a taxi."

"His name is Kal and he drives a Maruti."

"That dude—you won't find him here. He's always in demand, always cruising, always being flagged down."

"What makes him popular?"

"Wish I could figure that out, Madam. Some folks have the interestingness. They B.S., they network, they make fast friends. I don't have those skills. But our popular guy has been looking quite upset in the last few days."

"Any idea why?"

"How would I know?"

"Would you know if I asked you for a lift and paid you double the going rate?"

"That'd improve my memory, Madam. From what I've heard, and

this is all secondhand, Kal's flat was broken into day before yesterday. Poor guy. Lives alone. He wasn't there and nothing was stolen. I imagine it made him angry. Or scared him to hell. Everyone's scared since that American gentleman was murdered."

Nothing was stolen. Maya noticed a pattern here—that like Rory's murder—and wondered why Kal might have been tagged. Had he helped the murderer? Had he failed to stop the murder? Or did he possess a crucial piece of data about the incident that someone wished to quell?

"Can you put me in touch with Kal?" she asked.

"No, I can't, but keep your eyes open. He hangs out at big hotels. He's been seen at another rest spot in the evening, quite a distance from here." He shared the address. Maya made a note on her cell phone.

He motioned toward a parked car. "Where to, Madam?"

FOURTEEN

ON THIS SUNNY MORNING, AT NINE-THIRTY A.M. the following day, Maya occupied a booth in her hotel coffee shop. Breakfasters jammed the place, a pleasant little nook, despite the whirr of a loud appliance coming from the kitchen. Other than burlap coffee bags lined up against one wall, the room had no décor. Through the windows facing the beach, Maya viewed the scenery. The ocean was a blur of blue, the sky threaded with gold. Seagulls shouted. Waves crawled to the shore, murmuring, frothing.

Despite the ambience, a sense of discomfort skittered through Maya. She recalled the latest incident: that of Kal's flat being broken into and how that made the cabbie vulnerable, whether he was guilty of a crime or not. To protect his life was one of her primary goals.

Esme, the town's head honcho, sat across the table from Maya. Her eyes were brown-rimmed, eyelids covered with a smoky shade and lips highlighted by a cherry-tinted hue. In her mid-forties, Esme looked younger than her age, but held a cheerless expression. On the glass-topped table between them rested oversized cups of aromatic coffee and appetizing stuffed parathas. Esme asked the waiter for an extra pitcher of cream and he obliged right away.

"Anything else I can get for you, Madam?" the waiter asked, voice imbued with respect.

Esme shook her head in a regal dismissal. The waiter bowed and departed. Amidst the clatter of silverware coming from the kitchen and a whiff of pastry baking there, Maya thought: How nice that she'd showed up. Maya wanted to have more facetime with her. She wouldn't ask about Rory, not a direct reference of any sort. However, this VIP might be able to provide Maya with information about the murder inquiry.

Esme put three sugar cubes, poured a splash of cream into her coffee, and stirred the cup, a drink more for comfort. Her eyes observed the room. "Lovely place to caffeine up."

"This beautiful town. I have had a hard time imagining any criminal activity here—"

"We don't have much crime here."

Someone stirred a spoon in a mug. "Unless you consider a recent murder," Maya said.

Hearing footsteps, she stopped speaking. A well-dressed man sauntered over to them and settled into a third chair facing the window. Maya recognized him as Jorge; she'd seen him from a distance. He acted as though that seat belonged to him. Maya hadn't expected company. She offered a smile.

"My brother Jorge," Esme said. "He wanted to meet you."

Jorge shot Maya a foolish sort of grin and said, "Enchanted."

Maya gave him a once-over without making it obvious. Tall and balding, forehead mapped with wrinkles, Jorge had green eyes and a prominent nose. He couldn't be more than forty. His most significant feature—Maya thought this facetiously—was his smile, creepy, even a little malicious. A sharp dresser, he exuded a smell of excess—drinks, indulgences, and late nights. He'd be difficult and aggressive, which became evident from the way he moved forward toward her.

What choice did Maya have? Esme's acquaintance would give her access to the community. She'd have to hit it off with Jorge. "The pleasure is mine," she said.

His glance flitted over her. They were blood-shot eyes, with lashes so long as to be protecting some secrets. "You're a private detective?" he queried. "Taking time out from your investigating this morning?"

What if I told you this was part of my investigation? Instead, Maya said, "I'm always open for a chat."

"You don't look like a private detective to me."

"What's a private detective supposed to look like?" A put down. Maya tried not to sound insulted, having heard that comment before.

"You don't scare me, a petite person like you." A trace of mockery showed in his voice. "I could pass by you on the street and not even pay you any extra notice. Worse yet, someone could knock you down with a blow of his hand."

Maya stared at him, dug deep inside herself, and brought out a smile. "To speak the truth, I don't intimidate easily. And it appears as though I don't intimidate you. Wouldn't you find it easier to enjoy a cup of coffee with me?"

Esme, who had been sitting and listening, interrupted. "My brother has a strange sense of humor, Maya. You'll get used to it."

Maya watched Jorge's reaction. And he did, indeed, have a reaction to her last comment. A look of apprehension flickered in his eyes. He stirred in his seat, having lost his composure. "It's different here," he said in a chiding tone. "It's Andaman."

"Please enlighten me, both of you—I'm new here," Maya said. "Why would Andaman be any different when it involved social interactions?"

Jorge must be struggling with an answer, for his breathing became shallow and perspiration beads showed in his temples. It was clear to Maya, as clear as the sky visible through the window, that his mental faculties weren't as keen as his sister's. How Maya wished Jorge hadn't shown up to disrupt the rapport between Esme and herself.

Esme's lips were pressed tight. She frowned down at her coffee, then raised her eyes and sent Jorge a sharp look. "Don't you have an appointment?"

"Yes, yes," Jorge replied to Esme curtly and switched his face toward Maya, with cold hard eyes. "I have to dash. We'll have to meet another time. Soon."

"I'll look forward to that," Maya said, wondering what Jorge meant.

He frowned, excused himself and hurried to the door. Before exiting, he turned and gave a stone-cold glance at Maya, indicating there was more to him than met the eye. She took a few seconds to regain her calmness.

"I apologize." Esme, with her shrewd gaze, concentrated on Maya's face. "Please don't mind him. He's a sweet guy."

He had more than a weird sense of humor, Maya observed. "No need to apologize," she answered.

"You're such an interesting person. I'd like to be better acquainted with you." A slight tone of authority showed in Esme's voice. "Tell me about yourself. Where did you grow up?"

"In Kolkata." Maya left out the part about her late father, not wishing to mention another detective in this conversation. "Raised by my mom, who was a single parent."

"In a happy environment?"

"Quite. Even though we didn't have much money, my mom filled our flat with music, laughter, books, and company. I couldn't have asked for a better childhood or more simplicity." Maya found herself shuttling back to those days and cheered by them. "Going for a kulfi ice cream would have been the high point of my week."

Esme's eyes were wistful as she listened to Maya. "That prepared you for bigger adventures in life?"

In between bites of her paratha, Maya responded: "At least it gave me a direction. Then again, it wasn't always so easy. An uncle of mine who managed our finances swindled the money my father had left us. That put my mother in debt, and it devastated her. She liked him and trusted him. It took her years to forget the incident, if she ever did."

"But you managed to go to the States to study?"

"Yes, my mother paid her last penny to buy me a plane ticket to the States. I enrolled in a college, but had to be on my own, which meant I had to pay my bills. At one point, believe it or not, I was holding six part-time jobs."

"You learned to depend on your wits?"

"Very much so. While studying nutrition, I took classes in criminology and worked part-time for a detective agency. In the end, it worked out. After a few years of running a business as a nutritionist and saving my paychecks, I could venture out as a PI, which is what I wanted to be."

"What makes you a good PI?"

The roar of conversation from the next table distracted Maya. "That's a tough question. I'm still learning the ropes. Once invested in a project, I don't let go till I have the answers."

Esme looked away for an instant, then said, "Your mom must be proud. You love your mom, I suppose?"

"Yes, very much," Maya said. "We're close."

"I didn't like my mother." Esme rounded her chest. "She was cold and distant, died when I was young. I had close relatives and they did their best to raise me properly, but I missed the loving attention that . . . that . . . I'd liked to have had . . ."

"I'm sorry."

"I pulled through it, but Jorge never did," Esme said. "Do you have a partner? A lover? A significant other?"

Maya didn't care for this question. Too private a matter. Shouldn't be any of Esme's concerns. "Yes," she said, but kept her head low to hide her expression.

"Why isn't he here?"

"Because of a job assignment."

"You must talk a lot on the phone."

Maya put her fork down. "We're missing each other's calls."

"Sorry to be intrusive," Esme said. "It's the habit of an islander. We're nosy, we like to know everything about everybody. Only then, we become chummy."

Well, then. *Take advantage of this opening, Maya.* "Believe it or not, I'm the same way. How're you occupying yourself these days?"

"Not much on the romantic side. I'm forty-five and on the shelf. The other day, I mentioned to you about my work with abused women, didn't I?" Esme leaned back in her chair. "That's my life now."

"Tell me more."

"Every year I host a tea party at my house to honor those brave women, to show we care. Our local newspaper calls it the 'best feed in town.' It's coming up later this week." Esme paused. "Would you like to attend? I'd love to have you."

A wonderful opportunity. "Why, yes," Maya said. "That's very kind of you. I'm a stranger."

"You've already made quite an impression."

Esme's voice had an edge; her comment wasn't complimentary. She pried a business card from her purse and handed it to Maya. Done on white silk paper, the gilt-edged card with stylish lettering spoke of money, power, and exclusivity.

Esme watched Maya's reaction and said, "Give me a ring. My assistant will answer. She'll handle any questions you might have and will ask for contact info. She'll send you a formal invitation."

Esme had other reasons for making this invitation, not all of it altruistic. Maya would have to puzzle that out later. Right now, she envisaged Sophie, how her cheeks shone at the sight of a feast, how she would say, "Fab," in a light voice, when informed of a party. This event would be her cup of tea, so to speak. The next moment Maya deliberated over whether it would be safe for Sophie to attend.

"May I bring a friend?" she asked Esme.

"Of course."

They pushed to their feet and said goodbye to each other. It was past ten-thirty by then. In parting, Esme's voice and expression had become unreadable.

As she strode out of the café, the sound of the waves matching her heart's rhythm, Maya found her mind working overtime. The entire conversation radiated mixed messages, with little indication of what was going on underneath. She couldn't quite place what bothered her. Even so, she wouldn't pass up this opportunity to show up at Esme's bash. With Sophie.

FIFTEEN

MAYA PERCHED ON A CHAIR by her bedroom window, the laptop in front of her. It was the same morning, about eleven a.m. Almost two weeks had passed since her arrival, without any major breakthroughs, the seriousness of the situation uppermost in her mind. She sifted through the material gathered thus far, which included her list of suspects, Lee being among them.

Maya's next move would be to check up on Lee's whereabouts. She didn't feel good about doing this. Lee was her closest friend and they texted each other several times a day, but she didn't have any choice. She picked up her cell phone and called Bipin Chandra, Manager of Emerald Villa, where Lee stayed.

"Anything unusual about Mrs. Thompson's comings and goings?" Maya asked Bipin.

"No, she doesn't go out much."

"Has she received any visitors this past week?"

"That she has. Several male guests. They all visited her for a short time, but one gentleman stayed for about two hours."

"His name?"

"Nemo Pal." He paused. "We now make it a requirement for all visitors to sign our registry, like you asked us to do. My staff likes it since the murderer of Mr. Thompson is on the loose and everyone's nervous."

The intriguing author had visited Lee. Not a total surprise, yet Maya startled. She'd called him and left a message, emphasizing that she was a friend of Rory. The call had remained unanswered.

Maya thanked Bipin, hung up, and decided she must get in touch with Lee. Her attitude wasn't one of judging. Regardless of what Lee might have done, Maya would respect her as a person and continue to nurture their friendship.

She phoned Lee. They chatted for a few minutes, following which, Maya said, "Would you like to come over to my place? Catch up, do a mini-hike, have a meal?"

"Sure, I'll be there within the hour."

After hanging up, Maya checked her online mail, only to find a flurry of messages from her clients, the telephone company, friends and neighbors, but no reply from Alain. What had happened to him? With an eye to the turquoise ocean stretching out before her, Maya decided not to overtax herself with worry.

Her cell phone shrilled. The desk clerk at her hotel announced the arrival of a woman visitor.

"What's her name?" Maya asked. "Send her up here."

"She refuses to give her name. She wants you to come down to the front lawn to meet with her."

How strange. It couldn't be Lee. They'd talked only a short time ago. If Lee did come over a little early, she wouldn't hide her identity. It preyed on Maya's mind, the recent phone conversation she had had with the hotel manager about a fishy character. It was as though she couldn't breathe easy in this luxurious resort. "Have you ever caught her hanging out here?"

"Yes, we've spotted her a few times. To be on the safe side, our security will keep an eye on her from inside the lobby when you meet."

She thanked the clerk for the safety measures. After taking a long inhalation, she rolled her shoulders up and down, hurried out of the room, took the elevator to the main floor, and exited through the front entrance. Her slippers made a crunching sound on the hotel's gravel drive, which matched her concerns.

Zarina hovered near the gate, clad in an over-the-top pink chiffon sari in geometric print, a beaded choker necklace and sandals. She'd come for a visit? After the abrupt way their last encounter ended? How strange. What did she want? Despite the colorful outfit she wore, she looked dour.

Maya locked eyes with her, took a few more steps in her direction and said a warm hello.

"I only have a few minutes to speak with you, Lady," Zarina said. "If

Mr. Pande finds out that I . . .

"What would he do?"

"He'll stop giving food to me and my son. He'll take away my afternoon shopping break at the Women's Market, the only free time I have. And he'll curse me, day and night, like I am *saitan* itself."

"Quite a person, this Mr. Pande, isn't he? Shall we sit down?" Maya slid onto a wooden bench under the shade of a Pema tree studded with lilac-colored flowers and gestured Zarina to join her.

"No, no, I'll stand," Zarina said.

"You cut our talk the other day," Maya said. "What made you change your mind and visit me?"

"Look, Lady, I didn't tell you everything," Zarina said. "But first, I must apologize. I insulted you, our honored foreign guest. I feel terrible, like a little insect. I can see how much you love your friend and how you stand ready to help her. You came to visit me, which must have been difficult for you. And I . . . I misbehaved . . ."

"Are you prepared to talk about Rory?"

Zarina spared no word. Maya shuttled back to the last time she'd seen her. Animated and outgoing, she now peered to the ground, standing like a statue, hesitant and withdrawn, as though weighed down by a million concerns. Reticence didn't fit her, a creature who pulsed with life.

Maya decided to cut to the chase. "You knew Rory, if I were to make a guess."

Zarina, about to speak, stopped herself and must have thought the better of it, for she nodded.

"Tell me about him if you would, if you wish for his killer, who is still among us, to be tracked down and brought to the court. We don't have much to go on."

"Why did he have to die?" Anger and sadness laced Zarina's voice. "He was kind, kinder than most, and respectful."

"You had strong feelings for him. Perhaps you loved him. You're mourning his loss, am I correct?" Maya braced for the reply.

If for an instant, a blissful look rippled on Zarina's face. "Yes, right. Of course. He was big, bigger than our tallest mountain and I loved him. Was he ever ashamed of being with me? I never felt that. We were happy in the few hours we spent together. And you know what? He adored my son, too. Called him Krishna. Didn't ask him to run errands like the majority of customers do. Gave him pocket money to buy chocolate bars and asked about his studies."

Not unexpected. Maya took a deep breath before asking a heart-breaking question. "Is Krishna . . .?"

"Rory's child? Yes, it's the absolute truth. He loved his son very much."

Maya wished she had misheard. *Rory, you didn't have a one-night stand. You'd been involved in a more serious affair. You even had a child, a flesh-and-blood heir of yours. Being that I'm close to Lee, I find it hard to accept your philandering.*

An insect screeched somewhere. "Were paternity tests conducted?" Maya asked.

"Rory didn't ask for one. Why would he? He could tell Krishna was his."

Maya wondered for the second time: how to reconcile this new perspective about Rory, who lived a double life, who had fooled everyone, including her? She couldn't deny that he might have had loved Zarina, a woman so natural and full of life, unlike anyone he'd ever met. This, despite the fact she was a street walker and he was married. An image of Lee stole over Maya: red-eyed and swollen-faced, solitary in her sadness, one hand covering her mouth to stifle an outburst. How would Maya ever be able to disclose these findings about a deceased husband to a wife already so shattered? Yet, the case demanded that she dig into the truth, however much that slashed her insides, however it burned her.

She blinked away her feeling, gained command over herself and said to Zarina, "How many times over the years did Rory come to see you?"

"What a question. As if I keep a diary, like some lazy broad who has nothing better to do than to put her big butt in a café chair, open her journal, scribble a few words and stare out the window."

Zarina could retreat from her again when confronted with another question. Despite that, Maya couldn't help but repeat, "How many times? Think hard, please."

"More than a dozen times. He came by several times a year, always asked for me, if he didn't see me standing at the window. Paid for the full service. Always paid me extra."

Rory, how could you? How could you possibly have hidden all of this from Lee? What didn't you get from her? "When was the last time you saw him and for how long?"

"Last winter." This confession must have eased her burden somewhat, for Zarina's eyes danced. Her shoulder relaxed. The edge of anger in her voice, displayed only moments ago, subsided. "He came over several times," she said. "We enjoyed ourselves. He always visited me in winter."

"Did he promise he'd be back again this year?"

The voice went down a notch. "He did."

"But he didn't call you this time, I take it?"

Zarina, her face a mask of disappointment, studied a tall, graceful fern for a moment. "Someone let slip to me he'd been spotted at a watering hole in Port Blair," she said in a voice laden with hurt. "I stood at the window that damn evening and waited. No sign of him. I wondered why he wasn't showing up with an engagement ring or a bracelet. My son asked about his father. I lost my appetite."

Maya composed her next question, a difficult one that tangled in her mouth. "Does that mean he'd already proposed to you?"

Zarina put her face in her hands for a few seconds. It was as though she was going through a trunk full of goods, searching for a hidden heirloom, and located it. She raised her head, her pouty lips trembling. "Oh yes, he wanted to marry me and spend his life with Krishna and me. He made big plans for us."

Heaviness behind her eyes, Maya clasped her hands together. Disillusionment lingering, she admitted to herself that Rory was a man of big appetites. Could it have been his nature to want more? And more? Try to pack up that void within him that could never be made whole?

"Go on, please," Maya said. "I'm listening."

"Last year, about this time he promised to take me away from here. He told me, 'You're as pure as snow on a mountain peak, Zari. You're too young, too pretty, and too smart to be turning tricks to make a living. You deserve better. So does Krishna. He should be able to go to a better school, bright kid that he is, and he shouldn't forever be bullied as a 'Child of the Night.' He has rights.' I asked, 'Do you mean that? Do you?' He replied, 'Yes, I'll pay your bail to Mr. Pande for him to release you.'"

"Mr. Pande wouldn't object?" Maya asked.

Somewhere a truck roared, causing Zarina to stir. "No, he doesn't like me. I'm too much of a bother, tribal and a hick.

"What is your bail?"

Zarina replied and Maya keyed the amount on her cell phone. A huge sum in Indian currency, Maya could afford to pay that. For now, she said, "I'm with you."

"Rory said to me, 'We'll relocate to Delhi and start afresh. How does that sound? I'll put you up in a two-bedroom luxury flat, with big windows. We'll take long walks, my lovely girl, in the Lodhi Gardens.' He called me a girl because I was fifteen years younger. I asked him if we'd get married, have a big ceremony with friends, feast, flowers, bright lights, loudspeakers and a priest, and he said yes to that, too. I laughed, I cried, I held him tight, I kissed him. I could picture it, the good life we'd have together."

Maya couldn't face sitting there any longer. She felt an urge in her to rise from the bench and run back to her room but forced herself to stay seated. Did Rory take into account the effect his affair would have on Lee?

To Zarina she said, "He said he'd marry you? Didn't you know he had a wife?"

"He said he loved me more."

"You believed him?"

"Why wouldn't I?" Zarina's voice was laced with regret. "In my community we speak the truth. People look different when they lie, and we can tell at a glance."

Maya paused for a moment and wondered anew about a tribal connection to Rory's death. "Did Rory look different?"

"Yes. But, staring at his handsome naked body lying next to mine, I ignored it. I was smitten, happy and light-headed." Zarina giggled, showing her teeth, like pomegranate seeds, the reddish cast coming from munching paan. "All day long I sang folk songs. It didn't matter that I'd heard all sorts of gossip about him."

Maya became extra alert. "What gossip?"

Again, Zarina giggled. "That I'm not in his league. That he was too bookish for me. That, besides having a lovely wife, he had other things going. That he would let me down and stop showing up. I didn't believe any of that. His words were like pure honey. I drank it."

A girl's romantic dream. Cotton candy under the burning reality of the day. "What other things did he have going?"

"I don't know."

Rory—quiet, good-looking and attentive—offered space. Women filled it with their narratives. Was that how he justified his actions? "If you did know it, what would it be?"

Zarina threw a severe glance at Maya. "You ask too many questions."

Struck by the heat of her gaze, Maya persisted. "How did you feel when you found him dead?"

Zarina's lips curled in pain. "I went nuts. I wanted to feel his pulse, kiss his forehead, and bring him back to life. I wanted to tell him again he was a real man. He was my hero. But the police came and carted off his body. There went my heart, my tears, my tenderness and all my dreams. I haven't been the same since and neither has my son."

"Where's your son?"

Zarina's eyes flared. "Don't bring him into this."

"I'd like to meet him."

Tight-lipped, Zarina sat.

"Who do you think was behind the murder?" Maya asked.

"I don't have the foggiest."

"What about your tribe?"

"They have nothing to do with it."

"Look, Zarina, we have the same goal. Someone has taken away what you hold precious. We must track that person or persons down. Wouldn't you like to give me a hand with that?"

"It's not one of us, that much I can tell you. Neither my tribe, nor any woman in our house did it. We're the lowest of the low, happy to have another sunrise to look at, happy to hold onto what little dignity we have. People hate us, curse us, call us the scum of the society. But . . . what I mean to say is we don't go after people with a machete. We give pleasure. That's all we do. Look higher, Lady, look higher."

Maya sat with this confession for a moment. She had more questions for Zarina. To trace the crime-doer, she now understood, she'd have to cast a wider net. She heard the crunch of gravel on the pathway skirting the lawn as a yellow-black taxi cruised into the driveway.

Zarina swiveled her head around, took one quick look at the vehicle and said, half-turning, "I must leave now."

Before Maya could speak a word of gratitude, Zarina waved a hand and vanished behind a grove of trees in a whirl of color.

SIXTEEN

LEE DESCENDED FROM THE TAXI, her steps careful, and paid the driver. She displayed much grace and beauty in her outfit of a pearl white fine cotton sari and silver necklace. On a closer look, however, Maya noticed despondency around her mouth, creases of confusion at the corners of her eyes, and lines of distress on her forehead.

Could it be that Rory's infidelity might have given Lee enough motive to take his life? No, no, Maya didn't wish to color her attitude with suspicion. With arms open wide, Maya rushed toward her friend. Lee gave a quizzical look toward the direction of the vanishing woman, then flung herself into Maya's arms. As they sank into each other's embrace, Maya felt a welling of sadness inside her.

Once they separated, Lee said, "Who's she?"

Maya shrugged and put on a lighter tone; she hoped to keep the correct answer from emerging in her voice. "Someone I met."

Lee studied Maya's face. "Why do you look upset?"

"It's nothing. Let's go stretch our legs."

Despite an unsettled heart and musings about Lee's innocence, she couldn't be more comforted by this reunion. Together they promenaded the periphery of the well-kept lawn. They paused before the flowing contours of a stone sculpture, that of a mother and child, and a row of flowerbeds bursting with reds and yellows. A honeysuckle scent emanated from somewhere.

Remembering how much Lee loved flowers, Maya said, "Do you know some local tribes have an interesting custom? They name their daughters after flowers blossoming in that season. "

Lee's face cleared. "I imagine girls with the same name form life-long bonds."

"Correct."

Lee kept busy inspecting the flowers and commenting on them. A warm, gentle, and enveloping breeze blew, bringing in the earthy aroma of a native variety of grass. In the momentary pause, as they seated themselves on the wooden bench, Maya couldn't help but replay her conversation with Zarina in her mind. And which led to Maya's wondering about the relationship between Lee and her late husband.

Behind closed doors, were they lovey-dovey and tender, or cool to each other? How much did Lee know about Rory's infidelities? If Zarina's tear-filled statement—delivered in a convincing manner—was accurate, Rory lived a double life. His friends saw him as a scholar, an entrepreneur and a family man, refined in his appearance. Strong and flexible as the wind, always with a book in his slender hand, he had a way of filling the room. Yet he cavorted in the seedy part of Port Blair. In a miserable house. Taking advantage of a young tribal woman, a tragic figure who had fantasies about him, who had invested her future in him. Maya couldn't bear the thought anymore. She shielded her eyes with a hand, as though to wipe the Rory-Zarina episode from her mind. A moment later, she asked Lee how she was.

"I'll live." Lee's tone was heavy. "When the person closest to you is gone, all you're left with is nothingness. A day goes by, like a bird flapped its wings. The night creeps in dense and dismal. I can't eat. I can't sleep. I can't stay awake, either." She paused. "Remember that one time we were both complaining about something, must have been months ago. You said, 'Let's stop bitching about what happened yesterday. Let's focus on what could happen tomorrow.' Remember that? That lifted my morale."

"Is there anything I can do for you, anything at all?" Maya asked.

"No. You've done so much already. It's been only a short time since your arrival, so I hesitate to ask. I know how long it takes to get your bearings here. But I was wondering if—"

"If I've made any progress? Right now, I'm in a data-gathering mode. I have interrogated a few people and talked to the police—not a lot to go on quite yet. I do have a question for you. Have you heard from any of Rory's authors?"

"Yes, I have. His authors are from all over. A number of them have called, some more than once. A few have flown here and dropped around to see me. They all have given me comfort aplenty."

"How about Nemo Pal?"

"Of course, of course, the big-name author—I met him, after all. Rory used to say, they were "share the same toothbrush" type of buddies. He would spend hours gabbing on the phone with Nemo long distance. Rory was ecstatic when he signed Nemo up for a book. 'With all the skills the guy has in creating characters out of thin air,' Rory said, 'he'll be able to make his nonfiction soar, too. He has his shit together when it comes to putting words on the page. It might be the mega-hit I'm waiting for.'"

"What did they have in common other than books and writing?"

Lee knitted her eyebrows. "Nothing off the top of my head."

"How difficult it must be for you to have to drag up painful memories. I apologize."

"No need for apology," Lee said. "For your sake, I'll do it."

Maya recalled the YouTube interview of Rory in which the subject of finances had come up, causing his cheerful expression to disappear. "What was Rory's business story, if you don't mind telling me?"

"My dynamic husband dreamed of expanding his publishing enterprise," Lee said. "He wanted to incorporate video, build multimedia and create a digital platform for consumers. For that, as you might expect, he needed funding—the involvement of venture capitalists and angel investors, which is never easy."

"What about your family? Could they not have—?"

"My family has already helped us. Rory didn't want any more funds from them. You know him. He'd stop at nothing. He hunted for investors first in Seattle, then in Silicon Valley, but was bypassed each time. He would stay upset for days. At some point, despite being demoralized, he turned his mind to India."

"India? Investors? You never mentioned that."

"I didn't know what all it involved. The news was the Indian government had increased the overseas investment ceiling, which meant funding from India could flow outward to foreign shores for monetary support to projects. I remember how excited Rory was when he first began to explore that possibility. His face was flushed. His eyes were like stars. 'India is ready,' he said. 'She's making her debut on the world stage, which might mean a pile of cash for my business.'"

"I suppose Nemo was instrumental in making Rory aware of this new governmental policy?"

"Spot on."

"My own nutrition consulting business was small, but I owned it 100% and I didn't look for investors, as such. But my understanding is that you give away an ownership stake to your investors. You must also share the vision."

"You're up to something. However, that didn't stop Rory from exploring."

"It's possible then that Nemo might have put him in touch with prospective investors."

"Don't hold me to it, but that's quite likely."

"Did Rory divulge any further details about his investment scheme?"

Eyes downcast, Lee shook her head.

"Did you ever wonder about that, since you took care of the fiscal end of his business?" Maya asked.

"I did the number-crunching, yes, but that was so like Rory," Lee said. "He'd grown up quiet, lonesome, and bookish, used to keeping things to himself, not confiding in anyone, even me. 'On a need-to-know basis,' was a common phrase he used. I'm rather patient."

"Did you ever notice any unusual deposits or withdrawals from his bank accounts?"

"Let me think. Yes, he did make a quarterly deposit to a bank in Andaman, not a huge sum. When I asked about it, he didn't reply to me and I let it go."

"Can you give me the name of the bank and the account number?"

"It's business confidential."

"I must have it as part of my investigation."

"Okay, I'll text that info to you. Who do you think the money went to?"

"Not sure," Maya said. "On another note, was Rory ever . . .?"

"Unfaithful to me? No. Never. How could you even ask?"

"My apologies." Maya wondered if Lee wasn't holding back. It was her too-prompt delivery, acidic tone, and slouching posture. Best to try a different tack. "I'd be interested to hear more about this Nemo Pal."

"I've read one of his novels, *The Open Window*, and loved it. It was quite an honor for me to have him show up in my hotel room yesterday and offer his condolences. We had a nice long chat."

"He waited all this time for that?"

"He said he couldn't face me."

Due to what? Guilt? Could he have saved Rory's life? Maya filed that snippet of suspicion away and asked, "Why couldn't he?"

"He didn't say. I suppose that's how torn he was. Anyway, it was a pleasant surprise. He's a bit of a figure in Delhi, a charming man, a sensitive soul, cut up by Rory's death. Told me Rory was like a brother to him. Promised to give me a hand, whenever that was needed."

"Did you believe him?"

"I did at the time, but to speak the truth, I don't trust my own judgement, given the mental state I'm in."

How Maya wished she could lessen Lee's pain. Bring some closure by nabbing Rory's murderer. And to forever decimate in her mind that faint suspicion about Lee. "Anything unusual about Nemo?"

"Yes, now that I'm rechecking my impressions, he did act a little paranoid, like . . ." Lee cut herself off.

"Like he's under extreme stress?" Maya said. "On drugs? Depressed? Suicidal? Or he thinks someone's gunning for him?"

"Could be all five. Given the circumstance, his behavior is understandable, is it not?"

"I don't suppose he gave you any warnings?"

"He did. Told me to be careful. Right after that, he jumped up from his chair. Said he had to go back to his cottage on the Rock to work on his manuscript. The only thing that kept him sane, he insisted, was his writing practice." Lee paused. "He couldn't be a murderer, could he be?"

"I'm not clear about his motivation, if he had any, that is," Maya said, "but I wouldn't let him off the hook either."

"My God. It's creepy. I was alone with him."

"What's his new book about?"

"Don't know." Lee's long-lashed eyes opened wider. "The truth is—I never thought to ask."

SEVENTEEN

U PON ARRIVING AT HANK'S HOTEL suite at nine a.m., a day later, Maya assessed the situation in her mind while waiting for him to answer the doorbell. Since receiving a text from Lee yesterday, regarding the name of the Andaman bank where Rory made quarterly deposits, Maya had asked Inspector Dev to delve into the matter. He'd done so and relayed to her that the recipient of the fund was Mr. Pande, the brothel owner. Maya was now faced with the unpleasant implication of that finding. Why would Rory send money to Mr. Pande? Unless, the money was destined for Zarina and she didn't have a bank account. Child support, in other words. Maya shook her head in shocked disbelief at Rory's perfidy.

Regardless, she must continue digging into the case. She had several leads to check out. First, the financial angles of Rory's business: Might there have been an investor in the picture? If so, what was his or her role in Rory's life? Second, Nemo Pal's new book and whether the subject matter might have been the direct or indirect cause of Rory's death. And third, Nemo as a suspect. What motive would the author have had in putting an end to Rory's life, if that was, indeed, what had taken place?

She heard Hank's voice saying, "Come in, Maya."

She greeted Hank and entered his suite. He pulled up a chair for her. After a few minutes of chitchat, Maya decided the time was right to broach the subject of the author. "Is there much press on that guy?"

"Yassss." Hank elongated his Yes when excited. He positioned himself at the desk and powered up his laptop. "Sophie and I pulled up a lot of stuff on him and made a profile."

"Walk me through it, if you would."

In a flat, reportorial voice, Hank ticked off his notes from the screen: Nemo Pal, age forty-one, a free-wheeling writer, was hailed from a family of means in Mumbai. A journalist-turned-author, he was considered to have potential by literary critics, with three best-selling novels to his credit. Believed to have experimented with recreational drugs in his younger days. Dabbled with stage acting. Well-liked by his peers, moody and reclusive at times, Nemo Pal socialized often enough. Once given to expensive liquor, he was now believed to be on a health kick. A ladies' man, who had never been married, his name had been romantically linked to several socialites and even a Bollywood starlet.

The guy sounded impressive, but not everything about him added up, such as his call to the police station on the night of Rory's murder. "Might he be what you'd call an unreliable narrator?" Maya asked.

Hank smiled. "I'd say so."

"What's the connection between him and Rory?"

"They were friends. His next book for Rory has scored him a big, fat advance against royalties. The Indian press had gone gaga over it. Nemo and Rory often bar-hopped together in Port Blair."

"Hang on. A fat advance from Rory? That's most unusual." Maya filed that information for follow up. Where did the money come from? Or was expected to come, since an advance was offered in installments? She asked herself anew: Had Rory secured any new funding? An additional point to note: Being drinking buddies, perhaps they confided in each other. Therefore, Nemo would be able to offer intelligence on Rory, not to be found elsewhere.

"Nemo has agreed to meet with me this afternoon," Maya said, "but only under the condition that I show up alone. I'm going."

She was about to say more when Sophie emerged from the bathroom. Freshly scrubbed and bare-footed, a slim-thigh girl, she wore red short-shorts and a rebellious dot-printed tank top with a too-plunging neckline. Her silver necklace in a basket-weave design created a flash-bulb aura about her. She flew across the length of the room. In one long, sweeping movement, she kissed Maya on the cheek, Hank on the lips, and switched the television off with the press of a jeweled finger.

"G'Day," she said to Maya, a child-like treble in her voice. "I've ordered brekkie. I assumed you were joining us."

"Oh, yes," Maya said. What to make of Sophie? Maya admitted that the girl had turned out to be congenial. Up to this point, she hadn't caused a whiff of a problem, only minor irritations. From the moment she woke, this reckless girl buzzed about, planning this and that and consulting with so-and-so, leaving Hank out of her planning process. She spearheaded the meal arrangements, chose the right spots, and paid for everyone. Hank would smile and proclaim that Sophie had a Ph.D. in food. Though only twenty years old, she demanded prompt service from everyone and, with a mere glance of those shiny black-rimmed eyes and flutter of long lashes, managed to get it. She couldn't handle too much alcohol, however. A glass of wine would turn her red-faced and wobbly; she'd be unable to walk in a straight line.

"I overheard you saying you're seeing Nemo alone, Maya?" Sophie lifted her chin, voice reflecting concern. "My God. You have a date with a suspected killer? Don't you think we should tag along? In Sydney, when I'm about to step out of the house to go trekking, my dad tells me, 'Take a friend along. Make that two. Three heads are better than one in the wilderness.'"

"As I said, I don't have a date with him," Maya replied. "It's a business meeting, maybe even an offender profiling, in police terminology."

Upon hearing a knock, the ever-alert princess skipped toward the door. A pair of hotel workers—wearing uniforms of loose, snow-white tunic, apron, and trousers—bustled in, bearing huge trays containing an Indian feast. From the looks of it, this must have been a special order, paid by Sophie, and the kitchen help must have toiled since early this morning. Maya's eyes widened as she examined the array of dishes: soups, crepes, dumplings, and grain concoctions, in shades of green, yellow, beige, and rich brown. On most mornings, Maya's breakfast consisted of a poached egg and lightly buttered raisin toast or a bowl of oatmeal topped with sliced bananas—simplicity itself. She now allowed herself to be mesmerized by the colors, freshness, and familiar spicy notes, which brought childhood memories of India to her.

The men—young boys actually—arranged the dishes on the sturdy, elliptical coffee table, one platter after another, a feast more suitable for ten.

Sophie's eyes brimmed with excitement. "A banquet for breakfast!"

With the waiters slipping out the door, the trio huddled around the table. Hank slid a bowl of idli-sambhar toward Maya.

Maya gave a thankful gaze to her companions. How thoughtful of

Sophie to have remembered to order her favorite combo: plump dumplings and a piquant lentil soup for dunking. "This'll hit the spot."

Hank transferred a large, crispy dosa pancake and coconut chutney to his plate, saying, "It's astral."

Sophie stared at uppama, a cream-of-wheat preparation garnished with fearsome, toasted red chili peppers. Maya tried to figure out whether Sophie's obsession with food had to do with her mother's death when she was young, whether food might be a love substitute for her. Worth noting in that regard was the fact that Sophie didn't gorge on food; she liked having it around.

"If Nemo wants to meet with you, Maya, then he must have checked out your social media." Sophie blew an unruly bang out of her eyes. "Must've drooled over your photo."

How does one handle a girl like Sophie? "As I mentioned—"

"Loosen up," Sophie said. "Where are you two meeting?"

"At a spot called Saddle Peak Park Trail."

"Wait, I've seen that trail mentioned in my guidebook." Sophie rose, fetched the book from the bedroom, reclaimed her seat, and thumbed through the pages until she came to the right spot. "Here it says you have a choice. You can hike the white sandy beach trail or go through dense jungles. Both are secluded."

"I'll decide on the route when I arrive," Maya said.

"He wants to meet you in the middle of nowhere?" Hank asked.

"Why, yes, he thinks the cops have him under surveillance."

"They've tagged him as a suspect?" Hank said. "Do you . . .?"

"I do," Maya replied. "At this point, it's not clear what Nemo's motives were in making that desperate call to the police. Was he an accomplice? Does he have intelligence on the subject? I don't have the answers. However, it's clear that he's a potential scapegoat for Inspector Dev, who needs to hand-cuff someone."

"Can't imagine what it'd be like to be locked up for something you didn't do," Hank said.

"My agenda here is two-fold," Maya said. "First, pump Nemo to extract detailed answers about Rory's murder. We might need to rendezvous more than once. Second, help him exonerate himself, if he's indeed the wrong party and is being framed. I'll have to be as delicate as possible—I don't want to antagonize the cops. Their cooperation is necessary for me to accomplish what I'm here for."

"Sounds risky," Sophie said. "Damn it, we'll go with you. We'll act like tourists hiking the trails. Otherwise, how will you make sure you're in one piece when you're with a potential slayer?"

"In my line of work, I often have to—"

"Mate, watch it," Sophie plunged in, a pleasant but authoritative ring to her child-like voice. "We'll drop you off and wait someplace close by. Yes, that's the way it'll be. You are family, as far as I am concerned." She put the guidebook down on the table with a big thud. Her bossy manner was in keeping with what Maya had gathered from Hank about her family background. 'No bro, no sis, no mom. Plenty of loose change. Sophie likes to spend it.' The father, a shipping magnate, who had remained unmarried and lived alone in a mansion in an affluent suburb of Sydney was indulgent, to say the least. The daughter, who attended college in Seattle and hung around Hank, not in that order, presided over the household in absentia. She went to see her daddy on holidays and held the staff accountable for all their actions. According to Hank, the household help called her the "velvet whip" behind her back. That Sophie, executive Sophie, "velvet whip" Sophie, now said, "What if he grabs you? What if he holds you hostage? What if he tries to kill you?"

Maya controlled her voice to hide her secret anxiety about that rendezvous. "I can handle myself. It's a job requirement. And the last thing I want to do is to expose you two to danger. You mustn't be seen with me. That could put you on the radar of the police and whoever else is trawling nearby. I'll hire a taxi. You two drive your car and park at the trailhead. When I'm done speaking with Nemo, I'll join you."

"Give us a time frame," Sophie said.

"However long it takes for Nemo Pal to open up," Maya said

"Not good enough, mate."

A brief debate followed between Maya and Sophie. Hank sat back and listened, interjecting a monosyllabic reply every now and then and once asking Sophie not to be 'cheeky.' How Maya wished he didn't always give the floor to Sophie. In the end, Maya won.

"I'll have to concede, I guess." Sophie looked at Maya. "You're old, I mean older than I am."

At thirty-four, Maya didn't judge herself to be ancient. Far from it. She didn't detect an abundance of lines on her forehead when she studied her face in the bathroom mirror. This girl would take some more growing accustomed to. On top of all that had been happening.

"One other thing I must tell you," Sophie said. "I ran into Kal, the cabbie, at the corner store. We chatted. He asked how your sleuthing was going."

"How does he even know about that?"

"Beats me. But he said he'd be showing up at this hotel often in the next few days. A hotel guest has hired him for the week."

"If you see him sooner than I do, then ask his last name or get his business card, will you?" There was more to that cabbie; Maya had a hunch all along.

EIGHTEEN

SEA BIRDS CALLED. A brown-bodied, white-spotted, silky butter-fly floated in the air. Amber rays of sun peeked from behind wooly clouds. Maya listened to the roar of the surf as she stood on the shore next to a gigantic coastal rock, with dense greenery at her back and silvery white sand under her feet. Dressed in a pale blue fleece sweatshirt, denim pants, and hiking shoes, she carried a lightweight backpack that held a few essential items. Except for an occasional hiker traipsing by, the area was deserted.

Thank the heavens. The high humidity of the afternoon was offset by a gentle breeze. As she looked up, sea mist caressing her face, an image of Alain fluttered up inside her. An adventure freak, he would have liked this ambience. Would have thrown his arms up in the air and started singing in one of the many languages he spoke. The fact that she hadn't heard from him weighed down on her. No contact at all since the day they parted. Didn't he miss the warmth and comfort that she provided? Her kisses and laughter and joy they shared? It felt as though he was slipping away. Then again, this time, the first time they'd separated since meeting eight months ago, Alain had opened the door for her to pursue her career. She'd have to do the same for him. Release him from her concerns and allow him the time to settle in his new environment and finish his assignment. At the very least she'd wait for him to make the next move. Only then. Only then . . . what? She couldn't answer her own question.

A whistling sound coming from behind startled her. She swung around. Nemo Pal, the author recognizable from the headshot on his website, took firm brisk strides. She measured him. Tall and skinny, with deep-set eyes, he seemed to exist on air. With an aristocratic oval face, curly hair, a high nose and an in-between complexion—neither fair nor dark-—he looked to be seasoned, sophisticated, and complicated. A party kind of a guy, who could turn serious when he needed to be. Dressed in denim pants, a short-sleeved white shirt and hiking boots, he had a moneyed aura about him. In her mind she could hear Alain saying, "Rory had a friend in Andaman," which turned out to be Nemo.

"What a pleasure, Ms. Mallick," Nemo said in a rich voice.

"The pleasure is mine, Mr. Pal. You can call me Maya."

"Please call me Nemo." Close up, his eyes were shadowed from a lack of adequate rest. His facial expression was taut, and his chin twitched. Here was a man under stress, doing his best to act normal. "Best to be on a first name basis, even when being grilled."

"You expect a grilling, Nemo?"

"Aye." He turned and glanced at her. His tone turning light, he said, "Why else would you meet me, a lovely woman like you? You'd surely be sought out for company by one of the town's eligible bachelors. I'd expect you to sit in a stylish bar at this hour, nursing a beer and having a Port Blair evening, all eyes on you."

How embarrassing, his hitting on her, a ploy which could add an extra layer of complication to her investigative pursuits. "Save the flattery, please."

He laughed. "Instead, you're here with me on this secluded beach trail, where no one would hear you scream."

A sixth sense whispered she'd be safe with him. She took a pace back and summoned a laugh. "You're not trying to scare me, are you?"

"Nothing like that, simple author that I am. Of course, as a detective you know that when someone is trying to scare you, they're scared themselves."

What did he mean? Best to postpone that inquiry for later. "Shall we do a trek?"

"Good idea—stay away from surveillance."

"Surveillance?"

"Pardon me—I must sound paranoid. Sometimes I think . . . it's only a guess on my part, mind you . . . they're watching every move of mine."

"Who are they? Do you care to talk about it?"

He shook his head. A shock of a black curl danced over his forehead. They set off, rolling hills on their left, and the navy water of the ocean to their right. A gust of wind, carrying the smell of the sea, accompanied them. Soon they hit a bumpy, gravely, narrow trail through an evergreen forest redolent with the cool fragrance of the trees. Somewhere a stone tumbled. A red-throated bird made a high-pitched sound as it hopped from one leafy branch of a tree to another.

"Is that an Andaman bulbul?" Maya asked to put him at ease.

Eyes dreamy, pride in his voice, hair tousled by the gentle wind, he replied, "Yes. Once it was popular as a cage bird. Now it's free. It has all the air in the world to breathe."

"That reminds me of a story from my childhood," Maya said. "A prince in ancient times was taken in by the song of a bulbul in a forest. He caught it, brought it home and gave it plenty of food and water, but kept it jailed."

"And then?"

"It stopped singing. Not a single sound. The prince waited and waited. He took it outside and much as he didn't want to do it, he freed it. The bird hopped to a tree branch and started singing."

"Right you are. A bulbul stands for liberation and that's what is most important to it."

"Who's threatening you?" Maya asked.

"It's common knowledge the cops are after me."

"Haven't you given them your statement?"

A sense of weariness laced Nemo's voice as he tackled a steep hill. "Then what makes me a person of interest, is that what you're asking?'"

"Yes." Because of the altitude gain, she found herself slightly out of breath. "Unless you've given them any reason to—?"

"They don't need reason, Maya. They want to throw a body in jail, so it looks like they're doing their job. That's about it. I hope you'll catch the hitman soon, so I can go on living my normal, carefree, even boring life."

Pushing on difficult terrain, she said, "I'm the new person on this island, Nemo. I've only met a small segment of the population and haven't a clue as to what goes on here. I could use some heads-up."

"I doubt . . . I'll be able to . . ."

"But you met me. Why? Given the risks you're taking?"

He smiled, the one-time actor. "May I make a personal inquiry? Do you have a significant other?"

He'd avoided answering her question. She noted the deep brown gaze trying to swallow her essence and unsettle her. "Yes, a live-in partner in Seattle."

"Ah! A little separation."

"A business trip came up for him."

"He couldn't cancel? He let you come alone to this remote island?"

"Let me remind you," she said, "this meeting isn't about me. It's about—"

"Okay, okay." A small frown appeared on his forehead. He hadn't accepted her explanation with ease. "Let me tell you something. Andaman can turn things upside down for you. You start seeing yourself differently."

Even though Maya had been raised in India, she couldn't quite believe him. "How so?"

"Andaman takes you away from yourself. You feel unbound, like you could try anything, be whoever you want to be, go anywhere. You lose touch with your previous life. Am I making sense?" He paused. "I'm sure you remember that the British had built a penal colony here to punish the Indian freedom-fighters. Those martyrs were tortured. Most died. Locals believe their ghosts are floating around. Hiding in the shadows and listening, trying to help us remove our shackles, mold us in a different manner and give us a new life. Or that's how a community elder explained it to me."

"How unusual, how interesting." Maya stopped speaking for an instant. This place might challenge her to grow. Maybe she needed that. It hadn't been easy to uproot from Seattle. She was managing as best as she could. A little tense, she used her hands to sweep aside the branches of an overhanging evergreen tree to make progress on the narrow path. A few branches cracked, a pulpy smell asserted itself, and an insect buzzed about her head. She became aware of the reason why she was here. With the afternoon light fading and evening descending, she'd have to clear out of these trails soon. Her hopes of finding out more about Rory from this author would vanish. She said, "You know, I miss Rory."

"Each time I pick up the phone," Nemo said, "I keep hoping it'll be him."

"I suppose over the years you've had many interesting conversations?"

"Yes, one of them being about the concept of infinity. Let me back up. When I was five, my beloved uncle died. I couldn't process his death. I cried and cried and asked my mother, 'Where did he go? I miss him. I want to play with him.' My mother replied that he'd gone to infinity. That he was gone from our midst but not lost. That he was now a part of the continuum. She was trying to console me, a sad little kid, and explain that which can't be known." Nemo shuffled, head bent, as though feeling the full weight of memory. "When she died about a year ago and my woe stopped me from carrying on, I recalled that anecdote. By imagining her as part of the ultimate, I was able to spring back on my feet. Later I shared the story with Rory. We went back and forth, playing with the idea of infinity—endlessness—which to him was a fascinating concept."

"In high school we girls used to tell our friends, 'I'll love you to infinity,' without understanding what the word meant," Maya replied. "But I can see that the idea of having no limits, existing in a boundless condition, ignoring the clock would have appealed to Rory. For him there was no 'That's all there is.'" She wiped the perspiration off her forehead with tissue and allowed Nemo a few moments to recompose himself, before asking, "How much did Rory share with you about himself?"

"He wasn't an open book by any means, pardon the pun. Rather, he was one of those who needed to have secrets. Each secret is another identity, another experience, another rebirth, he once told me."

For sure. Like Zarina. "You had one of the last conversations with Rory. What did he say to you? How did he sound?"

"He was on his way somewhere. He sounded . . . more than a little disturbed."

A gust of wind caused a wayward tree branch to tickle Maya's forehead. She shifted into a high alert mode. "Were you surprised?"

"Very much so. The following day, he was going to open the inaugural Andaman Book Festival, and that would have been any person's dream. The applause, the storm of praise, the wine, the feast, the camaraderie, and the substantial honorarium. Not to forget the fans standing in long lines to have a word with him, to ask him for his scribble."

"Whom did Rory wish to meet that evening when you last spoke with him?"

Nemo shrugged, as though saying, *Hell, if I know.* He continued his hill-walking and replied at last, "You're relentless. Rory said he'd call me back in about an hour, but when he didn't . . ."

A strong wind blasted her face. "Why did that panic you?"

"As a writer, I listen to not what people say, but what they don't say."

"What did Rory not say to you?"

He gave out a laugh, a forced one. "You're tougher than the local cops. I have no idea what was bothering Rory. But being a friend—it was one of those moments, when you grasp something about a person you're close to, without fathoming why—I could tell something was up."

"You were afraid for his life and so you called the police. Why did you do that? Who could wish Rory harm?"

"Like I said—there's more to Andaman than meets the eye. Accidents can happen."

"What on earth do you mean?"

He turned and held his gaze on her for a long moment. "I hate to wipe that pleasant expression from your lovely face, Maya, but you might as well know this. You're not safe in this town, either."

She felt her face freeze. "What are you talking about?"

"Your movements are being watched. There could be attempts on your life or someone close to you."

Maya pictured Hank and Sophie, her young, innocent companions, who were parked nearby. That unnerved her, brought out her protective instincts. "By whom? Why me and my dear ones? What aren't you telling me?"

He diverted his gaze from the fork they'd reached, checked the time on his cell phone. "Do you mind if we turned around? I have to shove off. Another engagement. Already late."

She halted for an instant, looked him in the face. "What's so important?"

"Any chance you might come to see me at the Rock?"

A bird chirped. Another made a melodic noise. "What do you have in mind, Nemo?"

"Even though this is our first meeting, I've heard about you from Rory. Never thought I'd meet you in person. I . . . I'd like to become better acquainted."

"Look, as I said, I'm unavailable. But it'd interest me to talk more. About Rory."

"Please allow me to extend a formal invitation to you," Nemo said. "I'm spending all of tomorrow in this town visiting and shopping, so it has to be the day after. If you catch the ferry to the Rock and come to my cottage, I'll show you around. It's the most beautiful island in this archipelago and quiet. I'll be able to answer your remaining questions without anyone looking over my shoulders. We'll have lunch. And, if you'll indulge me afterward, I'll read a passage from my manuscript for you. How would that be?"

Best to take a moment to review this offer, since she'd placed her feet on a glossy, slippery rock. She led the conversation to a new direction. "What's your new book about?"

"You're interested? It's supposed to be a top secret, but I'll give you a hint. The story took place before either of us were born, during World War II, when the Japanese occupied these islands."

"How far along are you?"

"I have a chapter more to go," he went on. "The last chapter, as you might know, is excruciating. Everything must pool together to a satisfactory conclusion, which might not turn out to be a happy one. On top of that, you must provide a killer last paragraph that puts the reader in a reflective mood. Like when a dance ends and there's a moment of deep silence."

"Go on, please."

"There are days when I pull my hair out. I can't wait to type 'The End' on the last page." He paused. "Please keep any knowledge of the subject matter to yourself."

"Why the secrecy?"

He gave a signal of recognition at an aged, slow-moving hiker approaching from the opposite direction. "It was one of Rory's superstitions. Mine, too. I don't like to talk about a book in public before the manuscript is complete."

"Could the subject matter have landed both of you in trouble? Is there anyone who might want to suppress this material?"

"You're coming to the Rock?"

All these bothersome evasions were annoying Maya. She'd now use one of her own. "I'm kind of busy—"

"Do you know a saying we have? 'There's more to life than upping its speed?'"

She said in a bold voice, "I've been advised to stay away from the Rock."

He made a sound of frustration. "That retired-in-place inspector warned you, eh? He's a moron. Don't you get tired of his bullshit? I'm not a dangerous man, Maya—rest assured you'll be safe. You'll even have a little adventure on the way. Damn—a recent rainstorm has wiped out the bloody road, the shortest route from the ferry landing to my cottage.

You'll have to take a detour, rough it, and do a little high-elevation rock-hopping, but you'll be treated to a spectacular scenery and a far better work-out than at the gym. Are you okay with that? You look the athletic type to me."

"Yes, I am."

"Once you arrive," he said, "you'll appreciate the social ambience. My neighbors are families from the mainland, a friendly bunch. They'll welcome you. And my landlady—you wouldn't believe the meals she prepares. People kiss her feet after they've tasted her spicy, flavorful dishes."

Maya stole a look at him, at the bright eyes, the eager expression and the magnetism he exuded, aware of the slight chemistry between them. It showed itself as a fleeting feeling of pleasantness one might experience on a sunny day at the beach. Soon to be forgotten. It bothered her to be so vulnerable, given that he was a potential killer. She listened to the musical flow of a nearby stream to compose herself.

"Can I bring a friend and/or a guide with me?" she asked.

He gave it a moment's thought, then said, "Okay, if that'll make you feel more comfortable."

"On another topic," she said, "I wanted to pick your brain about the Petersons. This evening I'm invited to a reception at their residence."

He exhaled, as though he'd been listening to her intently. His breath smelled of a cinnamon jar and cigarette. "The Petersons—they're the royalty of this town. Their mansion is labyrinthine, has at least sixty rooms. Rooms full of history."

"Does that mean you—?"

"Yes, she's an old flame of mine."

"Oh." Maya swallowed. An unexpected connection, which could be useful. She could see the two embracing, a fierce flame that burned hot and untamed, but died out. She couldn't be sure whether their hearts had since turned stony to each other or not. "Are you friends now?"

"No. She's another fucked-up heiress, but she has more power than the Lieutenant Governor of Andaman. She can snap her finger and accomplish things that others can't."

Maya's eyes lingered on a star-shaped white orchid growing on a tree. Might there have been a love triangle of some sort? "Have you seen her lately?"

He looked distressed. "No." After a pause, "You're coming, aren't you?"

She couldn't be sure of Nemo's innocence or guilt or what game he was playing with her, but she'd visit him to unearth some clues, Inspector Dev be damned. "Yes, you can count on it."

They'd reached the starting point on the shore. Nemo halted, recited his address at the Rock and gave detailed directions to his cottage. Maya jotted them down on her cell phone. At a distance she could hear the crack of thunder.

"Are we going to run into any wild animals there?" she asked.

"No. But if I were to give you a general piece of advice about these islands, that'd be this. Do carry a mini flashlight and a stick wherever you go. The stick is for stray dogs. And . . . and always be careful." He half-turned, looking exhausted and vulnerable. His eyes held a wistful light as he said, "Until we meet again."

"Will you call me in the interim, if you get into a tight spot?"

"You're most kind, *yaar*." He stared at her and his lips parted in a smile. "It's a deal."

Yaar. Friend. The beginning of trust-building. Through the pinkish-mauve shade of the sunset, she held a pleasant expression.

NINETEEN

"You know, Maya, I love being gussied up." Sophie's face took on a peach-blush color in the late afternoon light. Her eyelashes were made more silken by mascara. And, indeed, she looked gorgeous, if a wee bit risqué, in a lacy, scoop-necked, knee-length chiffon dress in a lime green shade. Emeralds sparkled at her ears, while her white-gold twist bracelet dazzled. "And all we have to do is show our faces and make nice to the Petersons?"

Maya smiled. She'd put on a purple-and-gold sari, wrapping it around her in a hurry; for it didn't matter how she looked. She didn't compare herself to Sophie, much younger than her and like a sister. Her concern was: how best to conduct herself, so she could sniff around a trifle in the Peterson residence and find clues to Esme's personality. What if her sari didn't hang right, if it had a slippery feel? With the details Nemo had supplied, she had reasons to be wary of the Peterson's.

Maya and Sophie sauntered together to Hank's rented Honda idling on the hotel driveway.

Hank stood next to his car. His eyes shimmered as he gazed at Sophie. "Girl, you're straight fire." Then turning to Maya, "You look very nice, too."

Maya thanked him. Clutching her bead purse, she slid into the back seat of the car.

Hank started the engine. He grumbled about not being invited to this "Women Only" soiree, admitting he could use the time to sharpen his short story. Then, assuming a gentlemanly voice, he announced, "Door-to-door service, ladies."

The massive hilltop classical house turned out to be an iron-gated estate. It had a flat roof, pillared entrance, columned porticos, and a teakwood swing. Spread out over a large compound, it sported a separate wing, perhaps for the household staff. The entire estate was fronted by a garden thick with ferns, creepers and jarul trees. Maya looked up at the sky. A lonely white slice of the moon had cocooned itself in the clouds. In the violet light of the evening, the whole compound took on a dreamy, almost unreal look.

"A garden palace." Sophie sounded impressed. "And a fountain, too." She threw out an arm and pointed to a stone fountain in the middle of the lawn. The water splashed down to a catch basin, glistened and made a soft music.

They swept to the entrance, which was surrounded by potted flower plants. Maya rang the buzzer. A woman attendant—young, vivacious, and dressed in an orange tunic-and-pants ensemble, so bright that it hurt Maya's eyes to look at her—welcomed them. She shepherded them up the stairwell to the second floor. As she traversed the long marble corridor, Maya peered at the black-and-white, framed portraits of distinguished-looking family members mounted high up on the walls. Among the European faces, there stood out that of a Japanese woman dressed in an embroidered mandarin collar blouse. She held a serene but determined expression. You didn't want to cross her, or so Maya suspected.

Following her escort, Maya entered the large banquet hall, which featured curtained windows, a marble floor, a chandelier hanging from the high ceiling and a wine bar. A long table draped with a maroon cloth and placed along a wall was loaded with crust-less sandwiches, cakes and pastries, samosas and other savory items, enough to feed a hundred people. The centerpiece consisted of a large, aromatic silver bowl filled with local fruit. Yellow flames flickered from tall candles placed on a large, swirled brass holder. Women dressed in technicolored saris and adorned with jewelry shone against the neutral walls. Faces lit, they fluttered in the space, their hands cradling gold-rimmed teacups filled with amber tea. Steam rose from the cups, fragrant with ginger, black pepper, and cardamom, creating an intoxicating atmosphere.

"What a feed." Sophie served herself a samosa and a piece of white cake.

Maya strolled through the room, nodding at whomever she crossed paths with, taking note of all the details out of sheer habit, hearing happy exclamations about this get-together, all the while remaining watchful. She could hear enthusiastic compliments about this gorgeous evening all around her. From a corner drifted sitar music, a passable melancholy tune, played by a young woman. The whole atmosphere, Maya concluded, had been designed to set the guests at ease, so that they would enjoy themselves and sing praise of their fabulous hosts.

A stir at the door and Esme and Jorge blew into the room, both in great form, their steps measured and deliberate. Esme's smiling gaze encompassed the entire area. Heads turned and a hush fell, followed by spontaneous applause. Esme wore a long ivory gown. A row of dazzling white teeth matched the double string of pearls around her throat. Eyes surrounded by glowing brown mascara, she sported a redder-than-blood lipstick.

Jorge, handsome in a custom-fitted suit and dress shoes, his sparse hair well-groomed, stood next to his sister. He had a look on his face, like the last time Maya had seen him. The folded edge of a sky-blue, silk pocket square, a work of art, billowed out of his breast pocket. He and Esme busied themselves floating from one cluster of guests to another. Greetings and good wishes, delivered in happy voices, floated especially toward Esme. Her hair glowed under the chandelier light.

As Maya reunited with Sophie, Esme and Jorge advanced toward them, uttering welcoming words. Maya, in turn, performed the necessary introductions.

"Don't mind me." Jorge came to stand beside Maya. With a wink and a grin, he referred to himself, the only male in the room, as the "bull in a glass museum."

He had the habit of disrupting, Maya remembered from the coffee shop incident. She watched him as he turned to Sophie, who appeared young and demure, and his eyes gleamed. He shook her hand, whispered a compliment, and clasped her arm, appearing to be taken with her. They floated toward the other end of the room, from where came the sound of wine being poured into crystal stemware. Maya, swapping polite sentences with Esme, kept an eye on them. Jorge poked his head toward Sophie. She had a gold-rimmed wine glass in hand, took a sip every now and then and looked engaged.

Esme, with her shrewd gaze, noticed Maya's concern. "Colorful sari you're wearing." she said. "I wish I could dress in one, but I look ridiculous."

"What a beautiful home you have," Maya replied, changing the topic.

"I liked seeing the pictures of your family on the hallway. Who was that Japanese woman?"

"A great aunt of mine, known for her beauty and charm." She let an instant pass. "You're busy with your investigation, I suppose? How is it going?"

Maya noted the pejorative manner with which her hostess had spit out the word "investigation," and this was the first time she'd mentioned it. Keeping her voice warm and inclusive, Maya said, "At this point I have more questions than answers. Since you know the lay of the land and I don't mean village gossip, may I ask—?".

"Oh, God. I think it's outsider's job, a random attack."

Yeah, sure. Despite the buzz of the guests around her, the food aromas, and the twang of sitar, Maya wanted this chat to continue. "You mean a mainlander or a foreigner?"

"Could be either. However, once a shady character has skipped this island, it's hard to track him down. Do you suppose you're spending your time in vain?"

"Not at all." Maya was now ready to overstep and ask a question that verged on being personal. This was perhaps not the proper time and place to do so, but Maya couldn't take a chance. She might never run into Esme again. "Did you ever meet the murder victim—Rory Thompson?"

Esme tempered an uneven breath. A hint of a blush appeared on her cheeks. "Yes, I've met him a couple times. A charming man. What a tragedy—must be his own folly—being at the wrong place at the wrong time."

"His own folly? You believe that?"

Esme looked toward a pair of guests who had entered the hall. "Let's enjoy the party, shall we?"

She turned, plastered on a big smile and drifted away. Maya didn't buy her explanation. She backed away, stood by the table, and watched the yellow candle flames jumping up and intensifying.

A nose-ringed attendant must have noticed. She flitted over and pointed at a platter of chocolate ganache. "Specially flown in from Delhi. Made by the best chocolatier there. Please try."

"Thanks, maybe later."

Maya turned away, her gaze drifting along the room. Jorge, standing close to Sophie, chitchatted with her. The glass of wine in Sophie's hand glowed. The best Maya could do was to leave them alone for now.

Without anyone noticing, she sailed out of the dining hall, not sure what she was looking for, only that she might find an evidence or two by snooping in Esme's abode. This was Maya's only chance. In her mind, she circled back to what Nemo had said: *Rooms full of history.*

She crossed the hallway, pushed the door open and slipped into a drawing room, which was furnished with a set of plush sofas, a sideboard, and a gilded coffee table. From here she could hear the hum of party conversation and the music. She closed the door behind her and landed into an adjoining room, which turned out to be a study. Small, uncluttered, shadowy and melancholy, it housed a desk, an executive chair, a window and a wooden bookshelf. It belonged to Esme, Maya could tell. Her touch was everywhere. Her scent permeated the room. The ruby-red coffee mug standing on the desk next to a laptop could only be hers. There reposed a green-and-white clay jug containing a bouquet of fresh purple leaves. A small ornate bowl held seashells. The walls displayed a series of Japanese-style canvas paintings of swans, forests, lagoons, and fish in purple, black, and green. The floor glittered with a hand-knotted, geometric-pattered carpet in blue-and-gold. Esme spent her mornings ensconced in this study, her manicured fingers flying across the keyboard as she did her e-mail; Maya could picture that. A piece of broken glass glinted on the floor. Where did it come from? She pushed it with her feet and shoved it under the desk.

A strong breeze blew against the window and made a racket, as though urging her to hurry. She drew open the central drawer and looked in it. Among address labels, pens and markers, and spare change, there lay a smartphone. It was unlocked.

Should she? Why not?

Putting the guest protocol aside, Maya tapped the phone icon, located the photo library and clicked through the first few shots. They were images of Esme and Jorge with family and friends, none of whom Maya recognized. Hearing a small noise, Maya looked over her shoulders, her breath on hold. Was anyone approaching? Did she see the flicker of a shadow, detect a movement? No, it was her imagination. She'd make an exit if anyone entered. She rolled through several more snaps of natural scenery: birds, beaches, rocks and boats. Then she navigated to an image that made her pause, her breath more rapid now and it hit her upper chest.

Rory slouched in a chair, gazed out of the photo and smiled a typical Rory smile. Shy and not too wide. Not giving much away. It shimmered in Maya's mind, brought back the tug of mourning. Esme must have adored Rory enough, treasured him enough to have snapped this shot of him.

The next photo caught a profile of Rory, shirtless and with a come-hither look in his eyes. *Rory, what was in your mind? What had you committed yourself to?* Several other nude and semi-nude images followed, images a lover would preserve.

Esme had had a fling with him. He was part of her "history." This physical evidence suggested so. Yet, only minutes ago, she'd admitted only to having been an acquaintance of Rory, a big, fat lie told through her scarlet mouth. Something weird here. This finding had given Maya a few things to run with and directed her to a new course of action. But it wouldn't be easy. She'd have to be able to command every ounce of her strength and intelligence to pursue this lead. Against a formidable opponent like Esme Peterson.

She was about to check the location data of the photos when the door swung open. Jerking back, she closed the drawer, pushed away from it and turned around.

A slight young male, a staff member, barged in. He frowned at her and said in a rough voice, "What are you looking for, Madam?"

She stiffened, but replied in a normal voice, "The ladies' room."

"This way, please." He led her back to the corridor, pointed to a room at the far end and sent her a fierce look before stomping away.

Maya slipped back into the dining hall buzzing with conversations and eased to a corner. The lights seemed dimmer now; the gorgeous soiree had lost its appeal to her. Esme, orbited by a group of women, noticed Maya's reappearance. She allowed a pause, turned down the wattage of her smile, cast a glance at Maya, and signaled Jorge with her eyes.

Best not to stay any longer. It wouldn't be safe. Maya could smell trouble. She looked across the room, spotted Sophie standing by the sitarist and dashed over to her.

"I've drunk too much," Sophie said. "Jorge left me alone to greet a relative. We were having such a nice chat about Sydney. He goes there to watch cricket games, you know."

Jorge had made a fast move. Maya didn't like the smell of it, having heard of his reputation as being a dude who chased young things. Sophie, vulnerable Sophie. A "what if?" danced in Maya's mind, bestowing her another reason for not lingering.

The sitarist took a pause. Applause followed. The room became vibrant.

"Hate to break up the party," Maya said to Sophie, her eyes toward the exit. "There are reasons why we shouldn't stay any longer. Shall we?"

TWENTY

A PRIVATE FERRY CHARTERED BY MAYA ARRIVED at the Rock at ten a.m. two days later. During her three-week sojourn in Andaman, she'd been asked to stay away from it. In her urgency to gather more details about Rory's stay in Andaman, she'd accepted an invitation from Nemo Pal to call in on him. She hoped to fill in some blanks and move the inquiry forward at a faster rate. With the perp at large, the safety of Lee and Kal couldn't be guaranteed. Maya feared for her own life and that of Hank and Sophie as well.

Accompanying her on today's journey were Hank, Sophie, and Hindi-Man. Dressed in capris and a T-shirt and carrying a mini-backpack, Maya alighted first on the deserted sandy shore, focusing her attention on where she placed her feet. Hilly terrain, covered with a thick tropical jungle, spread out before her. Areca palm, coconut, and kathal trees towered over a multi-layered green canopy shot through with golden rays of the mid-morning sun. She could hear the shrieks of animals, the symphony of insects, and the cacophony of birdsong. She'd never visited an isolated place like this, a speck in the middle of a mighty ocean, where humans had left little trace of their passing.

Abid, the mustachioed ferry captain—a calm, slight man in his thirties—announced he'd turn around, shuttle back to Port Blair and return in an hour. "To collect you before sunset."

"What?" Maya said to Abid. She hadn't intended to bring Hank and Sophie with her. As always, Sophie had insisted on being a part of the team. "You agreed to stay here with my teammates. That was my understanding."

"Sorry, I forgot I have an errand to run. Do not worry. I'll be back within a short time." With that he vanished.

"He's being difficult," Hindi-man said.

Maya's eyes drifted to the departing boat as it floated across an expanse of cobalt blue and moved away from the land, the wind pushing on it. A lifeline, gone. "What if he doesn't come back?"

"He knows why you're here," Hindi-Man said. "But don't fret. I can contact other cruise services via the cell service. They'll be more than happy to give us a lift."

"I'd love to have a picnic in this cool place," Sophie announced. "First, let me change into a bikini. Be a tourist."

"Please, no bikini, Sophie." Maya whispered. "A Western woman showing legs and belly button? Not sure how the islanders would take it."

Sophie pouted. "They sound like my Thai relatives in Sydney. Okay, I won't change."

She spread out a blanket on the shore and began unloading the picnic basket stuffed with silverware, candles, fresh flowers, a Frisbee, sandwich fixings and several magazines. Maya assumed that they'd munch, sunbathe, play Frisbee, and browse the periodicals to pass the time.

"Shall we?" Hindi-Man motioned to Maya in the direction of the jungle.

Aware of the time crunch, Maya waved goodbye to her teammates, adding, "Watch out for sand-flies."

Hank tensed his eyebrows. "My, my, you'll have to trek through that jungle, Maya? Be careful. Call for help, if you need it."

Sophie gave Maya a thumbs-up. With the ocean as her background, the young girl looked tiny, lost and uneasy.

Maya pivoted and plunged ahead on a narrow trail, twisting through groves of trees, with Hindi-Man ahead of her. The path soon vanished, and they had to pick their way through a lush coastal forest choked with vines, thorny bushes, and prickly leaves over ground made treacherous by bulging tree roots. Was this the right way? A fearsome sun winked through the branches. The beams flecked Maya's short-sleeved cotton top with pinpricks of heat and dashes of gold. Every sound became magnified, vibrated in her chest, and exploded. Instead of giving in to her misgivings, Maya paid attention to each step she took.

Further in, she bumped her head against a black-and-green butterfly clinging to a branch. Oh, no, that gentle creature. She'd have to be more careful. The next moment, a snake, indistinguishable from the detritus on the forest floor, slithered past her legs. Was it poisonous? She lost her footing and slipped into a mud puddle. When she regained her balance and stood, a spiky branch scraped her forehead.

"Please be careful, Madam."

Maya overlooked the sensation of swelling. She couldn't navigate this territory as effortlessly as her guide, a native of this area. But she'd make it, no matter how difficult it turned out to be. She expected so much from this day: to pop in on Nemo, learn about his book, and hear about Rory.

A sound of stomping feet grew stronger by the second. "What's that?" Maya could hear the dread in her own voice.

Hindi-Man turned to look at her. "Sounds like the Badung tribe is celebrating a special occasion."

"Are we that close to their territory? Are we even supposed to be?"

"No, Madam. I didn't expect it, either. I'm not familiar with this island. The directions were confusing and we must have taken a wrong turn somewhere."

Hindi-Man's reply unnerved her. With bruises on her arm, feet aching, the scrape on her forehead burning, she even wondered about Nemo's intentions in making this invitation. "What do we do?"

"Follow me." Hindi-Man ducked his head under a branch, emerged on the other side, and contemplated the challenge before them—a tall embankment. He went straight up. She struggled with loose rocks, hung on to the bushes for support and emerged on a plateau. Choking on her breath, she took in the 180° view: serene and beautiful. Deep blue ocean surf tumbled on one side. A lush green grassy clearing stood on the other.

She spotted human forms. A knot of people had congregated at the farthest end of the clearing, resembling stick figures from this distance.

"That's the Badung tribe," Hindi-man said.

"What can you tell me about them?"

"Only a few details." Hindi-Man elaborated: The tribe didn't use money and shared few material goods they had among themselves. Attuned to the weather, seasons, and surroundings, they were content to live that way. They worshipped the fire, water, earth, and sky and believed in ghosts and spirits. Although harmonious, they could turn ferocious if needed be. "Don't ever cross a Badung, or so went a saying."

"We shouldn't be in their territory then, should we?"

"That's correct." Hindi-Man fumbled in his pocket and held up a pair of slim-line binoculars. "Use these. I'll go see what our indigenous brothers and sisters are doing. I'll ask them for directions and be back before you know it."

"Couldn't I come with you?"

"No, they're not used to seeing modern women."

He trotted off across the plateau at an easy pace. She didn't like being left alone—she'd never be able to find her way back and that raised a shiver of dread on her back. But she had no choice. Lifting the binoculars to her eyes, she trained her gaze on the gathering below. With this wide field of view, she could scrutinize the tribe's members of both sexes: strong, ebony-bodied, and naked, except for leaves or decorated loincloths. Maya deemed it comical that the natives had a custom of nudity. Minutes ago, she'd advised Sophie against wearing a bathing suit.

She heard the sounds as two clansmen beat out a rhythm on a hollow log with the palms of their hands. Others danced around an open fire, stretching out arms, thrusting shoulders in and out, clapping hands on their thighs, and stomping their feet to the beat of the drummers. The flames leapt high and powerful and brought out merriment in the group. A child with painted cheeks weaved in and out of the circle of merrymakers. A wiry, grizzled, elderly man with a wooden headdress held a long bamboo pole fitted with a slender blade in one hand. He drifted away from the group to meet with Hindi-Man. Maya assumed that he was their leader. Soon they began arguing, Maya could tell from their gestures. She found the situation disconcerting. A sea breeze whipped above her head, almost knocked her off her feet.

Hindi-Man returned, looking disturbed. "I got more detailed directions. We'll be there in a short time, if we rush. They don't want us in their territory. Word has circulated around here that you're a private detective. You're here to see a murder case to an end. They mistrust the authorities. They could turn hostile."

"How fast can we leave their territory?"

"Not to fret—they won't follow us."

Maya experienced a sense of unease. Accompanied by Hindi-Man, she retraced her steps, taking a different track through the jungle and facing a stronger wind. They emerged onto a plateau. It housed a modern settlement that entailed a cluster of eco huts, pebbly paths, and an extensive flower and vegetable garden.

"We've arrived," Hindi-Man said. "This is where mainlanders make their vacation homes."

Her gaze alighted on a knot of people, mostly women, milling about a cottage, a few seated, several others standing. "I'll go ask where we might find Nemo," she said to Hindi-Man.

He stood aside, saying, "I'll wait here."

As she approached the group, Maya noticed a woman in her sixties, positioned on a stool, her hair arranged in a rope braid, gesturing with a hand and wailing. Several other women, settled in a circle around her, offered words of consolation in a tongue Maya didn't understand.

A man with silvery flashes at his temples, dressed in madras shirt and white trousers, must have caught sight of her. His face taut in distress, his black loafers coated with dust, he ventured forward from the group. Overall, he had a sensible look about him. He peered at her through thick glasses and spoke in an educated voice. "Hello. May I be of assistance?"

"Maya Mallick. I'm here to see Nemo Pal."

"He told me about you. My name is Amer. I'm the community leader here."

"Could you help me find Nemo?"

"That's not possible, Madam."

"Why not?"

"He has expired."

Maya stood frozen to the spot, so astounded that she didn't understand the words. Her eyes and cheeks burning, she saw red before her, then was drowned in deafness. What did he say?

"Are you all right, Madam?"

Her breath was caught in her throat. Nemo—alive only a day ago—a larger-than-life presence, like Rory. He'd wanted to meet with her in his favorite islet. Overwhelmed by what she'd heard, she managed to say yes, then, "Expired? But how?"

"Our beloved friend—God Shiva bless his soul—was murdered, pure and simple. Who would have imagined that?"

"Murdered?" A chill ran down Maya's body even on this meltingly hot day. She felt ill. The edges of her surroundings hardened about her. With effort she directed her attention back to Amer.

"Yesterday the police found his body on a deserted beach in Port Blair. He'd been dead for several hours. Tide coming in had already washed away the footprints. No evidence left." Talking gave Amer some stress relief. "The officer said, 'It must have been a mugger.' None of us can believe the news. We're all numb. My grandson's asking, 'Is it real death?' How do I answer him?"

The wind moaned. The trees swayed. Birds flew overhead. Maya struggled to put her conjectures about Nemo and the murder of Rory in order, but she couldn't yet. "How did he . . .?"

"God Almighty. He was struck in the back and the head with a machete. Bled to death."

As Maya imagined the last few agonizing moments of Nemo's life, every part of her body shook. She felt as if her heart attempted to climb to her throat, her stomach going queasy. No, she didn't believe the robbery story, given that a pattern had emerged. She closed her eyes for an instant, a feeling of regret flowing through her, and made a resolution. Once she returned to Port Blair, she'd gather all the details about Nemo's murder and immerse herself in the case, looking for connections to Rory. She opened her eyes. With a sad heart, she listened to the woman's wailing.

Amer must have understood her unspoken question. "She was Nemo's landlady. Loved him like a son."

In times like this, Maya lessened her own grief and gained command over herself by focusing on the victim's family. She would do whatever was necessary to bring them solace. Now she asked Hindi-Man to speak with the woman in her tongue and offer her condolences.

"Could you expand on what happened?" she asked Amer.

Amer, with his calm and easy manner, poured out an explanation. "Our dear friend spent yesterday shopping and dropping round to see friends in Port Blair. He should have returned here by nightfall, but never did. He didn't show up for breakfast, either."

"And then?"

"This morning when the police arrived from Port Blair, we received the news. By then, our community was in an uproar. The constables confiscated Nemo's personal belongings, sealed his cottage and interrogated us. We're not used to such questioning. Everyone is both sad and mad. We were told no one has been arrested. The hoodlum is out there. No one feels safe."

Maya shook her head. "I'm so sorry. I met him only this week, but . . . he made an impression on me." All she could do to console Amer was to say, "I'll speak with the cops and ask for an immediate full investigation.

I'll also see to it that they keep you in the loop."

Amer excused himself, went inside a cottage, and emerged with three stools. "Please have a seat. You've come a long distance. Would you like tea or coffee?"

Maya, feeling nauseated, replied, "No, thank you." She settled on the stool in a state of bewilderment. Hindi-Man took another stool.

With the wave of good will flowing between her and Amer, Maya felt comfortable to ask Amer, "I have a few questions, if you don't mind. To start with: What sort of person was Nemo?"

"Brilliant, articulate, full of life," Amer replied. "And a fine writer."

"Have you noticed anything unusual about him of late?"

"Yes. After the murder of his friend, Rory, it was a trying time for him, and he was distracted and fearful. Like . . . like he'd been caught in a web and couldn't find a way out."

"Could you elaborate?"

"'Friends are a blessing and a curse,' he told me, as if I didn't know that. I tell my children to watch out for whom they befriend. But do they listen?"

"Did he suspect his cottage was bugged?"

Amer's lips parted in a small, sad smile. "He did and moved to another cottage."

"What about his manuscript? Did he have concerns about that?"

"Ah, yes, I'm afraid of complications here, too. He told me that he'd found a reliable provider of cloud computing. You might be asking why. Well, he wanted to use cloud storage for a safe backup of his manuscript. Even if his laptop and thumb drives were stolen, he'd be able to recover his files."

"Why would anybody want to steal his files? Worse yet, why would anyone want to kill him?"

"Funny, isn't it? Publisher dies, then author dies."

"Please tell me about the story Nemo was writing."

"I'm a retired civil engineer and a bit of a history buff. I believe Nemo's exposé had to do with the horrible period these islanders underwent between 1942 and 1945."

"You're talking about the Japanese occupation of these islands? Are there locals who want to clamp down on that history?"

"That'd be my guess. I don't have the details."

"Did Nemo ever appraise the danger involved in exposing such history?"

"Yes, he did. 'Screw them,' he told me. 'I'll write what I want to write. Our history is our birthright.' It takes courage to do what he was doing. That's worth a lot in my book."

Maya saw a spider-web of complications before her. Someone did away with Nemo, which could be due to his knowledge about the circumstances surrounding Rory's death. His manuscript, which vilified the Japanese colonization of these islands, might have contributed to his demise as well. From the similarities of the two murders, the modus operandi, it could very well have been committed by the same assassin.

"And the local family, who might have had concern about the manuscript? Who are they?"

"I have no idea. I haven't read the manuscript, Madam."

"Did Nemo, who had worked as a journalist, ever talk about alerting the media about his new book?"

"Yes, I remember him saying something like that." Amer made a move to rise. "He was media savvy, had cronies who were columnists and talk-show hosts. If he did speak up about his subject matter, then my guess would be the news would spread like wild-fire."

Maya would have liked to hear more of Amer's insight, but his face had become a mask; his eyes were opaque. She slid out of her stool and thanked him.

She and Hindi-Man turned around and strode out of the settlement. Her breathing labored, sadness pressing on her, she began retracing her steps on the same rough terrain to return to the shore. Somewhere an animal moaned. Hair stood up along her scalp, but she charged ahead, wiping her eyes every now and then. They were a hundred or so meters away from the shore when she glimpsed a tall lit candle perched on a rock and spied Hank and Sophie reclining on a blanket. She hastened toward them.

Hank and Sophie munched on snacks, smiled and chatted. Sensing Maya's presence, they turned and perked up.

Hank bolted upright. "Back sooner than I thought."

Feeling empty, breathing from a place of deep hurt, Maya rehashed with them what she'd learned. "We must return to Port Blair."

Sophie sat stunned. Eyes rounding, she went quiet, trying to process the news.

Hank's vivid blue eyes glazed. "Gosh, I'm . . . flabbergasted. That's as bad as it can get. How does this affect what you're after?"

"Complicates it. Being here and losing the better part of a day means I won't be able to examine Nemo's body, do a walk-through of the crime scene, or collect any evidence firsthand. The cops will make it difficult for me."

"Do they have an Australian consulate in Port Blair?" Sophie asked. "My father knows a lot of important people. I can ask him to—"

"No," Maya replied. "There's no Australian consulate in Port Blair."

As a teary-eyed Sophie busied herself packing up the picnic stuff, Hank took Maya and Hindi-Man aside and said under his breath, "Mention of a murder always puts Sophie in a down mood. Has to with her mother being killed during a home invasion. If she looks sad, that's why."

Abid had returned and was perched on a tree stool near the boat. He came alive, got to his feet, and motioned to them. They boarded the boat. Maya, fatigued and grieving once more, settled on a bench. She texted Inspector Dev, asked for a call-back, and left a long message to her mother. Looking out over the turquoise water, she couldn't help but wonder: What would make Nemo the target of a violent act? Given the similarities of the two crimes, they were linked. Who would hold the same grudge against both the victims? It tortured her that the murderer had struck again, this time on her watch, as though yelling to her, *Go away. The game's over.* The culprit hadn't wanted her to speak with Nemo; that much was clear.

As the vessel dipped and soared, Sophie offered "lollies," her favorite Australian toffee to everyone. To Maya's palate, the candy tasted insufferably sweet, even though it gave her mood a temporary lift. *No, it's not over yet*, she silently yelled back to the invisible slaughterer.

Hindi-Man, sitting ahead of them, cried out: "A turtle! Make that two!" Everyone scrambled to the windows to catch the view of the gray-brown domes. "When the wind blows from the south, they come to nest."

Hank spotted a saltwater crocodile—about twelve-foot long, grayish brown with yellow spots—which sank from view in the blink of an eye. "Yassss," he said, his voice rising.

"I'm stoked," Sophie said, showing her agreement.

Maya sighed; she couldn't share in the gaiety.

"Look, a croc," Hindi-Man cried out. "We're terrified of them. They can swallow a whole person in seconds."

As the boat rounded a tiny, deserted island, Hindi-Man pointed to a silvery gray wood pigeon clinging to a tree branch and making a whoosh sound. "It's one of our favorite resident birds," he asserted. "Loves to feed on berries. Eats so much it can't budge. Kids have fun watching it get stuck."

Hindi-Man was doing his best to boost their flagging spirits, especially Sophie's. Maya studied her watch. Almost one o'clock. By the time they reached Port Blair, an hour from now, Nemo's body would be at the morgue. She wouldn't be able to have a last look at him.

An earlier conjecture asserted its presence in Maya's head: Could a sighting of Nemo at the Saddle Peak Trail in her company have contributed to his murder, or at least hastened it? If that was the case, she would forever mourn his loss and be overwhelmed by feelings of guilt. She would never have any consolation.

Rory's favorite author: she visualized Nemo's sun-bronzed face, curly locks of hair, and slender physique. His fears had been real, as real as the hard bench on which she sat. Whether an accomplice to a crime or someone with intelligence in the matter, he'd been hunted. By forces not entirely unknown to him. On top of that, he hadn't had a good enough rapport with the police, as he'd admitted so himself. She worried about the safety of Lee and all those close to Rory, and which included Hank, Sophie, Kal and herself.

TWENTY-ONE

T HE PAST OFTEN INTERFERED WITH THE present but harbored one or more clues. Or so Maya believed and as such she spent the remainder of the afternoon and the evening researching the period of Andaman's history related to the Japanese colonial regime. Accompanied by Hank, she made a trip to the local library. Together they browsed the stacks and gathered enough material. After returning to her hotel room, she phoned her boss, Simi, who provided her with the name of a respected local historian and professor: Dr. Nathu Nagar. Maya left a message for him, picturing the professor—tall and elegant—as described by Simi.

Taking a break, drawing the window curtains aside, she watched the evening descend, layers of black-violet silk extending from the sky to the sea. A flash of lightning raced across the sky, giving her a feeling of being stuck in this island, with the perpetrator nearby. She whipped the gauzy curtains closed.

She'd texted Lee earlier about Nemo's murder and had left a message for Inspector Dev, but it was Dr. Nagar who returned her call in less than ten minutes.

"You want to know about that dreadful period of our history?" he said, in a voice of authority in answer to Maya's question. "The craziness of it. I wasn't born yet, but I did hear the story from my parents and grandparents. I shudder as I speak. First, the Japanese bombed these islands. Our local militia surrendered and the Japanese moved in. You can only imagine the carnage that followed."

"Please explain what you mean."

"If you have the nerves to listen. The Japanese occupying force would kick a child. They'd torture any civilian for being a British spy. They'd abduct girls from the field to work as comfort women. They looted. They burned. My father told me, 'Those invaders did as much physical and psychological damage in three years as the British did in two hundred.' Mind you, not all Japanese were bad. But those three years of Andaman's history were written in blood."

"What can you tell me about a naval commander named Hara, believed to be responsible for countless atrocities?" Maya asked.

"The locals called him *shaitan*, the devil. His young daughter was believed to have married into a moneyed, influential local family.

"Were such intermarriages common in those days?"

"No, but she was well accepted by the kin and sheltered by them. On top of that, the local family sided with the Japanese. You can imagine how our people, already bitter toward the intruders, felt about that."

"Which means that the descendants, if anybody, will want to make sure the history of the Japanese invasion remain vague?"

"That'd be my guess, too."

Maya would have liked to inquire more about the family, but Dr. Nagar concluded their conversation citing a prior engagement.

MAYA PICKED UP LOCAL DAILY DELIVERED to her room the next morning at about nine a.m. The headline read:

Best-Selling Author Slain in Port Blair

And further down:

Andaman police confirmed the death of the 41-year-old Nemo Pal. No arrests have been made.

Maya couldn't stand it any longer. She put the paper aside and again called Inspector Dev.

"Sorry not to have returned your call yesterday," the inspector answered, with a note of regret. "I'm as appalled as you are. To have yet another murder in our hands—"

A trace of anger surged in Maya. She cut him off by saying, "Couldn't you have protected Nemo?"

"No."

"That's very disturbing to me. Do you suppose it was a miscalculation?"

"It sure was, on our part, Maya. However, this time we've harvested some genetic material, which is being analyzed. We'll, of course, share the results with you."

That didn't do it for her. She managed a calm voice and said, "For now, will you please provide Lee with 24-hour protection?"

"Isn't she on your list?" the inspector asked.

"Even if she is . . . as the person closest to Rory, she faces risk. Do you agree?"

"Yes," Inspector Dev said. "I'll do all I can." His standard answer.

MAYA CALLED SIMI TO GIVE HER a progress report. First, she thanked her boss for her help in researching the history of Andaman and providing her with contacts.

"Drawn any conclusions yet, Maya?"

"At least I'm beginning to see what might have happened with Nemo. He made regular trips to these islands and cared about the people. He couldn't help but dive deep into their traumatic history. He saw enough material for a nonfiction title. My guess is he mulled over the idea, then suggested an exposé to Rory, who jumped at the chance."

"You're saying that Nemo's book will serve a purpose, will bring to light the crimes Hara and other Japanese officers had committed?"

"Add to that the role Hara's daughter had played, her marriage into the Peterson family, and how much of the whole history had been hidden from the public."

"Okay," Simi said. "This is what I gather. Nemo believed the scars from that period were in the collective unconscious, bandaged but festering under the surface."

"You're right," Maya said, concluding the call. "Nemo wanted to bring those historical events to daylight, to allow healing to take place. He was that type of a person. It's unfortunate that he had to give his life for that."

HALF AN HOUR LATER, MAYA CONFERRED WITH LEE on the patio of her hotel, the Emerald Villa. The sea roared at a distance. Maya had already disclosed the news of Nemo's death to Lee via a text and a phone call. Teary-eyed, her long black hair billowing outward from her head, Lee sat like a zombie. Maya could tell that Lee found the incident raw and hard to accept. A strong breeze rattled the window behind them. Damn noise.

"How could this happen?" Lee said in a shrill voice. "I saw Nemo only a few days ago. You're telling me he's dead? I'm terrified. When are you going to hunt down that maniac with a machete?"

Maya registered the accusations. Her insides knotted up, but she couldn't blame her friend, a pregnant widow who'd already suffered much. "I have every intention to sort this out, but it'll take me—"

"Meanwhile, the killer is picking out his next victim, correct?" Lee's tone had turned sarcastic.

A wait-staff brought a tea tray, placed it on the small table between them, and backed out. Maya poured two cups, placed one in front of Lee and the other at her own arm's reach. She placed the platters of rich brown pakoras and glistening, sugar-sprinkled peda cookies in the middle.

Holding the hot cup lessened tension, if only temporarily. "I'm now even more concerned about your safety." Maya regretted the words that had escaped her mouth.

Lee picked up a peda, then put it down. "Do you think I'm next?" she asked, her voice strained.

"No. In any case, I've asked Inspector Dev to provide you with protection, but you must be—"

"I'll be careful. I won't venture out of the hotel without my sisters escorting me, I promise."

Despite the assurance, concern nagged at Maya. Her mission was to help find the criminal before more loved ones were knifed. "I've asked you this before," Maya said. "Any idea who might have wanted to do away with—?"

"You don't think it's me, do you? No, I didn't kill my husband." Lee paused a beat. "I wish you moved a little faster with your detective work."

"Look, I'm doing my best. A few new things have turned up, but . . ." She couldn't quite tell Lee about Rory's other family. To change the topic, she asked Lee about her mother.

"My mother has a suite downstairs," Lee said. "I told her of my pregnancy."

"How did she take it?"

"She's beside herself with shock, practically bed-ridden, my mother, who so much wanted a grandchild. Everyone disappoints me these days. Even you. You lied to me the other day." Lee's eyes reddened; she shouted in her face. "You were talking to a call girl when I came by your hotel."

"I'm sorry, Lee."

"Who do you think I am?" Lee said testily. "A naïve girl? Hey, I'm a businesswoman."

"And I'm a PI. I can't give away someone's secret."

"Even though I'm paying your salary?"

"Yes. And, if I may say so, there's a gap in your story about Rory's last evening. You were out of the hotel for about fifteen minutes. The surveillance cameras caught you stepping out. Why did you go out so late at night? Where all did you go? What did you do?"

"Heavens. They know about that? You want to hear the truth? Being in a tizzy, I took a short walk to clear my head."

Maya gave no response. Looking at Lee's crumpled face, she concluded that her friend spoke the truth. Yet the questions remained: Why did she lie about it earlier?

"Even you . . ." Lee broke into a sob. "Even you don't trust me." She covered her face with her hands and laid her forehead on the table.

Maya could only imagine the amount of pain behind those tears. How could she have hurt her friend this much? She leaned toward Lee, her heart filled with compassion and apology. "I love you, Lee. I hate to see you like this. Believe me—"

Lee raised her head. "Sorry to be cranky with you. Please don't take it personally. I'm like this with everybody. It's the hormones."

They chitchatted for a little longer and Lee's face brightened. Even so Maya sensed some things had shifted between them. Experience told her that Lee had been holding back from her. What did Lee know that she couldn't share?

You need to be patient with Lee, Maya. She gave her friend a hug and said goodbye.

As she exited the hotel lobby, Maya noticed a familiar figure. Kal, the taxi driver, who had picked her up at the airport, discharged a passenger. Sophie had mentioned the likelihood that Kal might be around this week. Maya wanted to speak with Kal, yes, very much. Even though he was a potential suspect, she feared that there could be an attempt on his life as there had been on Nemo's. She must caution him. This very minute.

Before her eyes, Kal pulled out of the driveway. She tried to flag him down, but he didn't notice her.

There had to be another way.

TWENTY-TWO

MAYA FLAGGED DOWN ANOTHER CAB that was waiting, a rather unusual one. Painted a loud indigo blue, it had custom-made upholstery inside that displayed a lotus pattern in green and orange. The driver waved her in.

She jumped into the backseat. "Could you please follow that taxi?"

The driver turned to look at her. He had an open face, innocent eyes, blotchy skin and an expression of cheerfulness, this boy, no more than nineteen. He wore a faded short-sleeve check shirt that displayed no character. However, a copper amulet, encircling his muscled arm, gave him pizzazz.

"That taxi, Madam?"

"Yes, please hurry. I don't want to lose him. I'll pay triple your fare."

"Jolly good." He pressed a glance on her. "It's your lucky stars—you're in good hands. I'm the best driver in town. My name is Param. I'm still a kid. You know what? I'm known for my quick reflexes. I've given this taxi a makeover. Hired a talented artist not too high up on the ladder yet. What's your take?"

Maya let her gaze express admiration at the showy quality. "It's blingy."

"Black and tan are . . ."

"So last year's tastes."

"You said it." Param smiled, faced forward, and pulled out of the driveway. "But why are you chasing that dude, Madam, if you don't mind my nosiness? He's a pauper like me, a simple cabbie, not a babe magnet. He wears the wrong hair style and doesn't have man boobs.

Unless, of course—"

"It's not what you think."

"Okay, okay, you have your reasons." Param set off into the traffic. "Most rides are boring—drunks, druggies, pissed tourists, and bad tippers, a dice roll, really—but you're full of surprises. However bizarre this might sound, I must say my juices are flowing."

"Why, thank you." If for a moment, Maya set her blues aside and enjoyed Param's company.

The taxi sped along, weaving through cars, minibuses, and trucks, always keeping Kal's cab in view. It slowed as it entered a narrow sooty lane, full of potholes, and where the sidewalks were littered.

"I'm good in arithmetic." Param kept chatting. "The other day I multiplied 3654 by 45 in my head in thirty seconds. Well, give or take a few seconds. Did my mom proud."

Before Maya's eyes, Kal, clad as usual in a clean white uniform, parked his taxi and hopped out. He headed toward a tin-roofed building.

"Stop," Maya said to Param from the backseat.

Param came to a halt. "Believe it or not, there's a tea lounge in that building," he said, pointing. "Even if it doesn't look deluxe from outside, it serves the best masala chai in town. Who knows what they mix in with their spices? I'm told it's habit-forming."

"I want to speak with that cabbie," Maya said. "But I don't want anyone to see me doing that."

"My, my. Why so?" Receiving no reply, he added, "Someone might clobber him? Okay, you don't have to answer. You see, I, too, am full of surprises. I may have a solution for you."

"Which is?"

"I can make you invisible, so you can carry on your responsibilities clandestinely. What do you think of my vocabulary?"

"It's excellent, but how will you make me—?"

"I'll lend you a burqa that I have stored in the trunk of my car for a tactical situation like this. You wear it and think of yourself as a princess in hiding. Imagine."

The idea sounded crazy, but Maya was willing to explore it. "Why would you do me such a favor?"

"Because you vibe with me. Once you slip into that burqa, no one will be able to see your face or body, but you'll see everyone and everything. You'll use your eyes to show your feelings."

Maya smiled. "It's romantic, no doubt."

"One caveat: It'll be hotter than hell inside that veil. Like my friends and I say—YGTI. You get the idea?"

"Sure do." Burqa—Maya was well familiar with the long, loose, full length outerwear that covered the entire female body and the head. Small slits in the fabric allowed the eyes to look out to the world. Clever, indeed. It'd be perfect for what she had in mind. But then, a burqa wasn't a common attire around here. "How did you happen to have a burqa in your car?"

"Long story." His voice turned heavy. "It belonged to—how shall I put it—my wild ex-girlfriend. She was beyond dope. Her religion didn't require her to wear a veil. She used it to conceal herself when she sneaked into my place late at night. Who knows how many other dudes she dropped over to see, wearing that disguise? She turned out to be shit—can I say that? We broke up. She forgot to take her disguise with her."

"Are you sure you want me to—?"

"Yes, it'll give me great pleasure to see you wear it." He paused. "Go, conduct your business, I'll wait for you here. The first thirty minutes are free. When you're done, I'll take you back to whomever you want to chase next. How would that be?"

"That'll be fine. Thanks."

Param found a spot, parked the car, opened the trunk and took out the burqa, smiling. In the heat of the day, in the oppressive humidity, Maya donned the long gown, feeling ridiculous, and at first had difficulty breathing. Then she noted: her eyes were able to take in more inside this garment than she'd believed she would. Dragging it behind her, Maya shuffled to the chai shop.

The shop was an immaculate one-room affair, medium-sized and square, with a cozy feel. It housed a few tables, chairs, and a service counter, all worn with use, and gave off a whiff of sugar and black pepper. A few other customers, all men, were scattered in the room. Two teenage boys seated at a table gossiped, with no one within earshot. A wait-staff bustled about in the back. A small window opened to the sidewalk outside.

Kal, his head down, was settled in at a front table. He had a gold-rimmed cup of tea and a glass of water before him. The monotonous whirring of a ceiling fan had put him into a meditative state. Maya crossed to Kal and dropped into the chair across from him.

Kal started and half-rose, a freaked-out expression on his face.

She made a gesture for him to sit down and whispered, "Maya Mallick. Please don't make a sound. Do you have a few minutes to talk?"

He kept staring up at her in surprise, breathless and unable to answer.

"You gave me a ride from the airport—remember?"

"Ah, the lady detective herself." He gave a whoosh of relief mixed with elation. "Yes, you do sound like her. But . . . but why would a classy girl like you slum in this part of the town, dressed in a burqa, no less? What's going on?"

"I wanted to speak with you in private, Kal. This was the only way."

"Of course, of course." He turned and gave a glance to the counter. "They make a first- class chai here, which is why I can't stay away. It's addictive. Can I buy you a cuppa? Or a short eat, which is what they call their sandwiches?"

"Tempting—but it won't be easy for me to eat or drink despite this mouth flap. I'll take a pass but thank you."

He smiled. "What made you hunt down someone like me, who's at the bottom of the food chain? I feel lucky, you know."

"I have some news." Her lower lip quivered as Maya outlined the calamity: Nemo Pal's unfortunate death, the fact that the killer was at large, and how anyone associated with Rory could be in danger, which was only a guess on her part, but which could include Kal. "Did you ever meet the author?"

Kal gasped. Face paling, he covered his eyes for a moment. "Good Ganesh! Nemo Pal is no more? Yes, I'd taken him to plenty of places. He even gave me a copy of his novel, which I haven't yet read. Celebrity author one day, dead the next. What's happening, man?" After a long pause, "I used to be a computer coder, you might remember hearing from me. What you have in your hands is what we call a hydra. It's a mean bug. When you try to fix it, it introduces new ones. You're here three weeks or so, trying to crack the Thompson murder case, and now you have another homicide to contend with? A hydra?"

"Quite." For an instant Maya listened to the soft buzz of an insect. Despite the ceiling fan, she found it suffocating to be inside the burqa. "Since you brought up Rory's name, you might as well confide in me. Did you ever drive him?"

"Yes, often." He took a steadying sip of his chai. "Every time he came over to this island. How did you guess?"

"A shot in the dark. That day when you picked me up from the airport, I had the notion that it wasn't by chance that you were there. Nor were you looking for any arriving passenger to pick up. You were waiting for me. If I'm not mistaken, it had something to do with Rory."

"Correct." His finger danced along his cup's rim. "I read in the daily about your arrival and felt compelled to meet you and transport you from the airport. I'll do whatever I can to help you catch Rory-babu's killer, so justice is done. You see, I respected him. Called him babu, because he was cool. He liked me, trusted me, and buzzed me on his cell when he blew into town and needed a transport on short notice."

A victim's final day often provided clues. "What about on his last day on earth?" Maya asked.

"It breaks my heart to say this, but yes, I did drop him off to where he wanted to go." Perspiration had gathered on Kal's forehead. "I wasn't aware of the fate that awaited him. Only the following day when I read the newspaper, I realized what had happened. I asked myself: Who was the real Rory-babu? What was he up to? Why did he have to leave us? I couldn't answer any of those questions. I was in such a shock that I didn't go to work for two days."

"Where did you drop him that night? And at what time?"

Kal stared into his empty cup, appearing to be worked up. "At an intersection. It was past eight p.m."

"Did you think that was unusual? This is an early-night town."

"No, driving a taxi, you run into all kinds of people, doing all sorts of things at all hours. Some fares start confessing, some cry, others are tight-lipped. It'd have been out of place for me to have asked Rory-babu about his plans. That'd have been too personal."

"Which intersection was it?"

He averted his eyes. "The street names escape me."

How convenient to have poor memory. "How did Rory seem?"

"The look in his eyes—he was a bit absent. He didn't speak much."

"Have you reported any of this to the cops?"

"Goodness, no, I detest the khaki." Kal's voice was tight with dread. "They're rude, lazy and corrupt. They'll intimidate me and ask for a bribe."

"Do you realize as one of the last people to have been in touch with Rory, you'll be looked on as a suspect?"

"God, no, I didn't kill him. In the name of Ganesh, I'm speaking the truth. Why would I do that? I loved the guy. He was exceptional. I miss him."

"You'd have to go to *thana* and lay the truth out to the police."

"No. I'm trying to hide from those dirty cops. I don't want to be locked up for something I didn't do. Please, Detective Maya, I need your help."

"I can only help you if you speak the truth." Being that Kal's face was filled with dread, Maya said, "Listen to me. Your connection with Rory makes you vulnerable. Not sure who's behind it all, but they could be stalking you because you were Rory's driver. They'd like to shut your mouth."

"That has already happened. My flat was broken into a few days ago. Nothing was stolen."

"I've heard that. Let me warn you. If possible, take a few days off from work. Don't show up at the usual places you go. Steer clear of your flat. Is that clear?"

"Yes, clear as this glass of water. Somebody will again try to break in my place?"

"Or worse. A guess on my part."

Kal sat with his mouth open. "I must thank you, Detective Maya, for taking the trouble to warn me. My uncle and aunt will put me up. They're retired folks, live in another section of the town. I'll only miss the lizards in my bedroom ceiling."

Maya smiled, gave him her phone number and stood up. "Do me a favor. Don't tell a soul about this."

"Ma Laxmi—shell-shocked that I am, I follow."

"Give me a shout if you see or hear anything suspicious, okay?"

"I sure will. Always believed if you stayed low, you wouldn't attract the wrong kind of attention. Now I see that's not true. I have no item of value in my tiny hole."

"Look, it's you they're after."

TWENTY-THREE

MAYA HAD BEEN REVIEWING THE NOTES on her laptop on this rainy afternoon, a day later. The wind howled. The doorbell rang about four p.m., and Maya answered it. Gaze full of anxiety, Hank stood in the doorway, dressed in gym shorts and a T-shirt with the logo: "Don't hate me because I'm a Millennial." Maya ushered him in and offered him a chair; he kept standing.

"What's up?" she asked.

"Sophie's gone."

The gloom in Hank's voice stopped Maya for a brief second. "Gone?"

"She's sneaked off. I returned to my room and found her note." Hank's blue eyes were wide in fear. "It said she's going out to lunch with a 'friend.' I drove to a couple places she might have gone. No luck. I went back to my room. She wasn't back and there was no text from her, either. I left her several texts. She didn't respond. It's been far too long and I'm loopy."

"Where were you?"

"Lifting weights at the hotel gym to break a little sweat," he said, regret in his voice. "Then I lingered in the hotel coffee shop and had a leisurely breakfast. I was gone for three hours."

"You left her all alone?"

"We had a nasty fight. I called her spoiled. She called me an infant. I'm so sorry. We're so close, it's like she's inside me and I'm inside her."

"Where do you think she might have gone?"

"Dunno, but I have a terrible feeling. Like she's in trouble. Someone has been buzzing her. It's not her dad. Whoever it is, she's tight-lipped about him."

Uneasiness spread through Maya. Her initial annoyance with Sophie had given way to a liking for her. How could anyone help but adore Sophie? There never were any idle moments with her. Maya had never had a sibling—an older brother had died as a child before her birth. She'd been acquainted with Sophie for a brief period but had developed a protective instinct toward her. Sophie, carefree and naïve, could put herself in trouble. Maya could no longer keep a rein on her concerns. "Someone she might have met in the last few days?"

"That'd be my guess. On the one hand, she's cool, not jaded at all. She talks to everybody, flirts with everybody, flies through the day. On the other hand, she can be too trusting, too careless." He paused. "I've exhausted all the possibilities. Have no idea where to go look for her next. I'm so worried that I can't even . . ."

A deep fear nudged Maya as a vision of Jorge at the party flitted through her head. Something sneaky was afoot. "I have a suspicion. Jorge Peterson might have been calling her. Can't stand the guy or know what his game is, and he's a bigwig."

"That motherfucker. That savage. Do you think he kidnapped her? I'll beat him to a bloody pulp if he did."

"We have to hurry, Hank." Her pulse quickening, Maya sized up the difficulties facing them and devised a strategy. "We can't go on this venture on our own. Let me have a word with Inspector Dev."

"Would he . . . help us?"

"He might. I'll ask for police support. Meantime, you and I will head out to the Peterson residence. There's a good chance Jorge and Sophie will be finished with lunch by now and he might escort her to his grand house. He's too well known in this town. He can't take her to any old place, without being spotted. Make sense?"

"It does. But . . . but . . . whatever that bozo has in mind to do with her . . . he won't have a chance to—"

"Not if we play the game right."

"I'll drive us over there. Then I'll strangle him with my bare hands."

"Aw Hank, pull yourself together." Maya looked at her assistant. His smart appearance belied the fact that he was young, emotionally vulnerable, and could turn hasty in action. In other words, he could do something foolish. She wouldn't let him. He meant too much to her.

"Whatever you say, boss."

She stared down at her T-shirt, shorts, and sandals. She needed to change. "I'll meet you at the parking lot in a few minutes."

"Perf, boss."

After Hank departed, Maya called Inspector Dev. She explained the situation, that of Sophie's disappearance and a few details about her, but didn't mention the Peterson residence as her destination. "I'd like you to provide me with armed manpower—two constables will do," she added.

"I can't do that, not if the girl is missing only for a few hours. She might show up. I'm short-staffed as it is. And where are you going to search?"

That's B.S. "At the Peterson residence. Jorge was a little too interested in her at Esme's reception. He might have designs on her. My guess is he's the one who's taken her to lunch."

"Are you insane, Maya? We can't barge into that residence. Do you know the kind of clout they have in this town? If I mess with them, I'm toast."

"For once, Mohan, you might want to do what your conscience tells you is right."

The line went silent for a long moment.

"Think it over," Maya said. "We don't have time to waste."

"We're stretched tight, as far as manpower goes. I can't waste resources." The inspector's voice was hard. "I regret we won't be able to provide you with police protection."

He didn't want to be on the wrong side of the town's royalty—that much became clear.

"Okay, then. Hank and I will be on our way. If anything goes wrong and the police don't show up, you can be sure the media will hear about it." Maya paused and assessed the situation. A stink in the media would raise Inspector Dev's hackles. So now as an added incentive, she shared a few details about Sophie's influential father in Australia. That he would fly here as fast as he could, once he received the news. That he'd stir up things. Money and position talk, or so Maya trusted. She was pushing her luck, pushing it too much. If she were to make a guess, that was what her father, the ace detective, would have done in a similar situation. She hoped her strategy would work.

"You don't want another international scandal in your hands, do you?" she asked.

"I'll see what I can do," the inspector said, his standard answer.

After hanging up, Maya stood for yet another moment. What if her speculation was wrong? She could be in trouble. But then she didn't want to take any chances as far as Sophie was concerned. The young girl, Hank's babe, was part of her team. Maya couldn't face another incident in which someone close to her was hurt.

Within fifteen minutes she and Hank arrived at their destination. The rain had subsided. Sun's rays filtered through clouds. Hank parked a few streets over so as not to be recognized by anyone in the Peterson family. Together they marched up to the front entrance of the mansion. The huge compound was all quiet and intimidating. She rang the doorbell and braced herself.

The door opened. A male attendant in white uniform looked Maya over. "May I help you?"

"We're here to see Jorge Peterson."

"Do you have an appointment?" The tone wasn't polite.

Maya said in a voice of authority, "No, but it's urgent that we see him."

"He's out."

"When do you expect him back?"

"Soon. It had slipped his mind he had a meeting this afternoon. When I called him and gave him a reminder, he said he'd be on his way."

"Where was he when you called him?"

He shrugged. "I don't know. At some restaurant."

"With whom?"

The attendant slammed the door shut, the noise reverberating.

"Moron," Hank said, as they descended the steps together. "Now I'm even more worked up."

Maya looked up at the cloudy sky. A movement caught her eye and she turned. Inspector Dev, with his bulk and badge and khaki suit, marched through the gate. A pair of uniformed constables—stony-faced, with muscled arms—walked behind him. The inspector had a scowl on his face, but she was glad for his presence. He acknowledged Maya with a brief wave. They all gathered on the abundant front lawn filled with trees, bushes, flowerpots, flagstone walkways, and a tinkling fountain glimmering in the late afternoon light.

"What's the story, Maya?" the inspector asked in a harsh voice. "It'd better not be a wild goose chase. Then I'll be in deep shit with—"

"Look, Mohan, don't you think it's serious, given that we have a second murder in our hands and no arrests? Almost anyone is a suspect at this point. On top of that, a girl is missing."

The inspector stared hard at Maya. "You suspect Jorge? What's the evidence that links him, the two murders and the missing girl?"

"I'll explain that later. Right now, we're looking for Sophie."

Peering across the lawn and over the tall fence, the inspector announced, "I see Jorge's car. It's turning this way. Someone's with him."

Indeed, Maya could see a Mercedes Benz slowing on the road, Jorge driving and Sophie on the passenger seat. "Let's all hide in the bushes," she announced. "Wait and see what he does." Everyone complied.

Jorge pulled in the curling driveway. He leaped out of the car, came around to open the passenger door, extended a hand to Sophie. She looked winsome in a sleeveless, blue mini dress. Her face had a reddish cast, a sure sign she had had too much to imbibe, and she wobbled in her high heels. Jorge put a hand around her waist and bent down to kiss her. Sophie whipped her arm back, shoved him away, turned, and shuffled toward the gate, her heels slowing her.

Hank jumped out from behind a bush and scrambled over to them. "Keep your hands off my girl," he shouted to Jorge.

Jorge straightened and turned. His eyes grew sinister as he fixed his gaze at Hank. "Who are you, punk?"

They stood facing each other. "You asshole, you one percent." Eyes glinting, Hank gave him the finger. 'You're an idiot."

Jorge, his mouth slack, was taken aback by Hank's tirade. He must have had no idea that Hank wrote short stories. Hank who believed that a pen could cut more deeply than the sword. That even a man of short stature like him could look a bully in the eye and speak out.

Jorge could only come up with, "When are you going to grow up, jerk?"

Hank's voice went higher. "When are you going to stop stalking my girlfriend?"

Jorge eyed Sophie, who stood near the gate as though in a daze, and his lips twisted into a sneer. "She came willingly, party girl that she is."

Hank shouted, "Shut up, she's not a party girl."

"She had a great time. You better bug off. We have—"

"Don't go near her. Or else—"

Seeing Hank's hand ball into a fist, and Jorge's gaze turning furious, Maya ran toward the pair. Standing between them, with Jorge towering above her, she shouted, "Stop. Both of you." In the brief hiatus, she heard the fountain water running over the pebbles.

"Ah, Ms. Detective," Jorge, smelling of alcohol, pulled a cell phone out of his pocket and shot Maya a glare. "So, this is your doing? You've brought this asshole with you? Do you realize you're trespassing on my property? I can have both of you arrested. How would you like to spend the night in jail?"

As Jorge turned away and fussed with his cell phone, Inspector Dev strode toward him from across the lawn. The two constables, emerging from under a hedge, followed him and flanked Jorge. Hank flung the middle finger at him before edging away to join Sophie.

Standing there, dwarfing everyone, Jorge gave a gasp of astonishment. His eyes widened, his fingers curled, and he directed a glare at the inspector. "My, my. Another happy coincidence? You, too, are lurking on my lawn, with an arrest team, no less, bracketing me? No sand-flies to watch?"

"We had to ensure the girl's safety," the inspector said.

"That's bullshit. It was an innocent little tête-à-tête in a public place over lunch. Aren't you getting ahead of yourself?"

"If it's an innocent lunch, then why didn't you drop her back to her hotel?" the inspector said.

"I don't have to answer you, you know."

"You must understand," Inspector Dev said. "Because of the recent murders, we have to be extra alert."

Jorge stiffened. "I have nothing to do with . . ."

Maya scrutinized Jorge's face. Anger had colored his cheeks an unhealthy red and clouded his eyes. He held his breath.

"I didn't mean to imply anything of that sort, Jorge," Inspector Dev replied. "We were concerned. Like we should be. Sophie's an Australian magnate's daughter, only twenty years of age. Any scandal—"

At a short distance away, Hank and Sophie were holding each other tight and kissing. Sophie was crying and apologizing. They were making up under a clear sky and bright sunlight, surrounded by soft sounds. If for a moment, Maya was relieved, elated even.

"Scandal?" Jorge said to the inspector. "Has everyone gone mad?"

"Since you've brought her back and she's now reunited with her boyfriend," replied the inspector, "I reckon the situation to be diffused. We'll depart now."

"This is a total misunderstanding and an invasion into my privacy," Jorge shouted. "No more of this. Understand? The next time, I'll call the Governor General and he'll sack you." He whirled around and headed toward the entrance; his steps were unsteady.

Both Inspector Dev and Maya turned and started to walk toward the gate, the constables following.

"We've made Jorge mad," Inspector Dev said. "As mad as I ever have seen him. Are you satisfied now, Maya?"

"No, not until I've seen to it that Hank and Sophie are back to the hotel. Then I'll call you and we'll have a chat. I must thank you for your assistance."

"All's well that ends well," the inspector replied.

"It's not the end, Mohan, not yet." She waved him good-bye and he waved back, with anger and a question in his eyes.

Maya, accompanied by Hank and Sophie, speed-walked to the parking spot. In the car, Hank, busy coping with the intense traffic, kept his hand on the steering wheel. Sophie sat on the passenger seat next to him, a little breathless, hands nervous on her lap. She twitched, fingered her hair and fluffed it.

"How're you doing?" Maya, perched on the backseat, asked Sophie.

"Thanks for rescuing me. I'm so sorry to put you through so much."

"I'm glad to have you back."

"I fucked up, made a stupid mistake, accepting that creep's offer for lunch. He knows I'm wild about food. Of course, it was a gigantic buffet and the place had an incredible ocean view, but—"

"What did he do?"

"He wasn't there to waste time. He sat next to me. Kept moving closer. At one point during the lunch, while smoking a ciggy and yabbering a lot, he slid his hand toward me and tried to touch my breasts. Can you believe it? The bastard was going bonkers. I'm sure the server caught it. 'Bugger off, ya old bloke,' I said and pushed him away. He didn't budge. I stuck my long fingernails—my weapon—on his neck. Not too hard. No blood. He jumped up. He backed off." Sophie paused. "He was—I don't know—rather restless. Like he was about to bolt. 'It's now or never,' he said to me."

"And?"

"'Take me home,' I said. 'I must show you my painting collection first,' he said.'"

"You got in the car with him?" Maya asked.

"No choice," Sophie said. "I had no idea where I was."

"Anything else?"

"You know what? His hanky, that showy, blue silk, work of art, was spilling out of his pocket and I pulled it out. Not sure why I did it, but it was like fun. He didn't notice it, rotten drunk that he was, but when he finds out his hanky is gone, he'll be mad as a cut snake."

Maya gasped. "Do you have that hanky with you? It has his DNA. We need his DNA sample."

"Yes, it's in my purse."

"Will you give it to me, Sophie?" Maya said. "I'll turn it over to the police. They'll run scans to see if there's a hit on the DNA samples. I suspect that Jorge is connected to both the murders. That has yet to be proven." She paused. "Please handle the hanky as little as possible. Let me give you a pair of plastic gloves."

Sophie turned to open her purse. "My God. It's that important, that cool little thing I flogged?"

"I'd say so," Maya said. Thank God. She always carried a paper bag, which would protect the DNA evidence, and a pair of plastic gloves for safe handling. She dug into her purse, retrieved both the items and smiled. "Thanks to you, Sophie, we might have a breakthrough, after all. But don't do anything like that ever again."

TWENTY-FOUR

IT WAS ABOUT TWO P.M., a gorgeous, if humid day. Maya needed a break on the case, a diversion after yesterday's drama at the Peterson residence, which would help her forget the tragedy of Nemo's murder. How much it haunted her. She arrived at the Women's Market on her first foray to the popular shopping mall, wishing to rejuvenate her senses. "Sooner or later, all ladies show up there," or so went a local saying. Rules to follow: Bargain, but not too much. Buy as much you can afford to. Keep in mind that much of the proceeds go to causes that help women in distress.

Maya stepped into the sunlit pavement. She was also on a quest. She wished to "accidentally" bump into Zarina, who liked to hang out here, and question her further, in light of the new development, a second murder.

A cloud of insects flew past Maya like a small comet. She navigated her way through the stalls, listening to the loud staccato hammering of a woodpecker poised on a nearby tree. Vendors in the first row had laid out an array of ruby and diamond jewelry, along with seashell ornaments. Stalls on the second row sold bamboo baskets, conch shells, miniature wooden canoes, and decorative palm mats. A handicraft emporium displayed embroidered purses and dress materials. She stopped at a book stall and bought two nonfiction volumes for Lee: *Flowers of Andaman* by L. Chowdhury and *Indian Ocean: A Geo-Political History* by Amit Ray. Next, as Maya arrived at the food section, her nostrils were tweaked by an aroma of hot oil wafting from a dosa joint. Located across, a vendor clothed in a cotton vest, an out-of-fashion Nehru cap hugging his fore-head, sold cookies and candies from his stall. Despite his aloof demeanor, he waved at her. It amused her, his motto emblazoned on a banner: "Right Belief, Right Knowledge, Right Conduct, and Right Refreshments."

All around her, women looked, meandered, bargained, yelled, shopped, and lunched, a sense of merriment prevailing, but Maya saw no sign of Zarina.

Half-an-hour went by. Ambling past the children's section and a "No Spitting" sign, she spied her target. Clad in an electric green sari, which sported a riot of embroidery, Zarina stood in front of a children's cloth-ing shop, bantering with the shopkeeper.

Maya sidled up to her, said hello and braced for a reply.

Zarina turned, her expression one of astonishment. "Fancy meeting you here, Lady."

"Do you have a minute to talk?"

"No. Stop harassing me. I've told you all I know."

Maya gave a closer look. Zarina's tight curls spoke of where she might be at mentally.

"Do you know that Mr. Pande found out that I've been talking with you?" Zarina said. "He's furious. I'm screwed . . . I'm on edge. I can't be seen with you." She waved toward the shops and said in an insulting tone, "Bhago." Go away.

"We will handle Mr. Pande separately, Zarina," Maya said in a calm manner. "For your information, things have turned worse and I'd like to make you aware of it, for your sake and that of your son."

Zarina's eyes widened in curiosity. "What do you mean?"

Maya pointed to the shade of a bamboo grove only a few steps away, which would offer some privacy. "Shall we go over there?"

"Okay," Zarina said. Maya shuffled over and bought two bottles of Limca soda from the Right Refreshments vendor. Zarina borrowed two stools from a shopkeeper and they settled on them. On this warm after-noon, the smell of roasted peanuts exuded from a nearby stall.

Zarina sat on the edge of the stool. In between gulping her drink, she licked her lips without any self-consciousness, indicating she'd began to feel at ease in Maya's company. In a sarcastic voice, she said, "You sound like you've found a dead body."

"Yes, someone did find a dead body. In case you haven't heard . . ." Lament pressed on Maya's shoulders and her voice thickened as she recounted the latest murder.

The Limca bottle fell from Zarina's hand, struck the ground and rolled to a stop against a bamboo stalk; it was nearly empty. She didn't try to pick it up. "No! That's terrible, terrible. How much it upsets me. Rory had mentioned Nemo lots of times—his good friend. But why would anybody...?"

"We don't know the motives yet. That's why I'm here. I hesitate to ask you a question, a delicate one that—"

"Since when have you been shy, Lady?"

Maya allowed a pause, then said, "Did Rory have other women?"

Zarina stirred. "No, no, didn't I tell you he was mine?"

"Rory was married. It appears as though Rory had been involved with another woman in town. He might only have flirted with her or it could have been that she fancied him."

Zarina lowered her head, struggling to let out that which was too painful for her. "It crushed me to hear it from Rory, but . . . he did talk about hooking up with someone."

"Please tell me what he said."

"It was last year and his last day in Andaman. He was going to fly back to America the next morning. He came to say goodbye. We were sitting in my room. I was all sad and crying when I noticed how worried he looked. I asked him and had to tease it out of him. He mentioned a rich bitch. 'She's after my cock,' he said in a voice full of disgust. "She's going after me with all she's worth. Wish she'd leave me alone.' What? Some uppity bird has designs on my lover? That hit me on the belly. No fucking way would I allow that. I was pissed, so pissed that my blood was up. I gritted my teeth and asked, 'Why do you keep seeing her?' He replied, 'It is you I love, Zari, but I need capital for my business. She'll loan me the money, but first she wants to put her hands on me. That horse-faced broad, as trustworthy as a snake, who wears a fake smile and beds anyone she meets, a tigress. Keeps insisting she's in love with me, can't live without me and will stop at nothing. She drives me nuts. At first, I thought it's a phase she's going through. Now I'm beginning to believe she means what she says.' I asked Rory, 'Is the money worth it?' He replied, 'No, it isn't, not her funds, my dear love. I've decided to cut my losses and beat it. What if I exist only as a tiny publisher? That's not so bad.' I was stunned to hear this. I asked, 'So when are you going to dump her? I'm asking you to.' He said, 'Since I'm flying out tomorrow, darling, it'll have to be on my next visit. Yes, for sure, the next time.'"

"Which would have put the timing to this year, this month," Maya said. "Did he return to you?"

"No. I was crushed."

A feeling of sympathy toward Zarina crept over Maya. A young woman, not wise to the ways of the world, who'd been taken advantage of, who had little to look forward to in life. *Rory, how could you have broken her heart?*

"Do you suppose he went to see that rich bitch?" Maya asked.

"Don't know. I don't have a mobile phone, so I couldn't buzz him."

"Hang on. What's her name?"

"I'm not allowed to—"

She was hiding a crucial detail; Maya was sure of that. "If you were allowed to—"

"There we go again. Look, I'm already in trouble with Mr. Pande. I'll be in bigger trouble if—"

"Zarina, please. A person close to Rory has been hacked to death. If you don't speak, you could put more people, including yourself, in danger."

"You're one smart lady. Do you even have to ask me?"

Maya wouldn't stop there. "Would you please tell the police what you told me?"

"No, never, I hate the goddamned uniforms. They stare at us like we're cockroaches."

Maya regarded the teary-eyed, shrinking woman in front of her. And yet she couldn't let the matter slide, one of life-and-death importance. "Would you like to see more bodies falling? Do you want to endanger the life of your son?"

Her gaze on the ground, Zarina took a long pause, as though trying to process what she'd heard, what was a dilemma for her. At the same time, and this constituted a new phase for her, she wanted to please Maya.

"Okay, I will," Zarina said. "What do I have to do?"

"Go to the *thana* and give a statement to the police. I'll ask Hindi-Man to accompany you. He'll be in contact." Maya paused. "Did Rory send you money from the States on a regular basis?"

"Why wouldn't he? He had Krishna to support. Do you believe it now? Since I don't have a bank account, the money went to Mr. Pande and he took a cut."

"How can Mr. Pande dodge the consequences?"

"He has his ways. Are you coming close to arresting the scumbag who killed my love?"

"Yes, I hope to wrap up the case soon."

"You'll put the bad guy in jail. Then, then . . ."

"I'll leave this island," Maya said.

Zarina shifted her position, a small move that showed hostility and discomfort, both so much of a part of her. She turned her face away for a second, perhaps to hide the tears that flooded her eyes, tears that were a sign of her blossoming trust in Maya.

"I'll miss you, Lady," she said after a while in a strangled voice. "I understand you much better now. You're a true friend of Rory. You've gone through much trouble for him. You found out his secrets, but you're doing your best to forgive him. And, after all this, you don't dislike me. You look at me like I count. That says a lot."

Secrets. Caring. Dislike. Forgiveness. These were huge elements in a relationship. Maya couldn't process them now. She could only acknowledge the gratefulness in her heart. "You've fed me loads of data, Zarina. I have had this in my mind for a while—I'd like to see that you and your son are free and living a better life. Away from that house, away from the shadow of Mr. Pande. You deserve it and that's what Rory would have wanted. I'd like to honor his wishes. Here's my plan. Tell me if this'll suit you. First, I'll pay your bail to Mr. Pande."

"Goodness gracious. You will buy my freedom?" More tears streamed down Zarina's cheeks. "That'd mean so much to me. But . . . it's a huge debt."

"I'll manage. Believe it or not, the process is already underway. Hindi-Man will handle the details for me. With your permission, I'll have him contact Mr. Pande and finalize the transaction."

"My permission? Yes, of course, you have my consent."

"Second, I'd like to find a shelter for you to move to. One possibility is an organization called Wings." Maya explained the services it offered, how much it had helped women in the past, and how it operated. "I've checked them out. They're okay. They'll provide you with room and board. They'll give you pocket money until you're ready to stand on your own feet. You'll be offered computer training. Krishna will be sent to a better school."

Hope bloomed in Zarina's face, a natural light that brightened her features. "They'll take me in? I'm so overwhelmed, Lady, by your kindness."

"Considering how much you've helped me and how much I've put you through, this is a small gesture."

"Other than Rory, you're the only one who has ever treated me like . . . like I matter. Do you know how much that means to me?"

Her eyes misting, Maya rose to her feet. "I have to go now," she said, her voice heavy. "Before I leave this island, I'll finalize most of what I've planned."

Zarina slid out of her stool, too. "I'm not supposed to touch you, I'm a fallen woman. But allow me to give you a hug before you go, *behen*." Sister.

A most unlikely sisterhood. Sadness pushed behind Maya's eyes. They held each other for a moment. The Right Refreshments vendor gave Maya a curious look from a distance.

Maya fumbled in her purse, produced her business card on which she'd scribbled Hindi-Man's number, and handed it to Zarina. "He'll be in contact with you. Call me if you like." She half-turned, her heart heavy from the sorrow of having to say goodbye.

"I'll always remember you, *behen*." Zarina's voice was thick. "You're helping me fulfill my dream. I'll do better than my best. And I'll raise Krishna so he'll do us proud. Do come back and visit me. Next time, you'll meet Krishna. And know this for sure, *behen*. No matter where you are, I'll always send you my love."

TWENTY-FIVE

Maya and Kal sat on opposite ends of a bench in a quiet corner of her hotel lawn, a few days later, around seven a.m. A light breeze rustled the tops of nearby trees, while a white-breasted swallow pecked on a tree branch. Morning dew shimmered on the grass. With hardly a soul around, quietness prevailed.

Kal's appearance had changed, which had had to do with the warning Maya had given him. Instead of his usual white uniform, he wore black trousers and a matching shirt. He'd pulled his maroon cap down to his eyebrows. His cheeks were gray.

"You saved my life, Detective Maya," Kal said.

She heard voices in the lobby. "How so?"

"I was at my uncle's flat when my next-door neighbor phoned me. He said that a masked man crept up the hallway to my door and broke into my apartment. It was around nine p.m."

"What did the intruder look like?"

"He couldn't describe the guy. He was so scared that he hid himself under his bed. After the thief left, he crawled out and checked my flat—I'd given him a spare key. Nothing was stolen or even touched. They'd come for me and left because I wasn't there. I must thank you, Detective-ji. But why me?"

"Like I told you before. It's because of what you know."

"Me? I . . ."

"You drove Rory to his destination. You were a witness, so to speak."

"It's spooky."

"But it's not over yet," Maya said. "Hide at your uncle's place for a few more days. Don't go to work, either."

"Does that mean you're winding down your snooping?".

"Can't say."

"Will you let me know when you're all done and flying outta here? I'd like to drive you back to the airport."

"For sure," Maya said. "One question. You gave Rory his last ride, correct?"

"Yes."

"You didn't want me to know that, Kal. Which was why you were avoiding me. Am I right?"

"You're right. Again."

"Did Rory make any calls on the way?"

"No, but he checked messages on his mobile."

"Where did you drop him off that evening?"

"I couldn't reveal this before." Kal lowered his head and mumbled an answer. The street names tallied with what Maya had expected.

"Did Rory ask you to wait for him?"

"Yes, he said he'd be back in half hour. I waited for more than two hours, became sleepy, assumed he was delayed, then drove off. I expected him to call me if he needed a pick-up, but no call came. If only I had understood what was going on. I'd have followed him. I'd have waited for him."

It wasn't quite eight yet when Kal departed and Maya retreated to her room.

A call from Simi came, her voice indicated more than a little reserve. After they'd swapped salutations, Simi said, "I have some news."

Maya steeled herself for what she might hear, her senses extra alert. "Yes, please, go ahead."

"You've talked about Alain on umpteen occasions. I feel like I know him."

Maya itched in her position. "Alain, how is he?"

"We try not to butt into the lives of our employees. Only because you asked me to track him down, I went to one of my informers. He supplied me with a bit of intelligence about Alain's situation."

Maya's chest tightened in anticipation. "Why can't I reach him?"

"He was kidnapped by a terrorist group," Simi said in a pained voice.

Maya drew a blank. "But why? He was there for humanitarian reasons."

"They mistook him for someone else. He has since been released."

In her shock, Maya couldn't see or hear any more. Nor could she find her voice. A cold sensation crept over her. "Is he alright? How can I visit him?"

"He's been roughed up by the terrorists, now recovering in an undisclosed hospital in Borneo."

"What?" Maya stammered out, even though she could make no sense out of this violent act. "Our government...?"

"Not sure of U.S. intervention on this," Simi said. "And I don't have the details, but our informer was granted permission to phone Alain. He sends you his love. Regrets not being in touch with you. Said he'll be back as soon as he's discharged, perhaps will meet you in Andaman." She paused. "Are you there, Maya?"

"I'm ... supposed to solve other people's problems. Here, look at me. I can't speak."

"Don't be too hard on yourself, Maya. You love him." Simi said goodbye and promised to call with updates, if she did receive any.

It took Maya a few minutes to calm her disturbed self. Her desk phone buzzed. Staring out the window, trying to make sense of it all, she picked it up. Due to rain the previous night, the sunlight had a watery quality.

The desk clerk announced, without mentioning any names that she'd receive a visitor shortly. Who could that be? Maya wondered, still recovering from the news about Alain. Within minutes, there came a knock at the door. Zarina stood, accompanied by a boy, about five years old. In a blue-bordered, white georgette sari, eyes smothered in kohl, her face made-up, but less so than usual, she looked more like a domestic or office worker.

"What a surprise." Maya welcomed both the mother and the son and closed the door behind them. "How nice to see you, Zarina. And this must be Krishna."

"Yes, this is my son. We came for a few minutes. Krishna wanted to meet his good auntie from America. He said he must do that." She bent down, met Krishna's eyes and said, "Will you say hello?"

Maya's gaze fell on the boy. She stopped breathing for an instant. Fair-skinned, oval-faced, tall for his age, he bore a striking resemblance to Rory. At first Maya didn't want to admit it, but it was there, another identifying mark on the boy's forehead—a brown patch, a birthmark, like Rory had, only slightly larger.

The boy beamed at Maya, extended a hand, and said in Hindi, "Pleased to meet you, Auntie Maya."

How sweet he sounded. How many times he must have practiced those words. Maya collected herself, smiled and shook his hand, then ushered them to the sitting room. "I'm happy that you stopped by to see me. Won't you please sit down?"

"No, no, Lady, we can't stay. I came to tell you how much we appreciate it that you've given us a new life. I've been offered a job as a housemaid. I work like crazy, but my patrons are nice people and I'm free in the evenings. And Krishna will go to a much better school." Zarina wiped her eyes with the back of her hand. "All of these happened because of you. Now we must go."

Words of protest came from Krishna. "No, Ma, I want to stay with Auntie Maya."

Maya heard another knock at the door. She rushed and opened it, only to find Lee standing there, carrying a bakery box. Maya managed a smile; inside she was aghast.

"Surprise, surprise, Maya." Lee breezed into the room. "My uncle from Kolkata brought this box of sandesh sweet. It's from the famous Sen Mahasay shop and I'd like to share it with you. You'll love them with your tea."

The fudgy white, dissolve-in-your mouth squares were, indeed, Maya's favorite, but under the circumstances, she had no taste for them. She motioned with a hand. "How thoughtful of you, Lee. Come in."

Lee gave a look around and took a step back, flustered. "Oh, you have visitors. Sorry to barge in like that."

It took Maya another moment to register the incongruity of Lee and Zarina being in the same room, like this. Rory's wife and Rory's lover. Two women, who should never have met, standing only a few feet apart. Who would have expected that? So far, they hadn't exchanged glances. A cloud of awkwardness had, however, descended in the room. Zarina, uncomfortable at being in a fancy hotel room, shrank against the wall, keeping her gaze low to the ground. Krishna stood; his eyes were big with curiosity.

Maya simmered herself down, said in a level voice to Lee, "No problem. Please join us."

Before Maya could make the introductions, Zarina signaled Krishna, grabbed his hand, and gestured toward the door, saying, "We have to go now."

"No, Ma." With a sudden, jerky movement, Krishna let go of his mother's hand. He turned and looked first at Maya, then at Lee, gaze full of expectation.

Lee's eyes were riveted on the boy. She bent down to meet his eyes, a pained smile playing on her lips. "What's your name?"

"Krishna."

To Maya, standing close by, the birthmark on the boy's forehead was visible, and she couldn't stop thinking about it.

Lee stood rooted, ever the poised woman, a crimson blush deepening on her face. Then she choked, trying to suppress rising feelings of pain and anger, even of being cheated by her late husband. And yet Krishna must have brought out her motherly instincts enough to overcome them, for she resumed in a warm, if trembling, voice, "Do you like sandesh, Krishna?"

"Love them." Krishna wore a winsome smile showing his pearly white teeth. "Can I have the whole box?"

He'd inherited Rory's sense of humor; Maya couldn't help but reflect on that. She peered up at Lee. "Let him have the box."

Zarina stepped forward, her face ashen, movements jerky. Perhaps by now she'd figured out that Lee was Rory's wife. Perhaps that had crushed her. "No, no sandesh," she said to Krishna, her voice shrill. "Let's go." With that, she dragged him by the arm.

"Please . . . stay," both Maya and Lee said in unison.

By then, Zarina and Krishna had exited through the door and was marching down the hallway, Krishna sobbing.

Only after they'd disappeared, and she'd shut the door, Maya felt the floor under her feet. She checked Lee's expression, one of both disappointment and relief, the sadness around her eyes more pronounced. Maya gestured her to sit.

They both dropped down on the sofa. At first, Lee appeared to be too shocked to speak. "Such a darling boy," she said after a moment, her voice strained.

Maya allowed a pensive moment to pass. Lee sat erect. In her mind, Maya gave her friend credit for handling this difficult encounter with delicacy and class. In the future, they'd talk in detail about this incident and what they both understood about Rory. Now was not the time.

Lee blinked a tear away and peered up at Maya. "What's the matter?

You look preoccupied, like you've already had a rough morning."

"You could say that." Maya switched to another topic, briefing Lee on the break-in at Kal's place, and adding, "Our taxi driver is safe for now. But in the long run, I'm not sure he can be protected."

"My heavens. That's serious." Lee looked bewildered. Consulting her watch, she added, "I must return to my hotel. My uncle and aunt want to take me out. They're here only for the day. Do keep me posted, Maya, will you? I want to hear everything."

TWENTY-SIX

WITHIN MINUTES OF LEE'S DEPARTURE, Maya's cell phone trilled. She picked it up on the second ring, only to hear Inspector Dev's excited greeting, far more cheerful than usual. He must have showed up at work on time.

"Guess what, Maya?"

Maya's mind raced. The inspector speaking in such an informal manner? That indicated he'd begun to value her effort. Could it be because she'd given him an inkling that the murder cases could be solved? On his own, he might not have come this far. Even though it had taken several weeks, he was coming around to the point where he appreciated her presence.

"The DNA results from the lab have arrived, I suppose?" Maya said.

"Right you are. Jorge's skin cells matched the unknown DNA profile we harvested from Rory's body and clothing. It matched the DNA evidence left at Nemo's murder site. And which, therefore, puts Jorge as the suspected killer of both Rory and Nemo, as you've already guessed."

Saddened by the reminder of the two murders, Maya still tipped a fist up in victory. "That's terrific. I'd like a copy of the results for my file."

"But there's bad news. Jorge isn't answering his phone. Nor is he showing up at his usual haunts. One of my constables bribed a member of the Peterson staff and was told in confidence. Jorge has left town. He flew out of here yesterday in a big hurry, perhaps aware of our suspicions."

"Where did he fly to?"

"Airline records indicated he'd landed in Delhi. That was a miss."

"What'll happen now?"

"I've alerted my colleagues in Delhi. They let me know this morning that he's checked into a hotel." The inspector breathed a sigh of relief. "They're keeping an eye on his movements and he'll be arrested within the hour."

"Our work isn't over yet," Maya said.

"I suppose not. The DNA scans have deepened the mystery of the two murders for me, stumped me, as a matter of fact. I don't mind admitting it to you. What logical justification did Jorge have for hurting both Rory and Nemo? He isn't a nice guy and not bright enough to change his modus operandi, but . . ."

"What if I came over to your office and discuss this matter?"

"I'll clear my schedule to see you, Maya. You can have as much of my time as you require."

"We'll have to take one additional step, which'll be crucial for our purpose. Could you summon Esme Peterson to the *thana*?"

"At your service. She knows me well enough that she'd comply. Do you mean to question her about Jorge's whereabouts?"

"Much more than that. I'll explain it later. By the way, do you have any recording facility?"

"For sure. My office is equipped with a micro voice recorder. Great little machine—it's a workhorse, runs for ten hours but is unobtrusive. Are we going to need it?"

"Yes, a recorder will be of tremendous help."

After disconnecting, Maya called Simi, saying, "I have news for you."

"I'm listening."

"The results of the DNA tests have arrived. We can now narrow the inquiry down to the Petersons."

"Lee isn't under suspicion anymore?" Simi asked. "She did have motives, didn't she, such as having to put up with her husband's infidelities, being lied to etc.?"

"She didn't leave her hotel room that night, except for a fifteen-minute period. It would have been impossible for her to carry on the act and transport the body to another location in that time frame. She didn't have an accomplice, either. In my opinion and I'm so glad it turned out this way, she's innocent."

"What about that smart taxi driver?" Simi said.

"No motives on his part to take Rory's life. I've gathered that much from my conversations with him. He liked Rory. He'd have helped save the guy if he could have done so, if he had enough knowledge on what was going on." Maya paused. "As for the indigenous groups in these islands . . . no evidence of them being involved."

"And that tribal chick?" Simi asked.

"There would have been no way for Zarina to escape and carry out the murder, either, locked up as she was in that miserable house all night by the brothel keeper. Besides, she loved Rory. The tragedy of it is she believed he'd marry her and give her a new life."

"That leaves the Petersons, as you've suggested," Simi said. "We'll talk about their motivations later. But how're you going to deal with that family? They're one of the most powerful clans in Andaman. They have influential friends in top positions. And you're going to accuse them of a double murder?"

Maya checked her watch. "I'm working with the local police inspector, who's on my side. Allow me to fill you in later, once the matter has unfolded. Now I must prepare myself for a showdown with Esme, which will determine the outcome of the case. Wish me luck."

Simi expressed her good wishes and added, "Be careful, Maya."

TWENTY MINUTES LATER, MAYA ARRIVED AT Inspector Dev's office. She'd donned a black pantsuit and low-heeled pumps, more formal than usual. She was well prepared, having decided to be tough when necessary and to always adhere to the law. Taking her seat on a guest chair, she listened to the patter of rain outside. Esme Peterson had walked through the door only moments earlier, gracing them with warm hellos, and was now perched on another guest chair. Clad in white blazer and black trousers, she had a multi-colored scarf wrapped around her neck. Her light make-up didn't conceal the black hollows under her blue eyes. Those eyes betrayed unease, but she maintained a stiff, regal smile.

An airplane buzzed overhead, and road noise was audible through the window. Maya's eyes flitted to the tiny recorder placed behind the framed family photo on the inspector's desk, invisible from where Esme sat. An attendant brought a tray of papaya smoothies and placed a tumbler in front of each of them.

"Could you bring me a cup of tea?" Esme asked the attendant.

"We don't have tea, Madam."

Esme frowned. The attendant exchanged a glance with the inspector and backed away, closing the door behind him. The door creaked.

"I must say, Mohan, I was surprised to receive your call," Esme said. "You sounded urgent enough that I stopped my errands and zipped over. What is it?"

"Thank you for taking the time, Esme," the inspector said. "You're a good citizen. We'd like to ask you a few questions, if you don't mind."

"I'll be happy to help you with your enquiries." Esme turned her gaze to Maya, her voice going down a notch, and said, "Ask away."

Maya made note of Esme's manner of speaking, which was dismissive. She was already underestimating both Maya and Inspector Dev—especially Maya. Could that turn out to be an advantage?

"Remember you have the right not to answer any question without consulting with a lawyer," Maya began. "Note that we're recording this session."

"Standard procedure," Inspector Dev added.

Esme sat upright, projecting an air of confidence.

"A story is going around in the media circles about your family history," Maya said. "We thought you ought to know. It's about a secret that—"

"Who's behind it?" Esme cut in. "What's the secret?"

"What if I told you it was Nemo Pal?" Maya replied.

"That scoundrel?"

"He'd talked to the media about his latest effort before he was murdered," Maya said. "His new book, *The Price of Paradise*, isn't out yet. But when it does turn up in bookstores, it'll showcase several little-known historical facts that have been kept secret. Facts you might already know—"

Again, Esme interrupted her. "What facts?"

"How your ancestors coddled the Japanese soldiers who invaded and terrorized these islands. How they rounded up and killed thousands of innocent civilians. In addition, there's an account of the marriage between a family member of yours and the daughter of the most brutal Japanese soldier, a man named Hara."

Esme's face changed as her eyebrows furrowed, and lines became visible through her make-up. "Nemo had the nerve? His book should have disappeared along with him."

"Did either you or Jorge make sure of that when you planned for him to—?"

"Jorge was supposed to have taken care of that."

"Does that mean you're admitting Jorge murdered Nemo?" Maya asked.

"No, no, I didn't mean that. Jorge is in Delhi."

"We know his whereabouts, Esme," Inspector Dev said. "We have DNA evidence that links him to both the murders—Rory's as well as Nemo's. The evidence is such that we can't help but react quickly to what we learned."

Esme looked at Inspector Dev, her blue eyes filled with contempt. "There must have been a serious mistake, Mohan. Jorge is—"

"Jorge is under arrest," the inspector said.

"Goodness, Mohan, I think, you've caught the wrong party," Esme said. "Your analysis is, no doubt, erroneous. It makes no logical sense to arrest my brother. He never had that much to do with Rory. Why would he want to kill someone he never spoke to? Have you lost your mind?"

"But you had dealings with Rory." Maya asked Esme. "You've said so yourself."

Esme clasped and unclasped her hands. She toyed with her drink, without taking another sip. "Yes, I did, business type contacts and limited at that. I was surprised, very surprised, to hear of his assassination."

"Which brings me to a new set of questions," Maya said. "Would you mind telling us where you were on the night of Rory's murder?"

Her arms crossed, voice turning fierce, Esme said, "What are you after, Maya?"

"As Mohan suggested, we're after facts."

"Where was I that night?" Esme sounded nonchalant. "At home, relaxing, watching a boring television show and eating a cupcake, as far as I can remember."

"What show did you watch?"

"I don't remember."

"And Jorge?" Maya asked. "You must know what he was doing."

"He was in his room, sitting before the television as usual. All these unnecessary questions. Look, I have a busy morning scheduled. I'm expected at a breakfast and later at a luncheon. I have to go."

"Did you watch the show in Rory's company?" Maya asked.

"I've heard from your friends you don't like to be alone, Esme," the inspector said.

"This is ridiculous." Head low, Esme spat out the words. "As I've said before, Maya, and you don't understand it, I didn't know that lowlife too well. He wasn't there. He could have been found, and I'm sure it's not a surprise to either one of you, at the whore house."

Maya wouldn't allow Esme to divert the argument, to take the spotlight away from her being questioned. "Not on that evening, Esme. We know it for a fact that he didn't turn up there. If we were to examine the cell phone records, they might indicate that you—"

"That I'd called him that night?"

Maya hid a tiny smile. She had Esme on the defensive. "You might have made several calls to him, asking him to come over to your place, even begged his presence."

Voice full of venom, Esme replied, "Be aware of your boundaries, Maya, if you are to live and work in this town."

"This is uncomfortable, no doubt, Esme," Maya answered. "But as a detective, I'm only following a routine procedure."

An attitude of superiority appeared in the way Esme held her chin. "Didn't I tell you it was a brief business meeting?"

"Yes, a business meeting at eight p.m. in your bedroom, wasn't it?" Maya said. "You were infatuated with Rory. As you had been for a number of years."

"Lies, a pack of lies," Esme shouted, her face turning an angry red. "You could be sued. You could be asked to leave this island. Look, he'd applied for a loan from us to finance his publishing house, which produced nothing but worthless books, but I decided to listen to his pitch one more time."

"Did Rory somehow cross you?" Maya asked. "Upset you?"

"Upset? Yes. He was a financial risk and we decided against doing any business with his company. I wanted to get that point across to him in person. Plain and simple as that." Esme's eyes had taken on an ashen color under the ceiling light. She glanced at her watch. "Now, if you'll excuse me, I need to get on with my day."

Seeing Esme start to rise, Maya said, "This is an investigation into a double murder case. You'd be well advised not to leave until we're done."

Hands clasped behind his head, the inspector said, "No one's above the law, I might add."

Esme's gaze diverted to the floor. Hands restless on her lap, she groped for words. "You're not suggesting that I'm a suspect, are you?"

"Let's say you're a person of interest," Maya replied. "It's common knowledge you have photos of you two together on your cell phone."

"So, what if I had been infatuated? Nothing but a passing fancy. Can you prove otherwise?"

"I sure can. We have testimony from someone who'd heard it straight from Rory. How you went after him. How he wanted to break it off with you. And he must have tried to do so on his last visit. We have a witness statement from a taxi driver who'd dropped Rory off at your house about eight p.m. that evening. Can you dispute that?"

Esme looked annoyed. "He did come over. We decided to part, and he left my house. Half hour at most."

"No, Rory didn't get a chance to leave. He'd be alive, if he had." Words that were bottled up inside Maya rushed out. "Allow me to summarize how I think the evening went. Rory came over to say goodbye. You were devastated, you hated being ditched. You argued, you called him names. When you couldn't change his mind and stand it any longer, you decided he didn't deserve to live. You used an accomplice and had your wish fulfilled. Rory was murdered that very night. You had his corpse transported to an alley in the red-light district, with the help of your staff, with the intent of putting a stain on Rory's reputation."

Esme stood up, stomped a foot on the floor, and gave Maya a disdainful look. "More lies. I don't have to put up with this shit." She directed her next comment to the inspector. "Are you going to go along with this rubbish, Mohan? She's an outsider, for heaven's sake. What does she know about our way of doing things? She shouldn't be allowed to—"

"Hold on a moment," the inspector said, interrupting Esme. "I trust Maya's abilities and I depend on her. And given that there's been a DNA match—"

"That Jorge's DNA. Not mine."

"If I'm not mistaken, Jorge took orders from you that night," Maya replied, the air dense about her. "He carried out your instructions, the way you wanted the job done, which makes both of you responsible for killing Rory."

Rage contorted Esme's features. "What's the big deal about the death of a sleazebag, who slept with call girls?"

"You wanted that sleazebag. My guess is you were willing to give Rory more funding than he'd asked for. If I were to make another guess, Rory wouldn't accept that, given the condition attached to the loan. He'd have to stop publishing Nemo's book, thereby covering up the history of wrong-doings of your family."

"Fool that he was," Esme replied with malice.

Maya closed her eyes for a brief instant, a strong response brewing inside her. "Rory had his own set of principles. He wouldn't go along with your demands. He refused to take any funding from you. Another fact, a sad one: Hard as it may sound, you couldn't win his heart. Each time you tried to touch him, kiss him, fondle him, Rory pushed you away, told you he had other loves. That was too much for you to bear. Am I right?"

"How can you pass such harsh judgment on me, Maya? You, a single woman like me?"

You can't always win in love, how well Maya understood that after working this case. Now that Esme had reached a breaking point, she said, "And this time, in your bedroom, when it dawned on you he'd never be yours—how much pain you suffered from that rejection, how it put you over the edge—you left the room, leaving Rory behind. You locked the door as you went out, since Rory would have resisted and walked out. You took the next step, which was to go to your brother's room and ask him to do away with Rory. Jorge, who's trained as a sword fighter, agreed. On that rainy night, Jorge took his machete out, walked into your bedroom and overpowered Rory. In no time, he fell, bloodied, moaning, taking his last breath, then he became quiet. His bright life was no more. Am I mistaken?"

Her eyes betraying her rage, Esme jumped up from the chair. "How dare you insinuate such a thing? I won't sit here any longer and take your wild accusations. I refuse to answer any more questions."

"Please sit down, Esme," Inspector Dev said. "We're not done yet."

Esme regained her seat. "Do you have any idea how lonely I was, Maya? How much I wanted him to be mine? How I could stand it no longer? A man who ignited a burning desire in me every time he walked into the room. But that bulge in his trousers wasn't for me. Can you imagine what I felt when I found out he'd rather sleep with a call girl than me?"

"A crime of passion is still—"

Esme cut the inspector off. "He risked his life for being the obstinate S.O.B. he was. Crushed my heart, dumped me, made me feel like I was nothing. He deserved it."

"My constables are at your home as we speak," the inspector said. "They're questioning your staff."

Esme turned pale. "What right do they have to question my staff."

"We have proof. Someone in a house in the red-light district heard the sound of a car in the early morning hours when the body was brought in by your staff." Maya paused. "Now about that second murder, Nemo's . . .?"

"You're going to blame me for that, too, you smartass bitch?"

"Yes. You asked your 'killing machine' to take care of Nemo, because he knew too much about what was going on between you and Rory."

"Should he have been meddling, that slimy little creep?"

"Nemo, an old love of yours, was aware of who'd killed Rory," Maya continued. "On his last phone call, his last one on earth, Rory had told Nemo whom he was going to visit that evening. Nemo didn't like the sound of it. Which is why he was disturbed. Which is why he made a pleading call to the police. Hours later, even after Rory's dead body had been found, Nemo couldn't divulge the truth to the officers. He was in fear of his own life, being tailed by your men 24/7. He'd have confided in me, I'm pretty sure of that, when I stopped in to see him at the Rock, but he didn't have the chance. He'd spent the previous day in Port Blair, and you and Jorge had the perfect opportunity to ensnare him and murder him. You silenced a brilliant author forever."

"Rory's sidekick, made of the same material," Esme screamed the words out. "He deserved to die."

"Nemo had an additional reason for being victimized by you. You didn't want his new book, *The Price of Paradise*, to be published. You hated him for writing the history of this island, which had been suppressed by your ancestors."

"My family is one of the most respected in this town. How dare he pick a topic that'd ruin the reputation my ancestors had built up over decades? No way would I have allowed that."

"This a free society," Maya said. "Anyone can write and publish what they want."

"No, not in Andaman. We have a different code of conduct here."

"Let's not forget Andaman is a part of the Indian dominion," Maya said. "It operates under the same legal system."

"The society here is changing, if you haven't noticed, Esme," the inspector interjected. "A new order—"

"Please, Mohan," Esme said. "You know better. We control this place. What we say goes. Don't you dare implicate me."

"You destroyed two lives, but you did more damage than that," Maya said. "You stole the hopes and dreams of the loved ones who survived them, who will take years to recover."

"I'll make no further comments without speaking to my lawyer." Esme turned to the inspector. "Are you recording this?"

"Yes," the inspector replied. "You were informed."

Esme looked around. "I expected better from both of you. You caught me off-guard, took advantage of it, and made me . . . I must ask you to erase the recording. Better yet, give me the recorder. Pretend like this interview never happened. There won't be any consequences for either one of you. Understand? Do it. Do it now." A note of command appeared in her voice. "Where is it?"

Both Maya and the inspector sat motionless, their faces reflected their strong belief about Esme's guilt as an accomplice; of that Maya was sure.

Esme's eyes glinted. A sure sign she was getting ready to take some action. Indeed, she looked as though she would strangle them both. Heart beating faster, Maya placed her feet on the ground and watched Esme, ready to react as necessary.

Esme picked up her purse from the floor, scrambled up to her feet and made for the door, saying, "Don't think there won't be any consequences for refusing to follow my order. You might not wake up tomorrow. Understand?" She placed her hand on the doorknob and tried to turn it; it refused to budge. She tried it again and cried out, "It's locked?"

"Afraid so." Inspector Dev picked up his phone. "You're under arrest."

TWENTY-SEVEN

MAYA AND INSPECTOR DEV SHARED A small table at a trendy café located at a short distance from the *thana*. After this morning's episode, the inspector had invited Maya to join him at his favorite hangout. They sat at the back window flushed with light.

The case was over. Time to wrap up. Maya, feeling a sense of relief, listened to Raga Bhairavi playing in the background. She'd dealt with her email before coming here and notified Alain that Rory's murderer had been found. A brief reply from Alain said, "Congrats. I'm doing better. Will send a longer email soon. Hope you're well."

Somewhat comforted, she now let her eyes travel this cozy room, which sported an eclectic mix of furnishings and decor: antique velvet chairs, vintage photographs, a slow-moving ceiling fan, and industrial lighting. A view of a raised bed speckled with pink blossoms and a shrub cloaked with white buds came through the window.

"I'm a habitué," the inspector said. "Whenever I make an arrest and need to leave the *thana* to de-stress, I make a beeline for here."

"After a month of working on this case, I need a break, too."

For an instant they didn't speak, both recovering, both lost in their reflections. The server, bearing a tray, drifted over and served them gingery Assam tea in gold-and-lilac bone china teacups. Accompanying the beverage was aloo tikki, spicy stuffed potato patties, and brown balushai sweets, whose cardamom scent filled the air.

"Have you heard our famous saying about tea?" The inspector's voice was filled with pride and informality as he picked up his cup. "It warms you, if you're shivering, cools you if you're boiling hot, and cheers you if you're down."

"Today we need the cheers." Maya clinked her cup with his, seeing him in a more humane light.

The inspector took a sip and exhaled a blissful "ahh" sound. "What an exciting morning, that showdown with Ms. Peterson. She thought she'd get away with it. I suppose that's what you would call the arrogance of power."

"First, I must thank Sophie," Maya said. "She led us to Jorge. It's because of her, we have the DNA samples. I'm glad she wasn't harmed."

"Yes, your young friend was instrumental. I think she's quite brave."

"I also wish I could thank Nemo," Maya said, not without a constriction in her throat. "He put a hint of suspicion in me about Esme, which did the trick, which changed my way of looking into the case."

"I was wrong about Nemo, which I regret, the biggest mistake I've made in my career."

"I must make a confession here, too," Maya said. "How I wish I could have saved his life. I was close to doing so. Then again, I'm not sure my strategy would've worked, given that he was a marked man."

"Indeed, he was. In my line of work, you do your best, and then . . . you move on. So much is beyond your control, but you carry the regrets for the rest of your life." He paused. "What's next, Maya?"

Maya's shoulders were weighted down. "Now that my part of the probing has ended and you'll take over from here, I can start packing."

"That fast? Wish you were here longer. But I can understand why you might want to return home."

With the essence of ginger warming her throat, Maya said, "Glad I took the assignment. I've developed quite an attachment to Andaman, even though I'll carry some painful memories with me."

"You know what my wife says? She hasn't met you but heard a lot about you from me. 'If I had a younger brother of marriageable age, I'd have liked him to meet Maya.'"

Maya laughed, took a bite of her balushai. Smooth, dense and delicately sweet, it improved one's outlook, if for a moment. "How easy it is to make these arrangements in India."

"At least in our generation it's not considered uncool to draw such a match. My wife and I—we had an arranged marriage decades ago—and it has worked. I'm a proponent of it, you might say. Our friends jokingly call us 'arrangers.' By the way, did you have a chance to try that lobster joint I suggested?"

"No, maybe the next time. You know how you must leave a few sights unseen, so you'd come back?"

"I might not be here when you come back. How about dinner this evening? Would you like to join me and my family at Lobster Mania? My wife would like to meet you."

Maya was warming to the inspector, now seeing his sentimental side, finding both the strong creamy tea and his company to be rather pleasant. "Why, sure, I'd love to," she said, elated.

"At seven, then."

"Do you, by any chance, have a job transfer?"

"Yes, back to Delhi. I'm burned out. And it's become obvious that I can't carry out my duties here—too few resources, far too many compromises to have to make at every step, always being a toy in the hands of the mighty. As you can see money and power are concentrated in a few hands. Yesterday we received a call from an old blind lady about a property crime. We couldn't even reach her flat till twelve hours later. She was inconsolable. That made me sad."

"Will it be better in Delhi?"

"No. They'll put me back on the payroll. However, they won't give my old position back . . . It'll be a step down. But then, my children would be happy. My wife would love to have her siblings living close by. My family's smiling faces—that's all I ever ask for."

Listening to the inspector, watching his wistful eyes, Maya understood an incident from decades ago: the police in Kolkata couldn't be of help when she and her mother were burglarized. They lacked manpower and funding and, as a result, were forced to prioritize.

She studied the bright surrounding with appreciative eyes. In hindsight she saw that as far as the Rory murder case was concerned, she had had a few losses but some gains, too. She felt a bit wiser and was more deliberate. She'd leave this place a different person, seeing everything in a different light—Andaman light.

"Policing here hasn't been easy for me," the inspector was saying. "Nemo was right. Paradise does demand a high price. Private interests try to ruin the public good."

"On another note: Did I stir things up too much?"

"You did, indeed, stir things up, Maya. That was needed. Andaman can't stay a sleepy little resort forever. To say it's geo-politically important is an understatement. Indian government, as you might already have heard, has established a naval command, an army brigade, and several air-force bases here, but those aren't enough."

"The islands that are unoccupied will be populated, correct?" Maya asked.

"Yes. I'd like to see our government beef up Andaman. Increase our population count, introduce more public services, reduce the legal bureaucracy and become more powerful. This is already a militarized zone. What better position for monitoring shipping trade routes and India's Southeastern flank better than Andaman? But that's for our government to deal with." He paused. "I can only concentrate on my law enforcement duties. Looking back to my years of service here, I see that these two linked murder cases will stick with me the most."

"They'll stick with me, as well."

"I must admit it now, Maya. You're from America and you're very thorough. At first, I didn't like that. You wanted things to move at a much faster pace than we're used to. That didn't please me, either. Then I noticed, how you applied a methodology and made use of your people skills, which you must have been endowed with while you grew up here. You had a broader vision and stayed focused on the real issues until a solution emerged. For example, the cabbie and the call girl—they'd been overlooked by my constables. But you drew them out as part of your investigative process, which led to the answers we'd been seeking. I couldn't have solved this case without you."

MAYA RETURNED TO HER HOTEL ROOM, where the citron-tinted walls appeared more welcoming now. Hard to believe she'd check out of here soon. She'd grown attached to this place. Moist breeze blew through the open window. Rain had been predicted.

Positioned at her desk, her laptop within easy reach, she called Simi and filled her in with the latest news. Her voice trembling at times, she talked about the sense of relief she felt. All the while she kept her eyes on the glassy, whispering ocean, a view she'd forever miss, one that had expanded her general outlook. She imagined all the life below the surface, existing in harmony.

Simi sounded ecstatic. "This was a tough one, Maya. Your performance review is coming up, by the way."

"Oh, okay, I'm happy to close the case. Hank is documenting the details."

"You deserve beach time. Or do you plan to fly back to Seattle right away?"

"Yes, to Seattle," Maya replied. "As soon as I can book a flight."

"Give me a call when you return. Send me copies of all documentation for our file." She paused. "Any last observation on the Rory case?"

"One lesson I've learned from struggling with the case is this," Maya said. "How hard it is to let go of anger, resentment, and remorse. Sometimes, you can't make yourself forgive. You have to keep trying."

"Righto. I haven't forgiven or forgotten my ex-husband. It's been thirteen years, you know. I see his face every morning when I wake up." Simi paused. "I have an appointment coming up. Let's touch base soon."

TWENTY-EIGHT

A ROUND FIVE P.M., LEE CAME OVER and joined Maya on the private beach of her hotel. They sat beneath a yellow parasol. Lee's eyes were dim, her expression subdued, and she was no longer as loquacious, having lost some of her spark. Hiding her own disillusionment from all that had happened, Maya watched the blue-green elegance of the waves as they crawled and drew away.

"I can give you the run-down," she said after a while. Then as the wind blew and droplets of salty water hit their faces, Maya supplied the details: how she'd looked into the case, arrived at certain conclusions and gathered confessions, the truth as she'd discovered it, the arrests that had followed. She felt a release, but not a full one. Her throat knotting, Maya held off, telling herself, *Maybe later. Stay close-mouthed about the Rory-Zarina affair for now.* She couldn't pile on more misery on Lee's fragile shoulders.

Lee listened motionless, struggled to speak, but no words popped out.

"There's a missing piece here that's bugging me," Maya said. "Can I ask you about that?"

"Shoot."

"How much of this did you already know?"

Lee's lips twitched. "Why do you ask? To humiliate me, the stupid wife?"

"No, that's not it."

"What can be worse? To love someone so much that you lose your own self, then find out that—"

"Please, Lee, it's time you told me Rory's story."

"You're my best friend. You came to help me, even risking your life, when I needed it the worst. But raised the way I was, ashamed as I was, I couldn't share any of it with you, even realizing I could have saved you much suffering, soul-searching and legwork. I'm sorry that I acted cold and distant."

"Look, Lee, even beyond the risks I took and the worrying I did. I mean much could have been avoided, maybe even Nemo's death, and only now, only now, you're telling me—"

"I failed. Please forgive me."

As if that was easy. Maya closed her eyes for an instant. She would have to face this challenge, process this new finding. She rested her hand over Lee's, feeling the shaky warmth and the hidden hurt.

"Believe me I found out about that shrew, Esme Peterson, only that evening—Rory's last. She kept ringing him."

"Did you try to stop Rory from—?"

"Yes, I tried my best, but that bitch kept calling and he kept running to the bedroom balcony to talk with her in private. I didn't hear it all, only the gist. When I asked with whom he was speaking, he wouldn't answer. It made me mad. I couldn't see straight. I screamed at him, threw a book at him, slapped him, and spat on him. I even threw up on the sofa." Face red, her fist tight, tremors in her body, Lee said, "In the end, he came clean."

"We can continue this at another time, if you like," Maya said.

"No, you must hear the rest, Maya. Then you'd know why I stayed quiet, crazily quiet. Rory said he'd slept with her a few times. Yes, he admitted that he'd cheated on me. Do you know how hard it is to hear those words from your husband? I even paid for his trips. I sobbed. He said he'd tried to break off, but that shrew wouldn't hear of it. 'Leave your marriage and move in with me,' she'd asked him. "You'll have the funds you need for your business."

"And . . . ?"

"He told me he had no intention of doing that. No, never, he'd made it clear to her, but she wouldn't accept it. That's how desperate she was. My husband, the light of my existence, looked guilty. Like a hangdog. He insisted he'd have to go see her that evening. One last time. You can imagine the state I was in by then. I didn't like the sound of it. I felt sicker. Went to the bathroom and threw up again. Came back and tried to talk him out of going to her place. He looked away, unconvinced. I'd failed to persuade him."

Maya gazed up at her. *What did you do then?*

Pain drifted across Lee's face. "I slapped him again, slapped him hard. I must have hurt him because he turned away and closed his eyes. I turned. I couldn't bear to look at him. He brought me closer, kissed me and said, 'This will be the last time, I promise. Only half-hour. I'll be back. You have my word, dear. I love you.' He walked out, shut the door behind him. I remember that sound. I remember the last glimpse I had of him. I remember the loving reply I had stuck in my throat."

A black bird flitted through the air. A young boy flew a red kite. A lace of foam met the ocean's edge. Listening to the music of the waves, Maya continued to hold Lee's hand. Through shared sorrow and despair and this final confession of Lee, through the difficulties they had both had to endure, they'd regained their closeness.

"I have good news for you," Lee said minutes later. "Can you guess what it is?"

It pleased Maya to be able to say, "It's a boy."

"I'll name him Rory, Junior. That's not the name I'd chosen earlier, but . . ."

"Did Rory . . .?"

"No, I didn't get a chance to tell him about my pregnancy, waiting for the perfect moment. How I wish I hadn't waited. How it breaks my heart now. You know, he always wanted a son, his heir. He'd have been ecstatic. Nothing would have made him happier."

Regret had shortened Lee's breath. Maya sat immobile, allowed her friend to unburden her feelings and put herself at ease.

"It was quite a coincidence that I met Rory's other son in your hotel room a few days ago," Lee said. "It was his son, wasn't it?"

"You figured that out?" Maya said. "But then, of course, you would."

"Yes, Krishna looks like Rory. He has the same birthmark, same mannerisms, the darling boy. You can imagine my heartache when I saw the uncanny resemblance, when I realized that my husband was a serial philanderer. But you know children shouldn't pay the price of their parents' poor judgment and actions." She paused. "There's more, isn't there so?"

"You're right." Now Maya revealed what she'd learned about Rory's affair with Zarina. It took a while and Maya didn't hide the fact that she'd grown to like Zarina, that she had helped rehabilitate her, in order that both she and her son would have a future.

After a long pause, Lee said, "You're doing what's right. For me, it's hard to accept. Throughout the day, I get mad at Rory. I want to hit him. But do you know what I've realized? He was never fully mine."

"What do you mean?"

"I loved him and tried to make him a homebody, but that didn't work. He loved many, never could love one or make himself commit to one. If I could speak as poetically as he often did, I'd say, 'He belonged to humanity, to the planet, he was too big to be contained.' And, true to his talents, he gave big. Also had an enormous ambition to be fed. What crushes me is that he paid for his ambition with his life."

"Sounds like you're on the road to . . ."

"Forgiveness? You're saying I'll be better for it?"

Maya nodded. Lee's eyes sparkled for the first time since this tragedy. She held herself upright and squeezed her shoulders. She was coming back to being who she was and moving forward in her acceptance of this tragedy. Lee—a strong woman, perhaps stronger now, undefeated and feeling free—now that she'd figured out the truth about Rory. Maya couldn't be happier to see this blossoming of her friend.

"Good news," Lee said. "It's been announced that Rory's latest book— *Poisoned Plate*—is this year's winner of the international JLM Prize, a most prestigious award. It beat out books by major publishers."

A light wind blowing, Maya watched the rhythm of the waves pounding on the shore. Her disappointment toward Rory began to soften. Like the ocean, always in motion, her opinions about him became more fluid. In her mind, she, too, recognized Rory for who he was and acknowledged the long list of his contributions. How he was there for his authors, readers, and friends, a multi-talented man. What if he had a few serious shortcomings?

"Congratulations," Maya said, meaning it with her heart.

"Rory would have danced in joy."

Maya gave a warm look at Lee. She would be weeping for her husband for a long time to come. "What's next for you?"

Dewey-eyed, Lee peered up at Maya. "I have my work cut out." Lee spoke about maintaining contact with Rory's authors and making sure that his publishing venture continued to operate. After all, that was Rory's legacy. She would honor it, do her best to preserve it, expand it the way he would have liked. Her voice rose, as though nourished by that dream as she said in conclusion, "His authors will form a cooperative and I'll oversee it. Not a done deal yet, we'll have to fund-raise, but I trust that we'd be able to make it a go."

"What about Nemo's manuscript-in-progress?"

"It makes me happy to say this, Maya. Amer, the community leader at the Rock, has claimed it. He'll finish the last chapter. And I think he's capable of doing a fine job. We have a meeting scheduled to go over the details. We'll have the book edited and published next year. It'll be launched first in the U.S., then worldwide, the way Rory would have liked."

"When will you return to Seattle?"

"I'll stay here another week or two, then fly back. My mother and siblings have promised to visit me in Seattle for the birth of my child." She raised her chin at Maya. "And I'm counting on you to be there."

Maya smiled, signaling her agreement. Looking out over the water glittering with diamond-like sparkles of sunlight, they sat in pleasant quietness.

"There's one last ritual," Lee said, "we must do together in the memory of Rory and Nemo. An *aarti*." In the breeze, a curl whipped around her forehead. "Like we did as school kids in Kolkata. Remember?"

"Yes, of course. An *aarti*." When a dear one died, friends and relatives performed a flower-and-light ceremony in the sacred waters of the river to honor the deities, who would then allow the departed to return to earth. There it would be accompanied by music, dancing, and incense burning and extend through an entire evening. Sadness would dissipate. Healing would make a quiet entry. Forgiveness, if it was necessary, would begin its lap.

Lee picked up a shopping bag lying next to her. She fished out two aromatic garlands made of fresh yellow blossoms, as well as a pair of candles tucked into leaf containers. She fumbled in her purse, scooped out a match and lit the candles. They emitted a sandalwood fragrance.

They walked past other beach goers lounging in the sun and stood together at the golden shoreline to do the *aarti*. In what would be a simple but heartfelt ceremony, they each launched a garland and a candle onto the water's surface, wordlessly uttering a wish and a prayer that the departed find peace. Waves crawled toward them and began to sweep away their offering. The flowers opened, the saffron flames danced with the waves, and both bounced up toward the pink-coral sunset. The last rays of the sun peeking through the clouds declared the ceremony had been blessed.

Water lapped at Maya's feet. A gust of wind blew through her hair and the sky began to don a purplish veil. It seemed to her as they turned around, each having to go back to their respective lives, that eerie as it might appear, Rory was right behind them—grinning and holding a book, his red hair tousled, saying, *Let's go*—and reassuring them in his warmest voice that despite his past failings, he'd never be far away; to which Maya smiled through wet eyes by way of a reply.

THE END

EPILOGUE

As her plane took off from the Veer Savakar International Airport, Maya looked out through the window at the rosy sunset. Down below the broken patches of white cloud, there rested the jewel-like Andaman Islands arranged like a necklace on the turquoise ocean. She could almost see the Petersons' estate, with its tinkling fountain, extensive lawn, and curved driveway. Both Esme and Jorge had been apprehended in connection with Rory's murder, which marked the beginning of the justice process.

This period was the culmination of what had been a dangerous month-long effort on her part, working in India under a different legal system. It had been a success, she declared to herself, a sweet taste in her mouth. She could visualize her late father, who had been a detective himself, blessing her. *You've chosen the right line of work, my dear daughter. I'm proud of you.*

As the plane reached cruising altitude, it rose within her, as it always did, the pain of leaving her birthplace. Heart aching, she whispered to herself, *I'll be back.*

Once situated in Seattle, she would await Alain's return. Limned by the afternoon rays, he would stretch out his arms and she would step into his embrace, a flutter in her belly. Yet she experienced a shiver of hesitancy at the prospect of bridging the gulf their month-long separation had created.

However difficult that might be, the time spent in Andaman had been fruitful in more ways than one. Zarina's face came to mind. Maya had been able to lift an exploited woman out of a distressing situation, the kind of effort that most motivated her in her professional life. Now Maya would ensure that a monthly stipend reached Zarina and Krishna. Cards and letters would fly between them, promises of a visit made, a new friendship in bloom.

Maya sat up straight, excited by the possibility of the next challenge that awaited her.

Dear Reader:

It is with great pleasure that I offer you my latest mystery story set in the Andaman Islands. My visit to the island has been a joyful adventure, filled with beauty and diversity, and made more pleasant by the hospitality of the people. In these pages, I've tried to depict what I experienced there. However, bear in mind that this is a work of fiction. The crime aspect of Andaman has risen from my imagination and as such the people, personalities, and establishments named herein do not necessarily exist. I've taken the liberty of creating the Peterson family, the Badung tribe, Soldier Hara and his daughter, Wings, the police department, the Women's Market, the hotels and a few other places.

Currently, Andaman doesn't host an international book festival, although an entrepreneur might consider initiating one.

Part of my research was conducted at the Suzzalo Library of the University of Washington, Seattle campus. In particular, I have been greatly aided by the volume *The Land of Naked People: Encounters with Stone Age islanders* (Houghton Mifflin Company, 2003) by Madhusree Mukerjee.

For their feedback, I thank Roxanne, Kevin, Lisa, Judy, and Jan, all fine writers.

As for the publishing side: I couldn't have been happier working with my editor Jennifer McCord. Thank you, Jennifer, for an excellent collaboration. Thanks also to the Epicenter Press for their many considerations.

Although not directly connected with this book, I'd like to express my appreciation for the following people. Their names (in no particular order) are: Rekha Sood, Santosh Wahi, Nalini Iyer, Curt Colbert, Alan Lau, Wendy Kendall, and Elena Taylor. My appreciation also flows to Ginny Crothers, Jan Hayes, and other members of our Bookworm book group.

And, last but not the least, my deep gratitude goes to my husband Tom for his love and caring and for being the First Reader. Couldn't have written yet another novel without your warm support.

Always yours,
Bharti Kirchner
Bellingham
Washington, USA

B HARTI KIRCHNER IS THE 2020 WINNER of the prestigious SALA Award in creative writing. She's the author of seven previous acclaimed novels and four nonfiction works, most published by major U.S. or U.K houses. *Goddess of Fire*, a historical novel set in India, was shortlisted for the Nancy Pearl Award. Bharti has written for Food & Wine, Vegetarian Times, Writer's Digest, The Writer, San Francisco Chronicle, The Seattle Times, and eleven anthologies. Her many awards include a Virginia Center for the Creative Arts Fellowship. She's a popular teacher at writer's conferences nationwide. She's been honored as a Living Pioneer Asian-American Author. Visit www.bhartikirchner.com.

CPSIA information can be obtained
at www.ICGtesting.com
Printed in the USA
FSHW011251220121
77908FS